DREAMS OF PERFECTION

BOOK 1

REBECCA HEFLIN

DREAMS COME TRUE SERIES

DREAMS OF PERFECTION

REBECCA HEFLIN

Cover Design by The Killion Group, Inc.

Published in the United States of America by:

Rebecca Heflin Books, LLC

Gainesville, Florida

Second edition

ISBN: 9780997181296

www.RebeccaHeflin.com

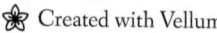 Created with Vellum

ACKNOWLEDGMENTS

To Lynda,
You ignited the dream.

Though this is a re-release of DREAMS OF PERFEC-TION, I still owe many thanks to my ensemble of beta readers: Lynda, Yvonne, Susan, Renee, Paul, and of course, Ron. Your feedback is invaluable. And Ron, thanks for advising me on all things Yankees.

I'd like to thank my beautiful my niece, Sole, who served as my guide to all things hip in New York City at the time of the original writing.

To my fashionista friend, Nina, thanks for keeping me up-to-date with fashion's most popular designers.

Thanks to Joan for submitting the winning worst first date story to my Best Worst First Date Story Contest! I hope you enjoy seeing your story in print.

Finally, thanks to my readers. You keep the dream alive.

QUOTE

"It is absurd to look for perfection."
– Camille Pissarro

CHAPTER ONE

Darcy Butler sat across the table from her blind date in a trendy new SoHo restaurant contemplating the fact that he was no Blake Garrett. Blake was . . . perfect. But why wouldn't he be? After all, she'd created him.

Listening with half an ear, she nodded at something he said. Her date was handsome, polite, successful, charming even. He had good taste in food, wine, and from the looks of his expensive suit, clothes as well. But the comparisons continued, and she found him lacking at every turn. Robert, or Russell, or something that started with an 'R' asked her a question.

She could hear her mother's well-deserved admonishment. He's buying you dinner. The least you can do is remember his name.

Focus, Darcy.

"What do you like to do with your free time?" He gazed into her eyes, clearly trying to make a connection.

"I love going to Yankees' games," she said, excited that the season started that week.

"Baseball? Really?"

"Yeah, do you like baseball?" Her excitement rose at the prospect of finding a fellow baseball lover. Provided, of course, his loyalties didn't run in the wrong direction.

"No. I find baseball boring. Too much standing around. I prefer boxing or hockey, something with a little action."

Okay—first—baseball boring? Her excitement fell in proportion to the rise in her blood pressure. Second, boxing? Hockey? Where guys beat the crap out of each other? Did she want to date a man with a proclivity for violence?

All right, all right. Down, girl. Maybe she could educate him on the subtleties of baseball, the beauty of a breaking ball, the rarity of a no-hitter, the excitement of a bottom-of-the-ninth-down-by-three-full-count-with-two-outs-and-bases-loaded game. Help him see the light.

"Do you like boxing or hockey?" he continued.

"No. Sorry. I don't."

The clatter of silverware against china, the clink of glasses, and the low hum of conversation from other diners did nothing to diminish the uncomfortable silence that descended. "So"—he cleared his throat—"Laura tells me you're a writer. What do you write, fiction, non-fiction? Murder mysteries? I love a good murder mystery."

He signaled to the waiter for another gin and tonic. His third so far, but who's counting?

"No, I write romance." *Was that an eye roll?*

"Seriously?" he asked, his highball glass poised halfway to his mouth.

That was definitely an eyebrow lift, and not the wow-that-intrigues-me sort of lift, but the you-can't-be-serious sort of lift. "Yes, really. I'm a *New York Times* and *USA Today* best-selling romance author," she said, with no small amount of pride in her voice. "In fact, my latest book, *The Doctor's Dilemma*, will be out in a few months."

"That's, um, great."

"You seem surprised, and not pleasantly." She tilted her head.

"Well, I mean," he stammered, "Laura said you had a B.A. in Creative Writing from Columbia, and, well, using it to write books about half-naked men and heaving bosoms seems . . . a waste." He made no further attempt to hide the disdain in his voice.

Her blood pressure soared, not to mention her temper. She set down her glass of Chardonnay so she could make her point without the risk of throwing the wine in his face, and propping her elbows on the table, leaned forward.

"Romance is serious business. Did you know that romantic fiction has the largest share of the U.S. consumer market? That romantic fiction generated over one billion, that's *billion* with a 'b,' dollars in sales last year? That almost seventy-five million people read at least one romantic novel a year? And that includes men."

He held up his hands in surrender. "Okay, okay. I get it. It's a money thing."

"No, it's not a *money thing*," she replied with a dash of snark. "I happen to love what I do. And so do my fans. All three hundred thousand of them." *Wow, I really need to get a grip.* She'd caught the unwelcome attention of neighboring diners.

Mr. R.—and 'R' didn't stand for 'Right'—glanced around as if seeking the closest exit. His phone rang—one of those sultry sax tones—and from the look on his face, he welcomed the interruption. Excusing himself from the table, he stepped outside to take the call.

Darcy snatched up her phone and texted Laura, the instigator of this blind-date-gone-wrong.

He hates baseball. How could u?

Momentarily her phone buzzed.

How am I supposed to know he hates baseball? And who cares? He's cute! And rich.

Darcy dropped her phone into her purse as Mr. R. approached the table.

"I'm sorry, I've got to go. My sister's in labor. Twins." He gave Darcy a lame smile.

She couldn't tell if he was lying or not, but if he was, he got an 'A' for creativity. Either way, she didn't care. The evening couldn't end soon enough as far as she was concerned. "Well, congratulations."

Darcy stood as he tossed a hundred dollar bill down on the table. "This should take care of it. I'm really sorry. Good luck with your new book." And with that, he left.

Well, another one bites the dust. She sat back down with a sigh, before signaling the waiter. "I'll have a Grey Goose Cosmo, and the Ahi tuna salad, with the dressing on the side. Oh, and the melting chocolate cake for dessert." Since Mr. R. was buying, she might as well eat.

D arcy tapped on the door as she jiggled the key in the lock. "It's me," she called out as she entered.

"Well thank God for that, since it could have been any one of the other hundred people who have a key to my apartment." Josh Ryan didn't bother getting up from his prone position on the couch. "How'd you know I'd be home?"

"It's Wednesday night. You never miss an episode of Survivor." Darcy dropped her purse and keys on the kitchen table before opening the refrigerator in search of her favorite diet soda. "God, my feet are killing me." She slipped off her shoes and padded into the living room.

"What do you expect? Walking around in those stilts?" Josh picked up the remote and paused the TV, before sitting up. He raked his hands through his tousled dark brown hair and turned his attention to Darcy. "So, what's up?"

Darcy plopped down into an oversized leather chair next to the sofa and draped her bare legs over the arms. "Oh, you know. Another blind date." She grimaced, then took a sip of her soda.

"You're a glutton for punishment," he said, shaking his head. He plucked the soda can from Darcy's fingers and took a generous pull, made a face, and handed it back to her. "How do you drink that stuff?"

Taking the can, she shrugged. "I'm a girl. Anyway, Laura made him seem so great." Her voice sounded petulant, even to her own ears.

"The fact that Laura set you up should have been your first clue." Josh sighed, propping his elbows on his knees, and hanging his head. He lifted his head and quirked an eyebrow at her, his warm brown eyes glittering with amusement. "What was wrong with this one?"

"Don't look at me like that. He hates baseball. And he disparaged my profession. You know I couldn't date anyone who didn't love baseball *and* respect my writing."

"Okay. Mr. Right isn't Mr. Right unless he loves baseball and supports your work. But why the desperate rush? How many dates have you been on the last two months, anyway?"

"You mean how many *first* dates? Fifteen, if you count that musician from the East Village." She grimaced. Shaking the now-empty soda can, she frowned. "According to mathematical theory, I should have found my love match three dates ago."

Josh snorted. "I repeat, why the rush?" He rose, and, taking the can from her, headed to the kitchen. "Want another?" he called.

"No." Darcy heard him pop the top on another soda. Why the reluctance to tell Josh the reason for her all-out hunt for Mr. Right? She'd always been able to tell him anything, even the gory details of Doug's infidelity.

Perhaps because she could barely admit it to herself. She, writer of nine best-selling romances, couldn't lay claim to a romance of her own. Now, here she was just six months shy of her thirtieth birthday, and not a Prince Charming in sight.

Josh resumed his seat on the sofa, munching on a pretzel, and gave her a direct look. "Ms. Butler, please answer the question."

She huffed out a breath. "It's just that, well, you know what happens this October."

"The Yankees win the World Series," he said, his face earnest.

"Well, that, too. But I'm talking about my birthday."

"Ah, the Big 3-0. And your biological clock is ticking, right?"

Darcy tried to hide her embarrassment by rustling the bag in search of a pretzel, then taking the soda can from Josh's hand to take a sip. "Like a time bomb in an episode of 24." She shuddered and glanced at the can of regular soda in her hand. "How do you drink this stuff?"

"I'm a guy." He reached out and tugged on her well-manicured big toe with its sin-city-red nail polish. "Darcy, you can't force chemistry or love. It'll happen when you least expect it." Josh stood, grabbed the half-eaten bag of pretzels from her, and leaned over to buss her forehead before heading back to the kitchen.

"I create chemistry all the time. Every time I write a novel. Why can't I create a little in my own life?" Darcy sulked.

"Oh, hey, speaking of novels"—Josh dropped down on the sofa, clearly leading the witness in another direction—"did you figure out that sticky plot problem?"

"Yeah, I had to kill off Ken."

"That's too bad. I really liked him."

"Yeah. Me, too."

Still sad over Ken's demise, she shook her head then flashed Josh a smile. "Anyway, are we still on for the Yankees season opener Friday?"

"Do the Yankees hate the Red Sox? Now, get out of here so I can find out who gets voted off this week."

CHAPTER TWO

After Darcy shut the door, Josh resumed his prone position on the couch and picked up the remote, then set it down again before dragging a hand through his hair. These conversations wore on him. He'd heard them a thousand times before. And now her upcoming birthday was making matters worse. Why did people—especially women—feel it necessary to mark their lives by some arbitrary number?

He couldn't pinpoint exactly when it happened, but he was in love with Darcy, and probably had been since the day she'd walked into his law school class and claimed the empty seat next to him.

She'd been young and fresh-faced, lacking the hangdog look of a third-year law school student. Professor Jacobs had introduced her as a creative writing major who was auditing the class to learn about copyright law. Little did Josh know then that at age twenty-one she'd already published her first novel, *Love's Sweet Revenge*, a break-out success.

Josh hadn't been able to concentrate the entire class. The delicate floral scent of her perfume nearly drove him mad. Rather than taking notes from the professor's lecture, he'd mentally catalogued the many endearing characteristics and quirks that had intrigued him on that first day.

How she'd flipped her long golden brown hair over one shoulder and tucked it behind her ear; the way she chewed her full lower lip before jotting something in her notebook; and the dimple that flickered at the corner of her mouth when she smiled.

But it had been her eyes, heavily lashed and moss-green, like the cool shades of a summer forest, that had captivated him. They'd sparkled with such energy and intelligence. When she'd introduced herself after class, he could barely get a word out around the knot in his tongue, a rare occurrence for a third-year law student with aspirations to litigate.

They'd become fast friends, much to the envy of the other male students in the class. Well, with the exception of Steven Birnbaum, who had been so focused on achieving top honors that an earthquake wouldn't have distracted him.

A few weeks into the semester, just when Josh had drummed up the courage to ask her out on an honest-to-goodness date, she'd come to class with an enormous rock on her left hand.

Engaged.

Josh had been devastated, especially since she'd never mentioned a boyfriend. By the end of the semester the engagement was off. Darcy had caught her sports caster fiancé demonstrating his version of the quarterback sneak with the TV station's bombshell meteorologist. Bastard.

Even though he didn't know Darcy well at the time, he could see the difference in her. Where a once sunny, confident Darcy had been, he saw someone filled with self-doubt, and her face bore a shadow of pain and heartache.

Josh wanted nothing more than to be the friend she needed.

So after her break-up, Josh gave her time and understanding to help her heal, to allow that vivacity to shine again. The next thing he knew he was studying for the bar and trying to make a name for himself at her father's law firm. Then, over time, things got comfortable between them, and he was afraid to shake things up for fear of losing her friendship. That, and you just didn't sleep with your best friend. It was one of the first rules of the Top Secret Guy Code, and, as the Code demonstrated, the consequences could be disastrous.

Friend. Baseball buddy. Shoulder to cry on. He'd never be more than that to Darcy. But he could be happy with that, as long as it meant she was part of his life.

Picking up the remote, he pressed 'play', thankful he didn't have to make that argument in front of a judge.

———

Darcy dropped her keys on the console table in her small foyer as she dug in her purse for her cell phone. The strains of "Promiscuous" alerted her that the caller was Laura.

"Hello," she huffed.

"Um, am I interrupting something?" Laura didn't sound the least bit sorry if she had been.

"No. I just got home." She wearily climbed the stairs to her bedroom, stilettos in hand.

"Eleven-fifteen . . . you two must have found *something* in common. How'd it go?"

"No, we didn't find anything in common. His sister

went into labor, or so he said, and he had to leave. I've been at Josh's."

"What was wrong with this one?"

"Is there an echo?" Darcy sniped.

"What?"

"Nothing," Darcy muttered.

"Oh yeah, he hates baseball," Laura continued with her third degree.

"And romance novels." Darcy dropped her purse on the bed before plopping down herself. "And apparently romance novelists."

"Well, he doesn't have to *read* your novels."

"No, but he has to at least respect my profession."

"I'll be sure to add that to the ever-growing list of candidate prerequisites."

Darcy could practically hear the eye roll on the other end of the phone.

"Jesus, Darcy, no one's perfect, so you might consider lowering your expectations just a bit."

"Kettle, meet pot."

"What's that supposed to mean?" Laura's voice rose with her indignation.

Darcy stood to pace the length of her bedroom. "Who is it you're madly in love with this week, Laura? Jonathan from Britain? That is until next week, when Philipé from Spain or Maurice from Lichtenstein comes along."

"That's not true."

"Right." Darcy snatched a nightie out of her dresser drawer and tossed it onto her bed.

"At least I get somewhere with the guys I meet."

"If by getting somewhere, you mean into bed, you're right."

"Boy, you really need to get some yourself—and soon."

"Good night, Laura." Darcy hit 'end' and threw the phone onto her bed in frustration. The phone bounced up, knocking over a delicate crystal water decanter her mother had given her, which had the audacity to shatter on the hardwood floor.

She flopped back onto the bed with a groan. "Super."

Her oldest friend, Laura Armstrong was an account executive for Giddings-Rose, one of Madison Avenue's oldest ad agencies, and had her sights set on a VP position. Not that Laura's father would notice.

Darcy thought of Laura as the female version of *Mad Men's* Don Draper—well, minus the chain-smoking, the infidelity, and the shadowy past. But still, Laura worked hard and played hard, especially when it came to men.

Laura had said she needed to get some, and maybe she did, but unlike Laura, cheap sex didn't interest Darcy, so until Mr. Right came along, she'd just have to remain celibate. And if Laura's opinion counted—which it did not —grouchy.

She groaned, rolling over onto her stomach and dragging a downy pillow with her. Hugging the pillow, she wondered again if Laura was right about her expectations being too high. She couldn't imagine settling for someone less than who she wanted, or spending her life with someone who didn't know her inside and out and love her in spite of her foibles. Or maybe even because of them. Someone who would never tell you he loved you and then cheat on you. Someone perfect. Someone like Blake.

She closed her eyes and drifted off to sleep, clothes and all, with visions of Blake Garrett, the Perfect Man, dancing in her head.

CHAPTER THREE

The crowd roared as A-Rod's two-run homer sailed over the outfield wall. Josh smacked Darcy's hands in an overhead double high-five.

Darcy, thumb and index finger in her mouth, let out a very unladylike whistle, while Josh hooted his approval.

From their seats along the first-base line, they'd watched the Yankees play season after season, hoping to catch a coveted foul ball, since Josh took a job in her father's law firm and could afford the tickets. It was the one activity he made time for in his demanding schedule as a law firm senior associate, and the fact that it involved Darcy made it all the better.

"Now that's what I'm talking about!" Josh clapped his hands.

Resuming their seats, they clanked beer bottles in a toast to their beloved Yankees.

Darcy closed her eyes and lifted her face to the warm April sun. "I just love baseball season," she said with a wistful sigh.

"Me, too," Josh said with a grin. "And the Yankees are in top form. Look out, Red Sox."

"Darcy?"

She opened her eyes to see a guy in faded blue jeans and a white T-shirt. "Steve. Hi."

He pushed his sunglasses to the top of his head. "You're looking good." He glanced over at Josh before leaning over to kiss her cheek.

"Thanks." Steve was one of the rare guys she'd dated more than once. Given her dating record since Cheating Bastard, one might have even called it a long-term relationship—two weeks. But things took a turn for the serious and rather than invest more time in a relationship that would likely end, she broke it off. Besides, she'd just begun writing *My Tender Passions* and laid-back Steve just couldn't compete with dark, brooding Derek, and it didn't seem right to string Steve along.

He'd appeared devastated when she broke it off, telling him she needed to focus on her work, which wasn't exactly a lie. She had been keenly focused on her obsession with Derek.

Darcy introduced Josh then tilted her head, considering. Steve was still a hunk. Maybe now that she'd gotten over her 'brooding hero' stage, she'd ask him for a drink. And he was a doctor just like Blake.

"Darcy, this is my wife, Shelley."

Doh! So much for that drink.

A beautiful blonde with a big smile and an even bigger chest extended her hand. Was it possible for someone's mouth to actually reach from ear-to-ear? Darcy took Shelley's hand and shook it briefly. She looked a little like one of those scantily clad models you see draped over the hood of a sports car in some tawdry motor oil calendar.

"You're Darcy Butler. I just love your books. I can't wait for *The Doctor's Dilemma."*

A fan. Maybe Steve had good taste in women, after all. "Thanks. It'll be out soon. Congratulations. When did you two get married?"

Wearing silly grins, the happy couple gazed at one another before saying in unison, "November twenty-second."

"Wow. That's, um, great." If memory served, that was two weeks after Darcy broke up with him. Either this was the world's quickest rebound marriage, or he'd been dating Shelley before Darcy broke it off. She narrowed her eyes at him.

As if reading her thoughts, Steve shifted uncomfortably on his feet.

"Well, it was good seeing you, Darcy. Josh." He nodded before practically dragging Miss November up the steps to their seats.

"November twenty-second."

Darcy cringed. She could see Josh's analytical brain working out the dates. He never forgot a thing.

"That was only—"

"Yeah, I know, only two weeks after I broke up with him." She slumped back into her seat, and, picking up her beer, took a gulp.

"Guess you really broke his heart. I can see the guy was just shattered," he said with a laugh.

"Shut up." A sharp elbow to his ribs produced the grunt of pain she'd hoped for. "I'm glad he's happy," she said, chin lifted slightly. "I wouldn't want anyone mooning over me with a broken heart."

Josh snorted, and Darcy elbowed him again. The crack of a bat and the roar of the crowd cut off any further gibes.

———

"Hey, batter, batter, batter, batter!" Josh grinned as he heckled, thoroughly enjoying himself.

Darcy swung with all her might as the ball flew past the plate. "Fudgesicle!" She glowered in response to Josh's taunting.

Before she could set her feet again, the *whack-thump* of the pitching machine distracted her. "What is this thing set on anyway, Mach 4?"

Josh laughed. "Don't be ridiculous. It's only on Mach 2."

Darcy huffed as another ball shot past her.

Kids and adults alike crowded the batting cages, post-game patrons inspired by the Yankees' winning performance to hone their own batting skills.

"Your stance is off. You've been wearing too many hooker heels on those blind dates of yours."

Darcy skewered him with her patented eat-shit glare. "Manolo doesn't make 'hooker heels.'"

He walked up behind her and, grabbing her hips, pulled them back into a slight squat. His hands burned as if he'd just touched hot coals.

Ignoring the sensation, he continued his critique. "You're leaning forward onto your toes. Sit back onto your heels. That's it." Nestled up behind her, he closed his hands over hers on the bat and swung at the next ball. Bat and ball made contact with a satisfying *whack*.

Now his hands weren't the only things burning. He stepped back before he gave himself away.

Darcy could still feel the imprint of Josh's hands on her hips. His hard chest had pressed into her back as his hands covered hers on the bat, and she wanted nothing more than to lean back into his strength and warmth. Had it been so long since she'd been touched by a guy who wasn't a family member that Josh's touch sent her over the edge?

The palms of her hands stinging from her efforts, she relinquished the bat to Josh, removed her batter's helmet, and shook out her hair. Confused by her reaction to the feel of Josh's touch, she stepped out of the way of the supersonic balls, and settled onto a bench to let Josh bat.

She'd always admired his form, and his rangy build gave him a long reach. He'd played baseball in high school—short stop—but had given it up to pursue an Ivy League education and become the first person in his family to graduate from college.

He'd worked hard to get where he was. *Whack.* Raised by a single mother, after his father died when he was only twelve. *Whack.* Now here he was, up for partner in her father's law firm. *Whack.* Even though she hadn't known that twelve-year-old boy, she was proud of everything he'd accomplished.

Whack.

"Hey! You hungry?" Darcy shouted to be heard over the din.

He turned as another ball rocketed past him. "Sure." He pulled off his batter's helmet and ran his fingers through his hair, before adjusting his Yankees cap. Rubbing his flat stomach, he gave her a grin. "I could eat."

Laughing, he threw his arm around her shoulders as they left the batting cage, the warmth of his body an unsettling reminder of her extremely long dry spell.

CHAPTER FOUR

I n deference to the old adage, "If at first you don't succeed . . ." Darcy put the finishing touches on her hair for yet another blind date. This one came with her accountant's stamp of approval—a recently divorced client of his.

She didn't generally date divorcees—too much baggage —and she had enough of her own, thank you very much. But she trusted her accountant and his taste in men. After all, who knew men better than another guy—especially a gay guy? That, and he'd been hounding her to at least meet the man.

A quick taxi ride later, she arrived at a coffee shop near the eligible bachelor's office in the Financial District where they'd arranged to meet. Grabbing a table in the busy establishment, she ordered tea to await the arrival of one Kempton Bell. Kempton. What kind of name was that? she wondered. According to her accountant, Patrick, Kempton had risen quickly through the ranks of an investment firm and had tremendous potential to one day occupy the position of CEO.

A few sips into her iced chai tea latte, a nice looking,

physically fit gentleman approached her table. Darcy sat up in her seat. *Not bad. Not bad at all. Thank you, Patrick.*

"Darcy?"

"Yes. And you must be Kempton." She flashed him her warmest smile. "Please, have a seat." She indicated the seat across the table from her.

He pulled out the chair but before sitting down, he snatched a napkin from the dispenser and dusted off the seat, then handed it to the waitress who'd approached to take his order.

Hmmm. A bit of a neat freak. That, or a germaphobe. Well, at least he wouldn't bring home any communicable diseases.

"I'll have a large soy with extra foam, split shot with a half squirt of sugar-free vanilla and a half squirt of sugar-free cinnamon, a half packet of Splenda. Oh, and put that in an extra-large cup and fill the rest with whipped cream with caramel and chocolate sauce drizzled on top."

Alrighty, then.

The waitress looked at him as if he'd just arrived from another planet.

Kempton finally returned his attention to *her*. He tilted his head in appraisal. "Pretty."

She smiled at his compliment. "Thank you."

"Yes, you'll do quite nicely, but you dress provocatively. Your blouse is cut too low."

Her smile faded as she glanced down at her scoop-neck blouse to confirm the girls hadn't popped out to say hello. *Nope. Still safely tucked away.* Frowning, she said, "I don't think—"

"And I understand you're a best-selling author. I'm sure it's lucrative."

"Yes, I'm an author, and yes, it's lucrative, but—"

"Of course, that won't be necessary once we're married. I'm quite capable of providing for you and our children. Besides, you won't have time for that with all the social and charitable commitments you'll be undertaking as my wife."

Can you say controlling? Before she could hit him with a pithy reply, he steamrolled ahead.

"Now, let me tell you about myself." He opened his briefcase and pulled out three files, laying them carefully on the table. "I'm looking for a mate, not a date. I don't have a lot of time to waste dating, and I understand neither do you, if you want to become pregnant before you're too old."

He glanced up, clearly mistaking her expression for awed speechlessness rather than horrified incredulity. He patted her hand. "Oh, don't worry, I am not opposed to children. I have a strong sex drive, so children are inevitable, but I don't believe in premarital sex, so marriage is mandatory and soon."

Aghast, Darcy looked around the coffee shop, expecting her family and friends to storm the table, laughing and teasing, certain this must be a joke.

He gestured to each file in turn. "This is my resume."

Resume? He did realize this wasn't a job interview, right?

"These"—he pointed at portrait size photos of happy, smiling, neatly dressed children—"are my three children, Kempton the Third, Angela, and my youngest, Thornton.

Children!

"And these"—he picked up a stack of paper— "are letters of recommendation."

Flabbergasted, and not a little intrigued, Darcy waited for him to continue. After all, she enjoyed a good joke, even if it was on her.

He placed his resume in front of her, which she noted

included his salary and net worth. *Seven figures—impressive.* Next came a description of his home on Long Island and his country club privileges.

Darcy suppressed a giggle, still waiting for the punch line. Let everyone think they'd pulled a good one over on her.

The photos of his children came next. "My oldest is in college. The other two are in boarding school in Connecticut. They're polite, well-mannered children, and I'm sure you will love them, although they spend most of the time with their mother when they're home from school, so they won't be a burden to us at all."

Feeling as if she were in a scene from an Austen novel reminiscent of Mr. Collins' marriage proposal, Darcy shifted uncomfortably in her seat, the possibility that this was not a joke quickly becoming crystal clear.

Last but not least, he collected the stack of recommendation letters, but offered an explanation before handing them to her to read. "Six months ago, my ex-wife and I realized our marriage was in trouble, so we spent a weekend in the Hamptons to either end it or save it. After the first night, we decided to end it."

Gee, I can't imagine why.

"But, we used what was left of the weekend to write recommendations for one another to facilitate remarriage. This is my ex-wife's letter of recommendation written in her own hand."

Stifling the laughter that threatened to bubble to the surface, Darcy took the paper from Kempton, never having read a letter of recommendation from an ex-wife before. The letter began by praising his suitability as a husband and father, and his aptitude as a provider.

Darcy's eyebrows winged up at the accolades she gave

his bedroom performance, using words like "stamina of a stallion" and "endurance of a god." It was a wonder she gave him up. Biting her lip, she read the two other letters from friends extolling his honesty, loyalty, yada, yada.

Darcy didn't know whether to burst out laughing or run, so she just sat there quietly, afraid if she did open her mouth, an unladylike snort would escape.

"I'm sure you see that I'm a perfect candidate, and with a few adjustments, you'd make a proper wife for me." With a few more references as to his need to find a mate, he packed away the file, set his intertwined hands on the table, and rested his case.

Ticking off his psychological disorders: obsessive-compulsion, narcissism, and possibly a touch of sex addiction, Darcy planned the quickest possible exit. She tried in vain to compose her features.

Very quietly she laid some money on the table for her tea, swallowed a chuckle, and said, "Mr. Bell, it has been very, um, entertaining, but . . . Not. In. This. Lifetime. I have not yet reached the level of desperation it would take for me to become your, er, Stepford wife."

For a moment she feared he was going to blow a gasket. His handsome face turned an unpleasant shade of purple, his eyes bulging, his mouth gaping in shock. Then he grabbed his briefcase and strode to the door, barreling into the UPS man in his haste to leave. He hadn't even paid for his coffee.

She didn't know whether to laugh or cry, so she did both. The pent-up laughter erupted in a series of snorts, giggles, and guffaws, until tears ran down her face. Wiping her face with a napkin, she resolved one thing: no more blind dates.

CHAPTER FIVE

K ids squealed, dogs barked, and the smell of grilled hotdogs and hamburgers filled the Sunday afternoon, floating on the soft spring air. Darcy carried an enormous bowl of potato salad to the table that would serve as the buffet for the family cookout.

Her five-year-old niece, Samantha, threw her arms around Darcy's knees with all the gusto of a Giants defensive tackle, practically knocking her and her potato salad over. Placing the bowl on the table among the other side dishes, she gave her niece a smile.

"Aunt Darthy." Sam's lisp had become even more pronounced with the loss of one of her front teeth. "Will keepths chathing me."

"Well, I bet if you stop running, he'll stop chasing you." Darcy knelt down to nuzzle the girl's neck. Her sunny blond hair smelled of the baby shampoo her mother still used on it, and Darcy experienced the now-familiar tug at her heart that occurred whenever she interacted with her nieces and nephew.

Josh snuck up and lifted a shrieking and giggling Sam in

his arms and blew raspberries on her bare belly. "Sthop, Joth." But her continued giggles belied her pleas.

Josh set her down and gave her rump a little pat as she ran off to torment her cousin Will some more.

"You're late. I was beginning to think you weren't coming," Darcy said as she turned to make room on the table for the rest of the food.

Josh waved a greeting to Anne and Brandon, Darcy's siblings. "Had some work to finish up at the office." He tucked his hands into the pockets of his khaki pants, mainly to keep them from grasping Darcy's face and kissing her. She looked so fresh and lovely in a sundress the color of the lilacs in her mother's garden. And smelled like them too. A breeze teased the silky strands around her face.

"Josh, 'bout time you got here, son." Darcy's father clapped his free hand on Josh's shoulder. In his other hand the spatula he'd been using to flip burgers. His 'Kiss the Cook' apron bore the brunt of the day's work, from splatters of his top-secret hamburger concoction to grimy handprints from his grandchildren.

Josh couldn't help thinking that Jeff Butler was still a handsome man, with a thick head of salt-and-pepper hair, a face tanned from his recent rounds of golf, and eyes so blue you'd swear they'd captured a summer sky.

"Got a minute? Step into my office," Jeff said, gesturing to the smoking grill.

"Sure."

"Jeff. No work today," Darcy's mom, Vanessa, admonished as she stepped out with an armload of desserts. "Josh, don't you let him talk about work. It's his birthday, and he's going to celebrate it even if it kills him."

Josh flashed Vanessa a smile. "No worries."

"Van," Jeff assured her, "we're not talking law, we're

talking something much more important—baseball. I want Josh's expert opinion on the new Red Sox shortstop."

Josh laughed as Vanessa rolled her eyes.

"If it isn't football, it's baseball with you two." Vanessa tolerated the sports fanatics in her family, including her youngest child, but that didn't mean she had to join in their obsession.

Josh knew that as a Jane Austen scholar, Vanessa preferred obsessing over Austen's letters rather than the Yankees' batting averages. And thanks to her mother's chosen obsession, *er*, profession, Darcy and her siblings bore some combination of the names of her mother's favorite Austen characters: Darcy Elizabeth, Anne Elinor, and Frederick Brandon. And because of his long-time relationship with the family, he knew more about Jane Austen than he'd ever wanted to know.

Van, as Jeff called her, dressed more like a Bohemian painter than a literary scholar. Her long, flowing skirts, silver gypsy hair and colorful tops would have been right at home in one of New York's many artist colonies. So different from Jeff's preppy look, but appealing in a natural sort of way. Even now, he could see what Jeff saw in her forty years ago.

As he and Jeff talked ERAs and RBIs over grilling meat, Josh watched the exuberant chaos that was Darcy's family. Being an only child, he'd missed that growing up. The roughhousing, the good-natured teasing, even the occasional disputes and sibling rivalry; he'd yearned for it all.

He had it now, though, or a close approximation of it anyway, and as far as he was concerned, better late than never. Jeff had become the father Josh had always wanted. From the moment he met them, Darcy's parents and older siblings welcomed him into their fold as one of their own.

Her parents scolded him, her siblings razzed him. And he loved every minute of it.

Not that he regretted his relationship with his mother. No. He loved and respected her too much. But he saw Darcy's family as an extension of that relationship, not a substitution for it.

Josh chuckled and drew Jeff's attention to his older granddaughter's skill at riding the family dog like a show horse.

Jeff let loose with one of his infectious laughs. "That's my little Tomboy-Princess, just like her Aunt Darcy."

Yep. One day, he wanted a big family just like the Butlers.

———

"I wonder what's keeping Gloria," Vanessa said as she glanced at her watch. "It's not like her to be late."

"I'm sure she'll be here any minute." Gloria Madison was not only Darcy's godmother, but her literary agent as well. Gloria and her mother had been best friends all through grade school, high school, and college. Other than her father, no one knew her mother better.

"And where's Laura? I thought you invited her today."

"She's probably still pissed at me for hanging up on her the other night."

"Darcy, why would you hang up on her? Did I teach you nothing?"

"Don't ask." Darcy grimaced.

"Aunt Darthy," little Sam called. "Come play printeth with me."

Happy for the reprieve, Darcy strolled out to the yard. She slipped off her sandals, enjoying the feel of the cool green grass of spring beneath her feet. The lawn, alive now with the antics of her siblings' two chocolate labs, her parents' border collie, and her two nieces and one nephew, sloped away to the banks of the Hudson River. Darcy laughed as Delilah, the Border collie, tried in vain to herd animals and humans alike into some semblance of a flock.

Darcy couldn't lay claim to a tragic childhood. In fact, she couldn't have asked for better. Her Westchester County childhood home held many fond memories for her. Trying to keep up with her older brother and sister, playing catch with her dad, watching the boats glide up and down the river, and just like Sam, playing princess on this very lawn, confident that her knight-in-shining-armor would come charging across the backyard at any moment to whisk her away to his castle.

Instead, the man she'd thought was her knight had ridden off into the sunset on someone else, *er, with* someone else, trampling her heart to smithereens in the process.

Doug had always called her a princess, but when she'd caught him with his, *um,* junk in the cookie jar, he'd turned that endearment into a criticism. Still, all these years later, she wondered what she'd done to drive him into another woman's arms. She snorted. It wasn't the woman's arms that attracted him.

Darcy bent over and plucked a dandelion, its fluffy remnants a perfect feathery ball. The experience had left her more determined to hold out until she'd truly found the perfect man. Just like the ones she wrote. She closed her eyes, took a deep breath, wished for her perfect hero, and blew with all her pent-up frustration, leaving one little parachute still clinging to the stem. "Phooey!"

Darcy discarded the stem and waved to her brother, Brandon, and his long-time partner, David. The two laughed as they ran after Will, their seven-year-old adopted son, as he in turn ran after a squealing Sam.

Clearly Will was sweet on Sam, and like all little boys before him, displayed that affection by pulling silken pigtails and giving chase with frogs and all manner of other slimy creatures.

"Sheesh." Even little Sam managed to find a boyfriend.

Darcy looked back at the house. The white colonial-style dwelling stood like a guardian over the ancient oaks and elms now brightly cloaked in spring green. Its proportions were modest in comparison to its more grandiose neighbors, most of which were rebuilds constructed during the McMansion craze.

The red-brick chimneys flanking the structure had been rebuilt about five years before, under the supervision of her architect sister, and the black-and-white striped awning over the porch was recently added, but otherwise the house endured the same as it had all her life.

As one of the founding partners of Butler, Lukeman, and Michaels, her father had done very well for himself. Especially considering where he'd come from. The only son of a factory worker, her father had been the first member of his family to go to college. Like Josh.

When he graduated from law school, he made a vow to take care of his parents, and he kept that promise until they both died, a year apart.

Jeff Butler knew the value of a dollar, and taught his children the same thing. Despite their professional successes, the Butler children continued to live a modest, but comfortable lifestyle. Investing their earnings wisely, saving for their retirement, and guarding against the unthinkable. Darcy glanced down at her new Tory Burch dress. Okay, so she caved to the occasional splurge.

"Hey, daydreamer!" Darcy's sister called to her. "I'd tell you to get your head out of the clouds, but there aren't any."

Darcy watched as Anne approached, Olivia on her hip, then looked up at the cloudless sky and smiled.

"I can always dream up a fluffy cloud or two."

She held out her hands for a willing Olivia and scooped her up, planting a kiss on that baby-soft cheek. The three-year-old put her hands on either side of her aunt's face, turning Darcy's heart to mush.

Darcy glanced back at Anne, noticing a new tightness around her mouth and dark circles underscoring her hazel eyes. "Where's Matt?"

"Oh, he's on a business trip."

Darcy heard the little white lie in Anne's voice, but before she could ask, Josh joined them, a pair of baseball gloves in his hands.

"Found these in the garage. Want to play?"

Darcy smoothed the folds of her sundress with her free hand. "I'm not exactly dressed for a game of catch."

"Oh, come on. Nothing hardcore. Let's just toss the ball around." He poked Olivia in the belly, making her giggle.

His boyish grin never failed to win over women, including Darcy. "Okay. Sure."

CHAPTER SIX

Gloria and Vanessa sat in chairs on the porch beneath the awning, protected from the sun, sipping on fresh-squeezed lemonade, and enjoying the kids, grandkids, and canines.

Gloria grew thoughtful as she watched Darcy and Josh take turns tossing the baseball to Will, the two adults in that picture laughing like teenagers. For all her princess dreams, Darcy had always had a tomboy streak in her. Pouring a healthy dose of gin into her lemonade, she asked, "Do you think Darcy's ever going to get married?"

"Hmph," Vanessa replied. "No one's ever good enough for her, especially since that no-good Doug Lansing—"

"Cheating Bastard," Gloria muttered.

"Broke her heart." Vanessa rattled the ice in her glass. "I've offered to fix her up with one of the professors in my department, but she wouldn't have it."

"Who?"

"Terrence McCulkin."

"That bag of bones? I wouldn't have any of it, either. Not even if he came with a fifth of Bombay Sapphire Gin around his scrawny neck." She took a healthy sip of her adulterated lemonade and released a gusty, satisfied sigh.

"He's a perfectly nice, stable guy," Vanessa protested.

"I'm sure he is, but what would they have in common? What would she do while he's off in some dusty library digging through medieval manuscripts?"

"Hey, what's wrong with dusty libraries and old manuscripts? That's what I do."

"Yes, Vanessa, but we're talking about your daughter."

"She's always going on those blind dates with men she has absolutely nothing in common with. Where *does* she find them?"

"BlindDatesRUs.com? Who knows? Darcy needs a man with her interests, who respects what she does, but who's also a steady influence. Someone with good judgment, high moral character, and maturity."

"Mr. Knightley," Vanessa murmured.

"What's that?"

"Knightley." Vanessa paused as she took a sip of lemonade. "You just described Mr. Knightley."

Vanessa set her glass on the side table and picked at the ruffle on her skirt. "I'm afraid I'm to blame for Lizzie's romantic notions of princes charming and knights in shining armor." Vanessa used the name she'd intended for her daughter. A name Darcy had always hated. As soon as she was able, she'd corrected anyone who called her Lizzie, until everyone finally gave up and used Darcy instead.

"You and Jeff always were soft on the girl."

"You're right. We've always let her take the easy road—to back down when the going got tough." Gloria remembered the neglected piano lessons, the forgotten gymnastics classes, and the abandoned golf lessons. Writing was the one thing Darcy stuck with. Then again, that had always come easy to her.

"Not to mention all those fairytales I encouraged her to read," Vanessa continued. "She loved them, and I thought it didn't matter as long as she was reading something."

Vanessa sighed. "I'm afraid she's never going to realize those men just don't exist—that relationships aren't all wine and roses. And I've been complicit in setting her up for failure."

"Nonsense. She's a smart girl. She'll learn. It may be a hard lesson, but she'll figure it out." No thanks to Cheating Bastard.

Vanessa glanced over at her own husband as he tossed a burger to Chuzzlewit, Brandon's portly chocolate lab. "Jeff is the exception. He's my knight, that's for sure, but still, he has his flaws. As do we all. Even Mr. Darcy, the most perfect of romantic heroes, has his share of faults."

Gloria glanced at Jeff, before returning her gaze to Josh and Darcy. Perfect matches didn't require perfect people. They only required love, respect, and understanding. But what did she know? She'd go to her grave a curmudgeonly, self-proclaimed spinster.

———

Late Monday morning, Darcy hailed a cab with an ear-piercing whistle. The weather had turned unseasonably cool, resembling winter more than spring. A light, bone-chilling rain fell, making the odds of the Yankees pitching a no-hitter this season better than finding an available cab at the moment.

When she finally arrived at Sardi's, Gloria's favorite restaurant, shaking the rain off her umbrella, she noticed through the window that Gloria already occupied her preferred booth.

"Sorry." Darcy slid into the seat across from Gloria, after breathlessly pressing a kiss to her godmother's cheek. Godmother or not, Gloria didn't tolerate tardiness and could be quite sharp in her rebukes.

Although Darcy doubted the existence of even the smallest romantic bone in Gloria's body, her representation in the world of romantic fiction was much sought after. Even seasoned authors vied for her services, but Gloria chose carefully, and because of that, Darcy counted herself lucky. In the publishing world, she was like Darcy's own fairy godmother—making dreams come true. But she knew Gloria wouldn't represent her based on their relationship alone. And authors didn't fire Gloria. Gloria fired authors.

"No matter." Gloria waved her hand dismissively as she sipped from a very dry martini—Bombay Sapphire, dirty, two olives—another of her favorites.

Darcy's brow lifted in surprise at Gloria's uncharacteristically nonchalant response. Her close-cropped preternaturally red hair stood out in spikes around her craggy face and her bold jewelry flashed against her customary black-on-black wardrobe. Eyeing the martini, Darcy asked, "How many of those have you had?"

"This is my first. Don't be fresh, girl." Gloria's address might be Gramercy Park, but her accent was pure Bronx. Her gravelly voice—the result of thirty-five years of chain-smoking—grated like glass shards in a blender. She'd given up the habit six years earlier, which might explain her perpetually waspish demeanor.

Appropriately contrite, Darcy picked up her menu. Gloria didn't need a menu. She ordered the same thing for lunch every time: steak tartar and a Caesar salad.

"I'm not drunk. I'm celebrating. Oh, Saul," she called, capturing the waiter's attention, "bring Darcy here a glass of champagne. Your finest."

Darcy leaned over the table. "What's gotten into you?"

"Wait for the champagne. Ah, here it is. Thank you, Saul. Now go away."

The crusty old waiter muttered under his breath as he shuffled off.

"I heard that," Gloria reproached.

Darcy knew Gloria loved to give the wait-staff a hard time, but made up for it with generous tips, always claiming she didn't have the time or the patience to wait for the change.

"Lift your glass for a toast. To the cover of your tenth novel." She pulled an advance reader's copy (also known as an ARC in the biz) of her latest book from the enormous Prada tote bag she always carried and presented it to Darcy with a flourish.

Darcy teared up, as she always did when she first saw her latest book cover. A blond-haired, blue-eyed hunk wearing a white doctor's coat stood, feet planted, a stethoscope draped his neck, his muscular arm wrapped around the waist of a dark-haired, dark-eyed beauty. An ambulance, a medical helicopter, and a hospital provided the backdrop. The words THE DOCTOR'S DILEMMA emblazoned across the top and DARCY BUTLER across the bottom.

Darcy's fingers traced the lines of the hero's face. "It's beautiful," she whispered.

"Of course it is. Now, let's get down to business."

The party clearly over, Darcy took a quick gulp of her champagne before the discussion began.

The book would be out in six months, so Gloria talked book signings, press releases, and television interviews, and making an event out of the release of Darcy's tenth novel with cocktail parties, book clubs, and women's charity luncheons.

Just listening to the upcoming schedule left Darcy exhausted. She hated this part of her profession—the public appearances. Not the book signings, she loved interacting with her readers, but the television and radio interviews still scared the bejesus out of her.

Saul brought their orders, and after preparing the steak tartar to Gloria's liking, took his leave.

Gloria set aside her notes, eyeing her raw meat with delight.

Darcy shivered with distaste, then delicately took a bite of her crab cakes. Unable to resist, she picked up the ARC again. "It really is beautiful isn't it?"

"Hmm," was Gloria's only response, as she took another sip of her martini.

Darcy skimmed her fingers over the hero's chiseled features. "He's perfect," she muttered.

"Harrumph. Nobody's perfect. Especially a man."

"He's perfect in my imagination," Darcy defended as she set aside the book.

"All right, what is it that's so perfect about the man you've dreamed up?"

Darcy looked thoughtfully at the cover again. "Blake is polished and sophisticated, yet all male. He's an adventurer, an athlete, and an intellectual—a superb dresser, an excellent dancer, and a connoisseur of art, music, food, and wine. And of course he's a gifted surgeon who saves lives through his heroic deeds." And once he found his true love, he'd never cheat on her.

"How old are you, girl?" Gloria's tone was biting as she leaned in to give more weight to her reproach. "You're not getting any younger, you know, and with expectations like that, all you'll ever see for your efforts is disappointment and an empty bed. Men like that only exist in the novels you write."

Gloria set aside her fork and leveled her most intimidating glare at her. "You'd better lower your sights, or you'll find you've imagined your life away, while real life, the one that counts, has passed you by."

Darcy lifted her chin. "Mr. Right is out there. I know he is. I just have to be patient."

"Mr. Right may be out there, but he won't be Mr. Perfect, and the sooner you get that through the fairy dust in your head, the better."

Darcy cringed as her phone buzzed in her purse. Gloria didn't tolerate these interruptions, so Darcy tried to ignore it. The buzzing stopped momentarily then began again.

"Oh for heaven's sake, answer the infernal device," Gloria hissed in annoyance.

Darcy rooted through her purse until she found the phone. "Hello."

"Is this Darcy Butler?"

"Yes."

"This is Metropolitan Hospital. Laura Armstrong asked me to call you. There's been an accident."

"What?" Darcy's voice rose an octave. "Is she all right?"

"She's fine, but she'd like you to come to the hospital right away."

"Of course. Of course. Tell her I'll be there as soon as I can." Darcy ended the call, and began gathering her things. "I'm sorry, Gloria, I've got to go. Laura's been hurt."

"That one. Probably tripped over one of her stilettos after one of her booty calls." Gloria waved her hand as Darcy leaned over to kiss the woman's cheek. "Go."

———

Gloria signaled Saul and watched Darcy as she fled the restaurant. She'd been harsh with Darcy, but someone needed to be.

Doug Lansing, AKA Cheating Bastard, had devastated her goddaughter with his infidelity, and if Gloria ever saw him again in person, she'd cheerfully stick a fork through his heart—if he had one. The verdict was still out on that.

As it was, she had to resist the urge not to launch the nearest heavy object through the television screen whenever she had the misfortune to stumble across one of his sports casts. But broken heart notwithstanding, that girl needed to learn that the perfection she sought wasn't all that.

CHAPTER SEVEN

D arcy dashed through the doors of the ER straight to the information desk. "Laura Armstrong?"

The receptionist tapped on the computer keys before looking up. "Through the double doors. She's in Room Nineteen."

"Thanks," Darcy replied absentmindedly, as she followed the woman's directions. Finding Room Nineteen, Darcy rushed in to find a slightly damp, bedraggled, and thoroughly pissed off Laura.

"Are you okay? Where are you hurt? What happened?" Her eyes swept Laura's disheveled appearance searching for injuries.

"I'm fine. Aside from a broken finger, bruised pride, and a mangled shoe." She held up the injured digit—the middle finger of her right hand—all black and blue and swollen.

"How on earth?"

"I was on my way to Barneys—they're having a fabulous shoe sale and I wanted some nude Louboutin pumps. Anyway, I was crossing Fifth at the light, when this cab driver failed to stop—"

"He *hit* you?"

"Well . . . not exactly." She chewed her lower lip. "It all happened so fast. I slammed my tote down on the hood of his car—"

Darcy gasped. "Not your new Vuitton?"

"That's the one. Anyway, he started cursing at me—at least I think he was cursing—I couldn't understand him, so I . . . I flipped him off." Laura lifted her shoulder in an insolent shrug. "I wasn't paying attention and I sort of . . . tripped over the curb," she finished lamely.

"You broke your finger because you tripped over the curb while flipping-off a cab driver?" Darcy's brows flew up as concern turned to astonishment, and astonishment became amusement. She pressed a hand to her mouth to suppress the giggle that bubbled to the surface.

"It's not funny! I not only broke my finger, I broke the heel on my favorite Louboutins." Laura looked as if she was about to cry.

"I'm sorry." Darcy continued to chuckle, her shoulders shaking with mirth. "You're right, it's not funny." She snickered, managed to compose her features momentarily then burst out in a full-fledged guffaw. "But it is." Between breathless attempts to stop laughing, she apologized to a red-faced Laura.

"Ladies, care to let me in on the joke?"

Laura's eyes widened then narrowed to the telltale slits of a predatory woman with a prime catch in her sights.

Darcy spun at the resonant sound of the male voice. A voice she'd heard in her head for the past six months. She looked at that handsome face, a face she also knew well, then at the name on his white doctor's coat. *Impossible!*

She couldn't get enough air in her lungs—like trying to inhale through a straw. Her head felt funny, as if it were filled with helium. The room began to spin and her vision tunneled.

The next thing she knew she was seated in a chair with her head between her knees and something icy on the back of her neck.

The voice, that sultry, silky voice, told her to breathe. "That's it. In through the nose, out through the mouth." His warm hand held hers in a firm, capable grip.

She wanted to look up, but was afraid of what she'd see. Or not see. The champagne and the anxiety must have gotten to her, made her dizzy, made her imagine things. *Yep. Visual hallucinations. That had to be it. That and maybe a touch of wishful thinking.*

Darcy lifted her head, slowly, hesitantly, and stared into the bluest eyes she'd ever seen, in real life anyway. A honey-blond lock fell over his forehead, hiding the scar she knew she'd find just above his right eyebrow.

He knelt in front of her, his gaze locked with hers. "Better?" He flashed a smile that almost sent her swooning again. "Your color's better, anyway."

She reached a tentative hand out and, holding her breath, brushed aside the silky hair. The breath she'd been holding came out in a gasp, and she dropped her hand as if it had been burned. *Whoa, Nellie!* The scar was there, exactly as she'd imagined it. From eyebrow to hairline.

His brow puckered in confusion.

Darcy felt as if she were having an out-of-body experience. Taking a deep, calming breath, she gazed into his eyes again.

"Um, excuse me, Dr. Gorgeous . . . hello. I believe *I'm* the patient here." Laura waved her injured hand in the air in an attempt to get his attention.

But he just gazed back at Darcy with something akin to amusement in his eyes.

Dragging her eyes away, she glanced down again at the name on his coat: *Blake Garrett, M.D., Department of Orthopedics.*

"Is this a joke?" That was it! Her friends were trying to teach her a lesson. Laura wasn't really hurt. *I mean, who breaks her middle finger flipping-off a cab driver,* she scoffed. Although . . . her hand *was* doing a pretty good impression of black and blue.

"Is what a joke?" he asked, brow lifted in confusion.

"You're . . . you're Blake Garrett . . . you're Dr. Blake Garrett," Darcy stammered.

"Very good, Ms. . . .?"

"Oh, um, Butler, Darcy Butler."

"I think you're going to be just fine, Ms. Butler." He patted her hand as he stood. "But, please, stay seated until the nurse brings you some water."

The nurse holding the ice pack left to do his bidding.

Dr. Garrett turned his attention to a now-annoyed Laura.

"About time," Laura grumbled. "I was beginning to think my injury had rendered me invisible."

He picked up her chart and skimmed over it. "My apologies, Ms. Armstrong. The X-rays show a fracture of the middle phalanx of your second finger. It's a clean break, but you'll need to wear a brace for four to six weeks. It should heal just fine." He tore off a slip of paper and handed it to her. "Take one every four hours as needed for pain. I'll have an ortho assistant fit you with a brace."

He set the chart on the gurney next to Laura. "The rest of your hand escaped unscathed. Can't say the same about your knees." He knelt down and examined her skinned, bloody knees. "The nurse will get these cleaned up and bandaged for you."

Darcy watched the interchange, still trying to get a grasp on reality. Blake Garrett, her hero, Dr. Perfect, stood before her in the flesh. Had held her hand, had gazed into her eyes. The nurse handed her a cup of water, which she drew shakily to her lips. This was a dream, and she'd wake up any moment now.

"Thank you, Dr. Garrett," Laura said with a predatory purr, pleased now that she was the center of attention once more.

"I'll return after the brace has been fitted." Dr. Garrett turned to Darcy. "Feeling better?"

"Yes, I . . . I think so."

"Good. I'll be back shortly."

Darcy stared as he exited the room.

"What was *that* all about?" Laura snarled as soon as he left. "I know he's gorgeous, but since when do you have fainting spells?"

Darcy shook her head, as if to clear it. "I don't know."

"Well, back off. I saw him first."

Darcy shot to her feet, and then regretted it when the helium filled her head again. She grabbed the back of her chair to steady herself. "No way." Her hero had somehow come to life, and she wasn't about to stand back and let Laura chew him up and spit him out like she did her other conquests.

"He's *my* doctor."

"Well, he's *my* hero!" Darcy stomped her foot for emphasis.

"Was that a foot stomp? Did you just stomp your foot?"

"Yes." Darcy lifted her chin defiantly. "He's my hero," she repeated.

"What? Because he swooped you up in his arms when you fainted?"

"He did?" Darcy asked, shocked, wishing she could remember *that*. "No. I mean he's *really* my hero." She reached into her tote bag and pulled out her ARC. "I get dibs on him."

Laura took the book with her good hand and examined the cover, then her injured hand flew to her mouth. "Oh. My. God. It *is* him!" She looked up at Darcy, eyes wide. "Your critics weren't kidding when they said your characters jump right off the page."

———

D arcy lugged her purse and tote, along with Laura's purse and tote, while Laura limped along behind her, the skinned knees and broken shoe making walking difficult. Laura had vehemently refused to wear the little rubber-bottomed socks the hospital offered.

Dr. Gorgeous, *er*, Garrett, stopped them. "Ms. Armstrong, perhaps I can help." He knelt down and, like Prince Charming with a glass slipper, removed the still-intact shoe with its signature red sole.

Before Laura could protest, he snapped off the heel. "There. Now you'll be even." He slipped the shoe back onto her foot as if breaking the heel off a pair of Louboutins was nothing out of the ordinary.

A speechless Laura stared at the dismembered four-inch heel he'd placed in her uninjured hand.

"Ms. Butler, may I have a word?"

Darcy frowned and glanced back at Laura's dumbfounded expression, before following Dr. Garrett into a nearby alcove. She could smell his spicy cologne, the same cologne she'd imagined he'd wear.

"Ms. Butler, Darcy, I'm not in the habit of asking out my patients, but then again, you aren't really my patient . . . technically."

He smiled, crinkling the corners of those deep blue eyes, making Darcy's knees go weak again. "I have two tickets to the Met on Friday night. Would you care to join me?"

"The Met? You mean the Metropolitan Opera?" She gave herself a mental dope-slap. No, the Metropolitan Museum of Art, you twit—of course the Metropolitan Opera. Just call me Ditzy Darcy.

His eyes sparkled with mischief. "Yes, the Metropolitan Opera. They're presenting *La Bohème*."

"Sure . . . I mean, yes . . . I'd love to go."

"Wonderful. I have to work, but my car service will pick you up at your place at six and then swing by the hospital to pick me up. Does that work for you?" Before she could respond, he placed a hand on her arm. "Leave your address with the charge nurse. And get some rest. Can't have you falling out again, can we?"

Her heart stammered in her chest, matching her less-than-stellar response. "Um, no. I mean, yes. I mean, the car service is fine, the falling out not so much." *Smooth. Real smooth.* She wasn't in grade school, and this wasn't Charlie Smathers, the first guy she'd ever had a crush on. She was a grown woman, for pity's sake. Just as Blake's pager went off, she offered up a tentative smile. "See you Friday, then."

"Looking forward to it," he said, striding down the corridor, pager in hand.

As if in a dream, Darcy drifted back to an impatiently waiting Laura.

"He broke the heel off my shoe. My *very expensive* shoe." Laura waved the heel in Darcy's face before narrowing her gaze. "So, do tell. Did Dr. Gorgeous pull you into a linen closet for a quick grope session *à la Grey's Anatomy*?"

"What? No. He asked me to the Met on Friday."

"Oh," Laura replied, her voice thick with disappointment, before it brightened. "Oh! Get you, Darcy. You're living your very own Pygmalion romance."

CHAPTER EIGHT

The lobby of the Metropolitan Opera teemed with patrons dressed in their best glitz and glam. Jewels glittered at the throats, wrists, fingers, and ears of the Met's wealthiest female patrons, all vying to see and be seen. The men, attired in either tasteful dark suits or tuxedos, networked with current and prospective business associates.

Josh stood back, watching the throng with something akin to dismay, trying not to look the small-town yokel that he was. He'd lived in New York for over ten years now, but he'd never seen so much affluence in one place in the whole of his life. The very air seemed to carry the scent of money.

These were the people he needed to rub elbows with if he wanted to raise money for the Women's Legal Fund of Harlem, the legal aid center he volunteered for, which helped single mothers with civil legal matters. Their big fundraising gala was set for late summer and as event chair, these were the people he'd like to attract. As marketing chair, Laura's connections would go a long way to make that happen.

A familiar laugh rose above the crowd, capturing his

attention. Surprised, he scanned the crowded lobby for its owner.

He spotted Darcy among a small circle of people, next to a guy who could have been on the cover of *GQ*. For her part, she put even the most glamorous women to shame. Dressed in some gauzy number the color of a ripe peach, her neck and wrists devoid of anything that glittered, she made the other women in the room look like a flock of crows in their unrelieved black.

She'd pulled her golden brown hair up and away from her face, revealing her long, slender neck.

Mr. *GQ* slipped his arm around her waist, pulling her closer, before whispering something in her ear. Whatever he said made her blush.

Another blind date? She appeared to be enjoying this one anyway. Josh groaned as he felt the familiar fangs of jealousy puncture his heart. Putting a lid on his emotions, he made up his mind to go over and find out just who this *GQ* jamoke was.

Making his way through New York's power elite, he overheard snippets of conversation, first about a dreadful week in Zermatt, then something about the jet being under repair, and finally the latest gossip about someone's botched plastic surgery. *Ah, the woes of the super-rich.*

Darcy and her date were just separating themselves from the group when Josh caught up to them. "Darcy."

"Josh! What are you doing here?" The expression on her face revealed not only surprise, but apprehension as well.

"The firm's box had an open seat. Thought I'd treat myself to some culture. Aren't you going to introduce me?" He lifted a questioning brow.

"Oh, yes. Josh, this is Blake." She flashed Josh a warning

look. "Um, Blake Garrett. Blake, this is my dear friend, Josh Ryan."

Josh's eyebrows winged up in disbelief.

The two men shook hands, sizing up one another.

"Blake Garrett? *Dr.* Blake Garrett?" Josh asked, cutting a glance at Darcy.

"Yes. How did you know?" Blake gave Darcy a quizzical look.

"Your reputation precedes you," came Josh's muttered reply. "Darcy, can I talk to you?"

"There's the Governor. I'll just step over and pay my respects." Blake walked away.

"He knows the Governor!" Darcy gushed.

Josh grabbed Darcy's arm, practically dragging her into a quiet corner of the lobby. "What the hell were you thinking? Writing a novel about a real person? Do you have any idea what kind of legal issues that creates for you, for your publisher?"

"I *didn't* write a book about a real person. At least I didn't mean to. I mean, I didn't know he was real."

"Then how do you explain that?" He jabbed his finger in Blake's direction.

"I can't . . . really," she faltered. "I met him in the hospital. He treated Laura after her accident."

Josh shot her an exasperated look. "You met a man with the same name as your hero, and he just happens to be a doctor?"

"It's true! I'm just as surprised as you are. But it's not someone with the same name who also happens to be a doctor. It's *him*. I can't explain it." She leaned in to whisper, "He even has the scar over his right eye," pointing to her eyebrow.

"The one he got rescuing the earthquake survivor?"

"Yes!" Her eyes sparkled in her excitement. "You're very handsome in your tux, by the way."

"Don't try to change the subject." He glared at her. "There has to be some explanation. It must be a joke, then. Laura! She must be playing a practical joke, and it's a doozy."

"It's not a joke. She didn't even know my hero's name, let alone what he looked like. You know she doesn't read my work-in-progress, and the book's not due out until October."

She glanced over her shoulder to see Blake striding toward them. "I've got to go." She turned back to see the frown on Josh's face. "Look, don't worry about me. My hero has come to life. I don't know how or why, and frankly, I don't care. I only know I've been searching for Mr. Right, and here he is, in the flesh, only he's *Dr.* Right. Who better than the man of my dreams, quite literally?"

An unconvinced Josh watched as Darcy joined Blake. Joke or not, he would get to the bottom of Darcy's *hero*.

———

Darcy floated on air. She didn't want the evening to end. As first dates went, this one had definitely rocked her world. The car service had arrived right on time. In the back of the limo there had been a picnic basket filled with gourmet treats and a bottle of champagne chilling in an ice bucket.

When they'd arrived at the hospital, Blake had come out in a perfectly tailored tuxedo that accentuated his broad shoulders and narrow hips, looking every bit as debonair as she'd written him. His spicy cologne filled her senses when he'd slid across the seat to kiss her cheek.

Since they wouldn't be eating dinner until after the

opera, he'd had Dean and Deluca pack a basket. They'd eaten juicy grapes, honey-drizzled brie and crackers, and fine Belgian chocolates, all while sipping the excellent champagne. Even she couldn't have written a more perfect start to the evening.

Running into Josh had been a little bump in the road. If she knew Josh, and she did, he wouldn't let this go. But the opera had been both breathtaking and heartbreaking, leaving her tearful at the end. Although her father's firm held a box at the Met, she'd never been to an opera.

On Blake's arm, she'd met some of the city's most influential people. Her ego got a boost when a few of the women recognized her name. Apparently even the rich and famous liked to live vicariously through steamy romance novels.

Following the performance, Blake had taken her to an intimate little restaurant for a sumptuous dinner accompanied by a crisp white wine and erudite conversation. Now, tucked under his arm in the back of the limo, she could hardly believe her fantasy had come to life.

The car pulled up in front of her Park Slope brownstone. Before the chauffeur could do his duty, Blake opened the door and helped her out.

As they climbed the steps up to her front door, hand in hand, she wondered if he would kiss her good night. The thought sent her pulse into overdrive.

He turned her to face him. "I had a lovely time, Ms. Darcy Butler." He smiled, crinkling the corners of those mesmerizing eyes. Cradling her face with his broad surgeon's hands, he leaned in ever-so-slightly. "You're not going to faint again, are you?"

She just shook her head no. Standing on the step above him, her face was almost even with his. This was it, she thought, as she glanced at his lips. The Perfect Kiss. A kiss that would be the ideal combination of heat and tenderness, seduction and devotion, need and fulfillment. She sighed in anticipation.

His lips tenderly brushed hers, testing, tasting, before diving into the kiss. His mouth was warm and inviting. Wrapping her arms around his neck, she melted against him, enjoying the feel of the athletic body she knew lay beneath that well-tailored tuxedo. God, it had been so long since she'd been kissed.

Then disappointment began to creep in. The kiss held warmth, but no tenderness; it hinted at seduction, but not devotion; and while there was clearly need, it left her unfulfilled.

Huh. Maybe they just needed practice. Something to look forward to.

He lifted his head and, gazing into her eyes, stroked her cheekbone with the back of his hand. "I would love to see you again. I have to fly to South America tomorrow to operate on a boy injured in a mine collapse, but I'll be back next week. Can I call you?"

"I'd like that." Despite the less-than-Perfect Kiss, she still felt lightheaded.

He took her key and opened the door for her before walking away.

"Blake?"

"Yes?"

"I had a wonderful time. Thank you."

A soft smile lifted the corner of his mouth. "See you next week."

CHAPTER NINE

The following Monday, Josh stared out the window of his cluttered office, absentmindedly tapping a pencil on his leg and ignoring the stack of cases on his desk. Who was this Blake Garrett? Obviously he wasn't the actual character from Darcy's book. Fictional characters didn't just come to life. Except maybe in the movies.

He wasn't above doing a little detective work. The law firm contracted with a service that could find the proverbial needle in the haystack. If there was any dirt to be found on this guy, they'd find it.

Feeling better now that he had a plan of action, he returned to the brief he'd been drafting. A few sentences in, someone knocked on his door. "It's open."

Mark Woodring, a fifth-year associate, stuck his head in. "Hey, man, you up for some hoops tonight?"

About to go with his first inclination to decline, Josh thought better of it. The physical activity and the male companionship might help relieve the stress and unwind the knots that had formed in his neck and shoulders since meeting Blake. "Sure. What time?"

"Seven."

"Great. See you then." The pick-up game gave him the incentive he needed to finish the brief before he left for the day. Then he'd be free to have a beer or two after the work-out. But first, he'd call the people locator service and get the ball rolling on Blake Garrett, M.D., if that was even his real name.

———

The doorbell buzzed, interrupting Darcy's train of thought. Since her first surprise encounter with Blake, she'd been lucky to keep that train solidly on the track. Something would trigger a memory of the sparkle in his eyes, his spicy scent, or the way his hair fell over his fore-head concealing the scar, and the train would derail, leaving mayhem in its wake.

At this rate, her latest manuscript might be finished sometime next year, instead of in the six months she'd contracted for.

She still couldn't explain the mystifying manifestation of Blake Garrett. She'd been up most the night trying to figure it out, but it defied explanation. While she believed in fairytale happy endings, she didn't believe that a pumpkin and mice could actually become a coach-and-four. She believed in love, not magic. She'd finally fallen asleep in the wee hours of the morning no more enlightened for her loss of sleep.

How could she wait a whole week before she saw him again? To confirm that he was indeed real and not just some illusion? Or *de*lusion, for that matter?

She glanced over at the ARC bearing his likeness. At least there was that, she thought.

She'd recently completed the renovations on the third-floor bedroom that now served as her office and writing retreat in her brownstone. She'd previously been sharing the downstairs office with her assistant, Millie, but Virginia Woolf was right, a woman must have a room of her own if she is to write fiction.

The soft yellow walls and bright white trim gave the space a cheery feeling. She'd found some great antique floral prints at the Hell's Kitchen Flea Market, and the colorful area rug at the GreenFlea Market.

Her antique Queen Anne desk faced the window overlooking her tidy backyard with its sizable elm tree, where a pair of mourning doves had built a nest. She looked forward to watching the pair incubate the eggs and then feed the downy-covered creatures until they fledged the nest.

But the pair of doves also acted as a bittersweet reminder of her own single, childless situation. Hopefully that would change—and soon. At least the single part.

"Sorry to interrupt."

"Oh, Millie, perfect timing." Darcy didn't glance up from her computer. "I need a million-dollar word for 'new.'"

"Nascent."

"That's it! Perfect." Her fingers clicked across the keys at lightning speed.

"Glad to be of assistance," Millie said dryly. "The reason I disturbed you in the first place was to bring you these."

Darcy finally turned to see her assistant practically staggering under the weight of an enormous bouquet of peach calla lilies that dwarfed her petite frame.

Millicent Stephens, with her dull brown hair pulled back into a severe bun, sharp facial features, and slight overbite, resembled the little brown mouse Darcy had once encountered in her parents' garage.

Millie, awash in browns from head to toe, including the eyes behind her brown-rimmed glasses, gave the flowers the appearance that they'd sprung from a patch of soil. But her attention to detail and dependability made her the perfect personal assistant. And there was no mistaking the intelligence in those dun-colored eyes. Plus, the woman was a walking thesaurus—a real bonus for an author. According to Millie, one should read the dictionary cover-to-cover at least once a year.

"Calla lilies are the symbol of purity and chastity among Christians, but the symbol of lust and sexuality among the Romans. I wonder which meaning he had in mind when he sent these." In complete contrast to her appearance, Millie's voice had a sexy bedroom quality to it, honey with a splash of fine aged whiskey.

Darcy snorted and, taking the vase, placed it on her desk and opened the card.

These calla lilies may embody your elegance and grace, but they pale in comparison to the real thing.
   Yours, BG

Darcy hugged the card to her chest, sighing wistfully, before grabbing Millie's hand to pull her into a dance around the little room.

After a couple of turns about the small space, Millie wheezed, "Darcy, I'm getting dizzy!"

Darcy released her and Millie pulled her sweater back into place before giving Darcy a skeptical eyebrow lift.

"Don't you find it odd that the man you just met is the personification of the hero in your upcoming release?"

Darcy adjusted the flowers in the vase, and gave a slight shoulder lift. "It's just a coincidence."

"Mmm hmm. Some believe there are no coincidences in life. Everything that happens, every person we interact with, serves a purpose."

"Well, maybe Blake's purpose is to make me happy."

"And maybe that's just wish fulfillment."

"Boy, Millie. You really know how to suck the joy out of something."

"Just being realistic."

CHAPTER TEN

S weat poured off Josh as he drove the ball in for a lay-up to put his team up by six, just two points shy of the win and a frosty cold beer. The tension he'd felt in the office flowed out of him with every drop of sweat.

Mark stole the ball from their opponents and dropped it in for another point.

"Yes!" Josh hissed with a fist pump. "Wooh!"

Their opponents managed to get a few more points on the board, but Josh and Mark pulled in the win. After high fives and a few backslaps, the guys dropped down on the bench, swigging water and talking trash.

"Hey, Josh. You coming to the Pound and Pence?" Chris Stewart asked as he dug a towel out of his gym bag and wiped the sweat from his ruddy face.

"That's the plan. Losers buying, right?" Josh elbowed Chris in the ribs before picking up his gym bag and heading toward the locker room.

"Before long, we'll expect you to buy rounds, what with your partner's salary." Martin Lemesh followed Josh to the locker room.

"Are you kidding? Once he makes partner, he's going to be too busy rubbing elbows with the other partners to remember we even exist." Mark gave Josh a good-natured shove.

"That's not true," Josh argued, his expression serious. "I'll remember your existence, I just won't acknowledge it." His face split into a huge grin, earning him a few more none-too-gentle shoves.

After showering, Josh threw on his dress pants and shirt, leaving the collar open at the neck, then packed the jacket and tie in the gym bag, before following his buddies out into the teeming city. The mild spring weather had drawn natives and tourists alike out to enjoy it.

The Pound and Pence, a favorite haunt of the firm's associates, was only a couple of blocks from the indoor basketball courts. Regulars already crowded the pub's bar. After ordering their drinks, the men headed for the mezzanine living room in hopes of a friendly game of pool.

Josh could hear the clack of the balls before they'd reached the top of the stairs, disappointed at the occupied status of the table.

Chris and Mark exchanged a look before their faces erupted in wide, wolfish grins when they spotted the three-some of knock-outs in denim and heels, cue sticks in hand.

"No sign of any male escorts either," Chris said.

Josh dismissed the whole interchange while he and Martin talked about an upcoming case involving a New York heiress.

The room resembled a large living room with groupings of sofas, chairs, and tables, along with televisions offering an assortment of sports to choose from.

Finding a table, the guys settled in with beers in hand,

Josh and Martin checking out the baseball scores, Chris and Mark checking out the women.

"Man-oh-man. Now that's what I'm talking about," Mark muttered as a tall brunette leaned over the table for a tough shot.

"Unlucky in basketball, but maybe lucky in love." Chris rubbed his hands together in anticipation.

"I don't think what you're feeling is called love," Mark shot back.

Mark flashed a smile at his buddies. "I've picked mine. Who do you have your eye on?"

"The redhead's mine," Chris murmured. "You know I'm partial to red."

Josh and Martin just shook their heads and went back to the baseball scores.

"Josh? Martin? There's one left." Chris gestured to the pool table where the women had just noticed their audience.

"No way, man. I'm getting married in a couple of months." Martin picked up a handful of pretzels. "I'm not getting anywhere near that."

"Josh?"

"Nope. Count me out."

"Fine. More for us." Mark picked up his beer and gestured to Chris to follow.

Josh watched the two men walk over to the table and introduce themselves. He'd never really gotten the hang of picking up women. When he dated, which wasn't often, it was usually the friend-of-a-friend kind of thing. The idea of making small talk with a complete stranger just didn't appeal to him.

"Damn."

Martin's muttered curse drew Josh's attention.

"The A's lost to the Tigers."

Martin's beloved A's were having a tough start to the season. Josh chose not to rub in the fact that the Yankees had won. Again.

"Hey, Martin. How did you and Cindy meet?" Josh tossed back a handful of the complimentary peanuts.

"Her sister works at the firm. You know, Vicki in Securities Litigation. Anyway, Cindy met Vicki at the office one day for lunch, and I ran into them in the elevator. Next thing I knew we were dating." Martin shrugged.

"How did you know, you know, that she was 'The One?'" Josh made air quotes with his fingers.

Martin grew thoughtful a moment. "I guess when I realized she makes me want to be a better person." He wore an expression of complete conviction.

Josh could only nod in response to such a simple, yet profound statement. What happens, he mused, when the one individual who makes you want to be a better person doesn't realize it?

"Speaking of the love of my life, I'd better go. She and her mother spent the afternoon at the florist, so she'll have lots to share when I get home." Martin gulped the remainder of his beer and grabbed his gym bag. "See ya."

Josh noticed that Martin didn't seem to mind that the evening discussion would revolve around flowers. He signaled the waitress for another beer. It *must* be love.

"Hi."

Josh looked up, startled to see one of the girls from the pool table, the one with the light brown hair, standing next to him.

"Hi."

"I came over to ask you and your friend if you'd like to join us."

Her accent had a soft drawl to it. *Definitely not a New Yorker.* "Yeah, he went home to his fiancée."

"Oh. How about you? Do you have a fiancée to go home to?"

"Um, no."

"Wife?"

"No. No wife either."

She sat down in the empty chair next to him.

"I'm Paige." She extended her hand to Josh.

"I'm Josh," he replied as he took her hand. It fit nicely in his grasp.

"We're visiting from Alabama." She indicated her two friends who were currently engaged in a boisterous conversation with Chris and Mark.

Josh enjoyed the mellow sound of her molasses-sweet drawl. "Really? I thought you were from New Jersey."

Paige smiled and shrugged. "It's pretty obvious, I guess."

"So what brings you to the Big Apple?"

"Ashley there"—pointing to the redhead—"is attending Columbia in the fall. Getting her Ph.D. in theoretical physics."

Josh's brows shot up.

Paige laughed. "I know, right? Beauty *and* brains."

Clearly, Chris didn't know what he was in for. "How about you? Are you in school?"

"I'm in the Ph.D. program at Alabama. Art history."

Another surprise. "So I'm guessing you've been to a few of New York's art museums."

Paige gasped. "You have art museums here?"

Josh laughed. Small talk was growing on him. "Surprising, I know. It's our best-kept secret."

"While Ashley's been apartment hunting, I've been

prowling the museums. Being a New Yorker, you probably get bored with all that."

No one had ever called him a New Yorker before. He kind of liked it. "Actually, I'm from the Mid-West, and I'm ashamed to say, I've only been to the Met once."

"I've been three times since Thursday." She shrugged in embarrassment.

"Oh, hey, can I get you a drink?"

"I'd like that."

Josh signaled the waitress again, and Paige ordered a beer.

"Looks like a little competition is in the works." Josh gestured with his beer toward the pool table. "Want to go cheer on your friends?"

"Sure."

After the introductions were made, Josh and Paige watched as Mark and Chris paired off against her friends, Sheila and Ashley. Bets were placed, and Mark racked the balls.

Paige leaned over and whispered to Josh, "You should probably warn your friends that Sheila was state champion in intramural billiards at Alabama, and Ashley is no slouch either. Her father once played professionally."

This just got more interesting all the time. Josh couldn't remember the last time he'd enjoyed an evening at the pub so much. "Nah. Why take all the fun out of it?"

The two women morphed into great white pool sharks, winning first at eight ball and then at straight pool. But the men didn't seem to mind the fact that they'd been hustled. Several games and a hundred bucks later, Mark and Chris were ready to cry 'uncle.'

Mark walked over to Chris, slapped him on the back, and loudly proclaimed, "I think I'm in love."

"Best fifty bucks I ever lost." They clinked beer bottles in a toast. "You ladies up for buying the losers a steak dinner?" Chris asked.

"Yeah, come on, ladies. We're flat broke now," Mark cajoled, looking convincingly pitiful.

Ashley and Sheila laughed and glanced at each other, then at Paige. "Sure. Why not."

The guys moved their gym bags to a bigger table, while the ladies went to the powder room.

Chris leaned over, rubbing his hands with relish. "This is our lucky night."

———————

CHAPTER ELEVEN

"Okay, spill it. Give me all the juicy details." Laura sipped from some mint-green martini concoction the bartender had dreamed up. Her ever-present smartphone sat on the bar so she didn't miss that all-important call, text, or email.

Their favorite midtown bar really packed them in even on a Monday night. The place fairly crawled with eligible young professionals looking to hook up. Darcy observed the sharks with a jaundiced eye as they circled Laura, calling to mind Jimmy Buffett's song, "Fins."

But who could blame them? Laura's long blond hair, tall svelte figure, and flirtatious personality drew attention wherever she went. They'd learn soon enough they had a barracuda in their sights.

"You're glowing." Laura leaned in, eyes narrow and assessing. "Did you get laid?"

"The mouth on you!" Darcy glanced around to see if Laura's vulgar comment had drawn the attention of the other patrons crowded at the bar. Fortunately, the noise in the place could cover a sonic boom. "No, I didn't sleep with him," Darcy replied rather primly. "He's a gentleman."

"This from someone who writes some of the steamiest love scenes just shy of X-rated." Laura rolled her eyes.

"What I write and what I do are two different things."

"Well, something must have happened to make you glow like that."

"Oh, Laura! I had the most wonderful evening." All misty-eyed, Darcy proceeded to regale her with every little detail, including the flowers, and, of course, the kiss.

"But . . .?" Laura nudged.

"But what?" Darcy asked, all innocence as she flagged down the bartender for another chardonnay.

"I noticed you lost some of your enthusiasm when you got to the part about the kiss."

"Well, the kiss was perfectly lovely, but not . . . Perfect."

"You and your Perfect Kiss. There's no such thing, you know." Laura took another sip of her drink. "Don't get me wrong. There are some guys that can really knock your Louboutins off, but most of them just fumble around like they're licking a sloppy ice-cream cone." She glanced at the bartender. "Too much tongue."

Darcy looked over at the tattoo-adorned bartender then back at Laura. "You and . . .? You're incorrigible!"

"He's from Ireland, and I have a soft spot for that lovely lilting brogue." Laura shrugged her shoulders. "Maybe next time you kiss Dr. Gorgeous you should give it some, you know, welly."

Darcy almost spewed her mouthful of wine all over the bar in her laughter. "I think you've been dating—what's his name?—Ewan, too long." Ewan was Laura's latest romance. A hunky model from Glasgow.

"I've been dying to use that phrase. Don't you just love it? I've got to work it into an ad campaign somehow."

The tattooed bartender brought over another green cocktail, giving Laura a wink as he set it down.

Lifting the drink to her blood-red lips, she asked, "Have you figured out where Dr. Gorgeous came from?"

Darcy sighed. "No, and I don't care."

"Maybe you should just ask him."

"Right. How about this: 'So, Blake, did a fairy godmother send you in answer to my prayers?'"

"Okay. I see your point. But aren't you the least bit curious?"

"Of course I am." Taking another sip of her wine, she played with her cocktail napkin. "But maybe I'm afraid of the answer—that he's not real." Or that he'd see she wasn't worth dating.

"He looked and felt pretty damn real to me." Laura took a moment to send a flirtatious smile to the guy who'd just walked up to order a drink. He smiled back, but the minute Laura saw the wedding ring, she gave him a dirty look and turned her back. She might be a modern-day *Doña Juana*, but she drew the line at married men. Even she had *some* morals.

"So when do you see him again?"

Darcy frowned. "I don't know. He's in South America performing surgery on a little boy." Her eyes became wistful. "He's so generous with his skills."

"I'm thinking if he's so generous with his, um, skills, you'd have been laid by now. Just saying."

"Jeez, Laura. Is that all you ever think about? Anyway, he's supposed to be home next week and said he'd call."

"Well then"—Laura raised her glass—"here's to a successful operation, a quick return, and . . . getting laid."

Checking his emails first thing in the morning, Josh noticed one from a 'pdobson' with a University of Alabama address. Guessing it was from Paige, he clicked it open.

Hi Josh,

I just wanted to tell you again how much I enjoyed meeting you. The museums weren't the only highlight of my trip to New York.

Anyway, if you ever find yourself in Tuscaloosa, give me a call.

Best, Paige

He'd really enjoyed meeting Paige, as well. After a steak dinner on Ashley and Sheila, he and Paige had strolled through the Financial District down to Battery Park and along the East River. They'd talked of art and law and life in general.

The evening ended with him walking her to her hotel and kissing her goodnight. And while it had been a very satisfactory first kiss, as first kisses went, with her living in Alabama and focused on her doctoral studies, there was no point in pursuing anything. She and her friends were headed home the next day anyway. But he did learn one thing from the encounter: Darcy Butler wasn't the only woman in the world.

He took a moment to reply to Paige's email expressing the same sentiment about meeting her and wishing her luck on her studies. He thought about giving her his phone number in case she ever came back to New York to visit her friend, and then decided against it. He wasn't interested in the occasional date.

He was already way ahead of last month's hours, and with the completed brief filed with the court that morning, Josh picked up one of the pro bono cases the Women's Legal Fund had assigned to him. One of the things Josh liked about Butler, Lukeman, and Michaels, was that it encouraged its attorneys to give back either by handling pro bono cases, or volunteering in their communities, and gladly gave them the time to do it.

Most of his cases were heartbreakers, but this one affected him more than most. Kelly Winters, the widow of an Iraq War veteran fighting to save her home from foreclosure. She had a son, about twelve, who'd clearly taken the death of his father especially hard. During the initial consultation, he'd never uttered a word. Just sat quietly, doodling in a notebook he'd pulled from his backpack.

Kelly had told him that shortly after she and Dan had married, they'd purchased a battered row-house in a Harlem neighborhood undergoing regentrification. They'd gotten it for a song, considering the price of real estate in New York. But they'd borrowed money over and above the purchase price to renovate the property.

Dan, a high school music teacher, lost his job four years ago due to budget cuts, and was out of work for almost five months when he enlisted in the Army. At least he'd be bringing in a paycheck to support his family.

Josh flipped through his copious notes. Kelly, an accounting major in college, kept the books for the butcher shop that had been in her family since her great-grandparents immigrated to New York from Ireland. Working for the family business allowed her the flexibility to be with her son after he got home from school.

She also kept the books for a couple of other small family-owned businesses in the neighborhood. Mickey and

Doris' flower shop, and Sal's Bakery. This she did in the evenings after dinner, either while her son did his homework or after he went to bed.

Dan had served two tours of duty, was injured in the second tour, but after he'd recovered, they sent him back for a third tour. He didn't make it back from that one. Died in a helicopter crash last year.

The phone rang. Josh glanced over at the number and, preferring to stay focused on the case, let it go to voicemail.

As if serving two tours of duty in a war zone wasn't enough, he and Kelly had been fighting a war of their own with their mortgage lender over the foreclosure of their home. Thankfully, their lender was so backlogged on foreclosures, it had bought them more time.

But their lender had also repeatedly lost their refinancing paperwork, and every time they sent new forms there were new requirements. No one could ever give them a straight answer.

Well, he'd find the answers if he had to break down a few doors to get them. Opening the file, he began pouring over the paperwork Kelly had brought him, determined to keep her and her son in the home she and her late husband had bought and lovingly restored with their own two hands.

CHAPTER TWELVE

Darcy's house phone rang once, momentarily distracting her, before Millie got it. Whoever it was, Millie would take care of it.

"Where was I?" she muttered. "Oh yeah, Dominic had pulled Larissa into his arms and—"

"Excuse me, Darcy, telephone."

Darcy never snapped at Millie, but her nerves were so frayed from lack of sleep, lack of communication with Blake, and the manuscript that just didn't seem to be working, that she turned to Millie with an exasperated, "What!"

Millie narrowed her eyes at Darcy's uncharacteristic reaction, but pulled it together and held her hand over the phone, "It's Blake."

Darcy's heart fluttered in her chest. "I'm sorry, Millie."

Millie simply sniffed in annoyance.

Reaching for the phone, Darcy took a deep, calming breath that she exhaled in a breathy, "Hi." Covering the mouthpiece, she mouthed another apology to Millie before she left the room.

"Darcy! You have no idea how good your voice sounds. How are you?"

"Great." Now that he'd called.

"Did you get the flowers I sent?"

Darcy looked around at the growing collection of vases filled with everything from calla lilies to exotic orchids.

"Yes. Blake, you really didn't need to send flowers every day you've been gone."

"Yes I did. I couldn't let you forget me, now could I?"

Right. She'd be more likely to forget her own name. "Are you back?"

"Yes, and I'd love to see you tonight if you have the time."

Hmm, let me check my calendar. Yep, all clear. "I'd love that."

———

Two hours later, Josh sat back in his chair, stretched, then scrubbed his fingers through his hair. He thought he could swing a settlement with the bank and keep Kelly's home. It would put all his negotiation and mediation skills to the test, but right now, he'd lay odds on a victory.

His assistant, Miranda, knocked before sticking her head in the door. "This report just came for you by courier. Figured it must be important." She handed him a large manila envelope with his name on it and the people locator service's return address.

"Thanks."

Anxious for the results that would reveal Blake as a fraud, but reluctant to tell Darcy the cold truth he knew the documents held, he drew the typewritten report and its exhibits from the envelope.

Skimming the pages, Josh couldn't believe it. Everything checked out; from Blake's prep-school education to his Harvard degrees; from his residency at Johns Hopkins to his fellowship at University of California, San Diego. And that scar, it was real, too. They had the medical records from Peru to prove it.

How can that be? Everything that Darcy wrote about the fictional Blake Garrett was true for the real Blake Garrett.

Josh didn't like to think of himself as a cynic, but he did think a healthy dose of skepticism had served him well from time to time. And this was one of those times.

Blake Garrett's very existence was a mystery, but Josh relished solving mysteries.

———

D arcy snuggled closer to Blake as they sat in front of the alfresco fireplace on Gansevoort's rooftop, the April evening still carrying a slight chill, especially on the roof. New York's hottest nightspot, the Gansevoort Park Rooftop boasted three levels of open-air terraces, bars, and dancing. After a fabulous dinner, the two settled in front of the fire, after-dinner drinks in hand.

Darcy thought she'd have to remind herself to ask Blake questions about his past, as if she knew nothing about him. When she developed a character, she knew everything there was to know, right down to shoe size. After all, you know what they say about men and shoe size. She'd been curious to see if his real past matched up to the one she'd written. But all evening, Blake kept her talking about herself.

She appreciated his desire to get to know her, and he really seemed to be listening, but she was beginning to feel like an honoree on a revival of *This Is Your Life*. She half-expected Regis Philbin to walk out any second. They were already up to Darcy Butler, the college years.

"So, you went to Columbia for college?" Blake's hand was making soothing circles on her back, and between the rich meal, the alcohol, and the cozy warmth of Blake's arm, she struggled a bit to stay awake.

"Hmm. Yes. Bachelor's in Creative Writing."

"And now you're a best-selling author. What's the name of your latest book?"

"The Doc—" Darcy bolted upright. *Holy cow! What am I going to tell him about* The Doctor's Dilemma? *The book from whence he sprung?* "Um, we're still working out a title."

"Oh. Well, I'll have to read it when it comes out."

No. You really don't. She had to put a stop to this topic of conversation. At least until she could work out how to best handle the fact she'd written about *him* before she even knew he existed. She covered a feigned yawn.

"Are you tired?" Blake asked.

"No, I think I'm just boring myself with all this talk about me." She smiled.

He chuckled. "I'm enjoying it." He tilted her chin up to look at him. "I could never get bored listening to you talk."

He really was perfect! What girl didn't want to hear that?

He leaned down, grazing her bottom lip with his thumb before closing in for a kiss.

She closed her eyes, and remembering what Laura had said, gave it some welly. His warm lips tasted of bourbon. A groan escaped her as he cupped her face, gently nipping at her lips. This was more like it, she thought.

She lifted her hands to his hair and slid her fingers

through the silky tresses. Still not Perfect with a capital 'P,' but you know what that say about practice. And unlike her childhood piano lessons, she'd gladly practice *this* until they got it capital 'P' Perfect.

Just as she thought about taking a major step and asking him back to her place, he pulled away. "I have an early case in the morning."

She held back a groan of disappointment.

He kissed her nose and, taking her hand, lifted her to her feet. Before they could reach the elevators though, he pulled her into his arms for a little twirl around the dance floor. And of course the guy could dance. She'd written him with an innate sense of rhythm and the grace of Fred Astaire.

"Maybe we could stay a little longer," Blake murmured against her cheek as they swayed to some inner rhythm of their own, ignoring the fast-paced music blaring from the sound system.

Ah, dancing on the rooftop under the stars. Two-for-two. Another perfect date. She felt like Ginger to Blake's Fred, and they were back in the heyday of Hollywood musicals. The only thing missing was the slinky evening gown and the white tails. Well, that and the big band music. The steady thump of Pink wasn't exactly Fred and Ginger material. Although, as Blake initiated a dip, she liked to think if Fred were still alive, he would totally get it.

CHAPTER THIRTEEN

D arcy still hadn't come down from her high. Dancing around her kitchen belting Pink's "Get This Party Started," she stopped short just before colliding with a disapproving Millie.

"Shouldn't you be upstairs working on your manuscript instead of acting like a love-struck teenager?" Millie admonished.

"Oh, come on, Millie, haven't you ever been head-over-heels infatuated with someone?" It was still too early to call it love.

Millie put her finger to her temple as if in thought, "Let me see. No." She brushed past Darcy with her teacup and set it in the sink before checking Darcy's datebook. "You have an interview with *USA Today* next Friday at eleven a.m."

Darcy sighed. "Why don't you use the iPad I bought you?"

"I prefer paper. Something I can touch and feel."

"You're a, an um, oh what's the word?"

"Your brain is drowning in love-induced dopamine, and

it's making you stupid. The word you're searching for is Luddite. And, yes, I am," she sniffed.

Darcy's phone began playing "Get Some," Laura's latest ringtone. "Hey, you!"

"My, aren't we chipper this morning. Did you get some?"

"We danced under the stars last night."

"Is that what you young people are calling it these days?" Laura replied.

"Did you call to talk about my sex life?"

"What sex life? No, I called to beg for your help."

"Why, what's up?"

"Brunch, Sunday, with Milt and Cherise. Come with me? Please? They like you better than me."

Laura's father had all the warmth of Stalin, while her mother gave more thought to her hair and wardrobe, than the feelings of her only daughter. Darcy could understand why brunch with her parents was not something Laura looked forward to. It was the only time Darcy saw Laura intimidated. No wonder she'd spent most of her childhood at Darcy's house. "Sure."

"Did I ever tell you you're my best friend in the whole world?"

"Not often enough."

———

D arcy threw a couple of twenties at the driver and told him to keep the change, then darted into the restaurant behind Laura. The sudden spring shower made finding a cab difficult and took the shine off Laura's previously well-groomed appearance. She fussed with her hair and brushed droplets of water from her lightweight suede jacket.

"Oh hell! They're already here. I wanted to stop in the ladies' room and fix my hair."

"Too late now, they've seen us," Darcy said.

"Well, my dear, don't you look like a drowned rat?" Laura's perfectly coifed mother gave her a disapproving glance. "Haven't I told you to always have an umbrella with you just in case?"

"It came up suddenly, Mrs. Armstrong," Darcy defended her friend, as she ran her fingers through her own damp locks.

Laura slid into the booth next to her mother, while Darcy took the empty seat next to her father.

"That's why you always carry an umbrella. And stop that infernal bouncing." Cherise referred to Laura's nervous tell—a jiggling leg.

A bad sign when Laura's agitation set in before her father even said a word, Darcy thought.

Laura had inherited her cool looks from her beauty-queen mother, Cherise, but where her mother was coifed within an inch of her life, Laura was polished, not plasticized. Her father, Milton, sat with his nose in his smartphone, barely acknowledging Laura's or Darcy's presence, other than to grumble that they were late.

From her father, Laura had inherited a workaholic propensity. The family's shipbuilding business had been around since the days of wooden ships. Then, luckily for the business, Mr. Armstrong's grandfather married the daughter of a steel magnate in the late-nineteenth century, just in time to switch from iron construction to steel. The business exploded, with shipbuilding operations all over the globe, making her father one of *Forbes'* "Richest Men in the World."

Laura had plenty of money. It wasn't wealth that drove

her, but a desire to prove her father wrong. Her screw-up brother had stepped into her father's shoes with the shipyard only because her father still clung to the view that women didn't run Fortune 500 companies. And even if they did, he'd never let Laura run his.

Laura signaled a passing waiter and ordered a Bloody Mary while Darcy scanned the menu.

"What brings you to Manhattan?" Laura asked her mother.

Darcy knew from experience that if you got Cherise talking about herself, she'd never stop. This greatly reduced the opportunity for Cherise to reproach her daughter over her taste in men, careers, clothing, and any other part of Laura's life she didn't approve of.

"Your father's seeing his tailor, and I thought I'd pop in to Barneys for some shopping and then to Guerlain Spa at the Waldorf."

When you spent the kind of money Milt spent on suits, your tailor gladly waited at your beck and call. Even on a Sunday.

Laura sucked down the Bloody Mary and ordered another one as her mother rattled on about the spa.

Darcy nudged Laura on the leg and shot her a look —*Watch the booze.* Laura skewered her with a look in return —*Bite me.* Darcy sighed, *right,* then signaled the waiter for another mimosa.

Milton ignored everyone at the table, too busy checking emails to interact, which was just as well. Unlike Cherise, Milton didn't criticize his daughter. He just acted as if she didn't exist. Better to be collectively disregarded than to be selectively ignored.

Cherise's one-sided conversation turned to a planned shopping excursion to Paris next month, then moved on to renovations at their home in Jackson Hole. A home they rarely used since Milton didn't like to be that far from the business' headquarters in Philadelphia.

By the time the waiter brought the food, Laura had drained her third Bloody Mary. Cherise's monologue finally wound down, leaving an awkward silence around the table, as silverware clattered against china. Darcy struggled for a safe topic of conversation, finally landing on her parents' upcoming vacation to Italy. She opened her mouth to speak—

"So, Darcy, are you dating anyone?" Cherise asked, skewering her melon slice.

Cherise could care less if Darcy were dating anyone. She had an ulterior motive for bringing up the subject. "Oh, well. . ." Pretending to swallow, Darcy telepathically pleaded with Laura to help her.

"Darcy's dating a doctor," Laura chimed in.

"Really? What's his name?"

"B–" Laura started to reply.

"Bill," Darcy interjected, "Bill Guthrie."

Laura's brow puckered in confusion.

"What's his area?"

"Proctology," Laura offered.

Darcy almost showered the table with her mouthful of mimosa.

"Oh, well, I suppose we should be thankful someone wants to practice in that, er, area."

Laura snickered, while Darcy bit her lip.

"Don't be juvenile, Laura," Cherise reproved. "At least Darcy is dating—and a doctor no less. You could do worse."

Laura rolled her eyes, shoveling a bite of breakfast crepe in her mouth.

Before Cherise climbed up on her boyfriend soapbox,

Darcy jumped in, "My parents are off to the Amalfi Coast in two weeks. They would appreciate any advice you might have."

"Oh, they'll love it, although I didn't particularly care for the . . ."

Darcy tuned out the rest as Laura mouthed a thank you.

CHAPTER FOURTEEN

The following Friday, Josh wandered the aisles of the corner grocer, mindlessly tossing items into his basket, still mulling over the enigmatic Blake Garrett, when his phone vibrated in his pocket and Queen began singing all about best friends.

"Hi, Darcy."

"Are we going to the Yankee Tavern for the Sox game tomorrow?"

"No, I'm having my peeps over." He dropped a jar of salsa into the basket.

"Am I one of your peeps?"

"You know it."

"Do you mind if I bring Blake?"

Josh cringed then realized this would give him a chance to put his cross-examination skills to good use. "No. Of course not. The more the merrier. Oh, and hey, can you bring your special pigs in a blanket? With the spicy mustard sauce?"

Darcy sighed. "Is that the only reason you're inviting me?"

"Well, not the *only* reason." Josh switched ears, readjusting his ever-growing basket of food. "What have you and God incarnate been up to lately?" As soon as the question left his mouth, he knew he didn't want to know.

"Josh, if you're going to be rude to him tomorrow, then never mind."

"You're right. I'm sorry. What have you and Dr. Perfect been up to?"

"He's been out of the country for the past week, but last Saturday night we went to the Gansevoort for dinner and then up to the roof for drinks."

"Oh. Sounds nice." Josh added a bottle of aspirin to the basket to avert a developing headache.

"Tonight we're going to a Broadway Show—*The Book of Mormon*."

"That show's sold out until like the next millennium." Josh had been trying to get tickets, and even his friend, Antoine, a concierge at the Plaza with major connections to the Broadway scene, hadn't been able to get tickets.

"I know! I'm so excited."

Josh's headache began to throb. "That's great. Listen, Darcy, I'm juggling a basket full of groceries, so I'll see you tomorrow about three."

"Okay. See you."

Maybe he'd pop a couple of those aspirins now.

———

J osh watched as Darcy staggered into his apartment lugging a tray of foil-covered pigs in a blanket, huffing from the exertion of her four-flight climb. "You have no idea the trouble I had hailing a cab with an armload of sausage. Next time I'm making them here."

She pushed past him and into the kitchen, blowing her bangs off her forehead and leaving the tantalizing aroma of Italian sausage and flaky phyllo crust in her wake.

Josh thought she looked so cute in her blue jeans and Yankees jersey, her hair pulled back into a ponytail with pieces escaping around her face.

"Where's the good doctor?"

Darcy made a face and waved her hand in dismissal. "Some excuse about having to save some guy's life. You know, same ole, same ole."

Josh laughed and rolled his eyes. "Yeah, people and their inconvenient life-threatening injuries." Although he wondered if Blake really saved lives, or if he just pretended to, the confirmatory report of his apparent stellar education notwithstanding.

"How was the show?"

"Oh, it was hilarious! I really wish you could have seen it."

Yeah, me, too, Josh thought, but without the good doctor.

"Where is everyone?"

"Oh, they'll be here soon." Josh scanned his messy kitchen. He should have stuck to the chips and dip, but he'd tried to put some other snacks together, and it kind of got out of hand. He never had parties at his apartment, unless you counted the occasional poker game with the guys, and they weren't picky. A few subs and some cold beer was generally enough to make them happy.

"Let me guess, you wanted me here early to make a plausible menu out of all this . . ." She picked up a jar of roasted red peppers and another of chocolate sauce "stuff."

Josh shrugged. "I guess I got a little carried away at the store yesterday."

"A little?"

Josh watched Darcy move efficiently around his galley kitchen as if it were her own, pulling down plates and bowls, some he didn't even remember he had. It may as well have been her own, since Darcy and his mom had furnished it. There were utensils in the drawer whose purpose eluded him. This is what it would be like if they were a couple, Josh thought, Darcy in the kitchen making order out of chaos.

"So why go to all the trouble with the food? It's just the usual crowd, right?"

"Well, Martin is bringing his fiancée, and I didn't want her to think I'm some sort of rube." In truth, he wanted to show Darcy he could be just as sophisticated as Garrett.

Darcy began plating the food in compatible combinations. The roasted red peppers joined the pickled green beans he'd also bought, along with the carrot sticks, olives, and celery he had on hand to make a nice a vegetable platter. Poking around in the refrigerator, she found some hummus and spooned it into a bowl and placed it in the center of the platter. "*Voila!*"

Josh plucked an olive off the tray and popped it into Darcy's mouth.

Munching on the olive, Darcy turned to raid the fridge again. "Ah! Strawberries. Perfect. Wash them and pat them dry, while I get the grapes out of the fridge and we can put together a cheese platter." Digging around in the cupboards, she pulled out a cheese board. "This looks as if it's never been used."

"It was a gift." Josh shrugged. "I think I have a cheddar in the fridge that came from a gift basket." Josh watched as Darcy opened the box of crackers he'd set on the counter and spread them on the cheese board.

"Now, put the strawberries on this plate, and pour the

chocolate sauce into a bowl. Who doesn't love strawberries dipped in chocolate?" Her eyes sparkled with enthusiasm as she bit into the juicy chocolate-covered strawberry she'd snagged.

He touched her arm. "Thanks, Darcy, this is great, really." The temptation to kiss the chocolate from her lips tested his resolve. He held her gaze a moment before the intercom buzzed, breaking the spell.

———

*W*hat was that? Darcy wondered. She thought for a moment Josh had wanted to kiss her. And she'd wanted him to.

Pfft.

Josh reached over and pressed the button, "Yeah?"

"Hey, man, it's Chris and Mark."

"Come on up."

Josh walked over to open his apartment door a crack before rejoining Darcy in the kitchen.

"Help me carry some things out," she instructed.

He grabbed the veggie tray and followed her to the living room, where she cleared away magazines and other clutter from the coffee table.

By the time the guys got to the door, a substantial spread greeted them.

"Brought some beer." Chris proudly held up a six-pack of what must have been on sale. "Whoa! Did you invite the Mayor or something?" he asked, taking in the smorgasbord.

"No. I just thought it'd be nice to have some *good* food for a change," Josh said with a hint of defensiveness.

"Are those strawberries . . . and chocolate?" Mark

reached over for a strawberry just as Darcy smacked his hand.

"Wait for the other guests."

"Hey! That hurt."

"It wasn't meant to tickle." She adjusted the strawberries on the platter.

"Heard from Paige?" Mark asked as he rubbed his offended hand.

"Who's Paige?" Darcy asked.

"A lovely little Southern Belle who picked Josh up the other night."

"Oh really?" Darcy raised a questioning brow in Josh's direction, surprised that he was seeing someone and hadn't told her. She pointedly ignored the hollow ache in her stomach at the thought of Josh and a girl. *Hunger pangs.*

"Yeah, but she's gone back to Alabama."

Mark began an off-key rendition of "Sweet Home Alabama."

The intercom buzzed again and Josh announced that Martin and Cindy were on the way up, effectively ending the Paige discussion.

"Laura's coming over later," Darcy warned.

"Since when does she like baseball?" Josh turned a jaundiced eye on Darcy.

"She doesn't, but she just broke it off with Ewan, and she's a little down, so I didn't want her to be alone."

"That's a new one. A shark who feels remorse for killing the meal it just ate."

Darcy punched Josh's arm. "Don't be mean."

Cindy and Martin came in and after the introductions were made, the party began in earnest with the first pitch from the Red Sox and everyone settled in to nosh and cheer on the "Bronx Bombers."

The Yanks were down by three in the bottom of the second, but no one seemed to mind as plates were filled again and again.

Chris, his plate piled high with goodies, said, "Okay Josh, I know you didn't pull this together, so I'm guessing we have Darcy to thank for this gastronomical feast." He held up one of Darcy's gourmet pigs in a blanket smothered with spicy mustard sauce.

Insulted, Josh shot back, "Hey, I did *buy* most of the food."

Mark reached for another strawberry, liberally dunking it in the chocolate, before popping it into his mouth. "I could get used to this. Thanks, Darcy."

"Don't expect this spread for the next poker game," Josh informed them as the intercom buzzed. "That'll be the great white huntress." He pressed the button. "Come on up."

One ball and two strikes later, Josh looked up from the game as Laura sauntered in. "Is it me, or is it getting colder in here?"

"Shark."

"Man-eater."

Darcy rolled her eyes at what had become the standard form of greeting between Josh and Laura. Even though Laura chaired the marketing committee for Josh's fundraising gala, they otherwise only tolerated one another's presence for her sake. She wondered how they managed to get anything done for the gala.

"Why won't sharks attack lawyers?" Laura directed the question at Josh.

"Professional courtesy," Josh replied blandly, never taking his eyes off the screen.

Laura muttered a curse and dropped down onto the sofa next to Darcy.

The rest of the gang was used to it, but poor Cindy appeared confused. Darcy would explain it to her later. They were also used to Laura's tendency to overdress for occasions.

This time she wore a pair of snug black pedal pushers, a turquoise halter top, and a bright pink pair of spike-heel platforms, accessorized with some bold jewelry . . . along with her hard-to-miss black hand brace. Her blond hair was pulled back into a sleek ponytail. She looked fabulous.

"Flip-off any cab drivers lately?" Josh asked, eyeing her brace and chuckling.

Laura gestured to Josh with the aforementioned injured digit before leveling an accusatory glare on Darcy. "You just *had* to tell him, didn't you?"

Darcy lifted a shoulder in response. "Oh come on. You have to admit now that it was pretty funny."

"No, I really don't," Laura muttered.

Darcy laughed and, draping an arm over her best friend's shoulder, asked, "Aren't you glad you came?"

CHAPTER FIFTEEN

A t the seventh-inning stretch, with the Yankees up by two, Josh muted the TV and everyone stood to sing "Take Me Out To The Ball Game" while Laura looked on as if she'd just entered *The Twilight Zone*. "You people really need to get a life."

In the end, the Yankees lost by one, but everyone's spirits were high as they took their leave.

"Man," Mark said as he rubbed his flat stomach. "That should hold me for at least another couple hours. Do this again for tomorrow's game?" he asked Josh, hopeful.

"Can't. Got to go into the office and work on the McMillan case."

Chris draped an arm around Darcy's shoulders. "Any time you need another best friend, I'm available."

"I'll keep that in mind," Darcy replied as she politely removed Chris' hand from her shoulder.

Martin took Josh aside. "Cindy was impressed. She thinks you're some sort of gourmand. Don't worry, your secret's safe with me." He slapped Josh on the back before grabbing Cindy's hand. "Let's go."

Cindy smiled and waved at everyone. "See you at the shower." Cindy had invited Darcy and Laura to her bridal shower next month, and the wedding the month after that.

Laura brought up the rear. "Well, that's two hours of my life I'll never get back."

"Yeah, that's too bad. Your clients probably say the same thing."

Laura stuck her tongue out at Josh.

"No thanks. Don't know where that tongue's been."

"You leaving?" Laura asked Darcy, giving Josh the evil eye.

"No, I'll help clean up. I'll call you later." She kissed Laura's cheek before closing the door quietly behind her.

Josh and Darcy worked companionably, putting away the leftovers—what little there was—washing the dishes, and wiping down his microscopic counters.

He'd just decided to ask her if she'd like to hit the batting cage with him, when her phone signaled an incoming text.

Snatching it up, she said, "It's from Blake. He said the surgery went well and the guy is stable." She texted something back, a soft smile triggering the dimple in her cheek.

Josh's chest tightened. Would she ever look at him like that?

Momentarily her phone chimed again and her face split into a big grin as she read the message. "He wants me to meet him at Annisa. My God, I must look a fright. Gotta go, Josh. I had fun. We should do this for away games more often. My place next time." She grabbed her purse. "I'll pick up my platter later." She bussed his cheek. "See ya."

"Yeah. See ya," Josh muttered to the now-closed door.

———

D arcy stepped out of the cab in the West Village where Blake said to meet him. She'd dashed home, and with no time to redo her hair, she'd pulled it back in a messy-chic twist, swiped on some makeup, grabbed a slinky little black dress out of her closet, and pulled on some strappy sandals. A spritz of perfume, and she was out the door in record time.

After paying the driver, she looked around for Blake, but Dr. Perfect was nowhere in sight. She glanced at her watch and frowned. Maybe she'd gotten the time wrong. Just as she'd made up her mind to check inside the restaurant, a sultry voice stopped her.

"Your date should be shot for keeping you waiting." Blake stood, hands in his pants pockets, a smoldering heat in his eyes.

"Perhaps, but he's a brilliant surgeon and I wouldn't want to rob the world of his life-saving skills." She lifted a shoulder. "That would just be selfish." She gave him the once-over, and liked what she saw. Navy slacks, white dress shirt, no tie. A man who was comfortable in his skin and his clothes.

"Then, by all means, let him live, if only to see you in that dress." Blake approached her, circled her like a shark circling its meal, and gave a soft whistle. "That's some dress."

He grazed his fingertips down her bare back, raising goosebumps on her flesh.

"Oh, you know," she tittered nervously, "just a little something I threw on." *Literally.*

He pulled her into his arms and kissed her. "I've been thinking about you all day. Sorry I missed the party."

Party? What party? Oh yeah. Yankees. Baseball. "It's okay. You were busy saving lives. How is he?"

"He's got a long road ahead of him."

"Better that than a dead end."

"No argument there. Shall we eat or would you like to take a walk first?"

Thinking of all the food she'd indulged in this afternoon, she requested the walk first.

Blake placed her hand in the crook of his arm, and headed in the direction of Hudson River Park. The tree-lined streets of the West Village, with their quaint brownstones and loft apartments, almost made you forget you were in New York. Residents strolled the sidewalks, some walking dogs, others with kids in tow. It was one of Darcy's favorite spots, aside from her own Park Slope, of course.

"Should we take up where we left off, Darcy Butler, college girl?"

Darcy giggled. "How about we talk about Blake Garrett, college boy? I bet you were cute in your Harvard tie." *Whoops!* She knew the minute she said it, she'd slipped.

He pulled back. "How'd you know I went to Harvard?"

"You seemed like a Harvard man, I guess."

"Good guess."

"You bet." Breathing a sigh of relief for having covered her flub, she continued. "Did you play sports?" Of course he did. Crew and lacrosse, as any self-respecting Crimson would.

"Crewed and played lacrosse."

"What else did you do for fun?"

"The usual college activities. Sports, women, and beer." He shot a glance her way.

"What about baseball?"

"What about it?"

"Did you go to any games while you were in Boston?" A terrible thought suddenly occurred to her. "You're not a Red Sox fan, are you?" She narrowed her eyes in suspicion.

He chuckled. "Yes, I went to some games, and no, I'm not a Sox fan."

Of course he wasn't. She'd never write a hero who was a Red Sox fan. *Sacrilege!*

"You like baseball, right?"

"More than life itself." The corner of his mouth lifted in a grin.

"Would you like to go with me to the Yankees game next week?" she asked, hopeful.

"Sure, if you'd like."

"Great. You remember Josh—you met him at the opera?"

"Yes," Blake said, a sardonic smile teasing the corners of his mouth. "He doesn't care for me."

"That's not true," Darcy protested. "You just need to get to know him. Anyway, I'll get Josh's ticket from him."

"Don't take the man's ticket. That only gives him even more reason to dislike me. I have a friend with a box."

Darcy wasn't sure about sitting in a box rather than the seats, but how bad could it be? She'd be with Blake watching her beloved Yankees smoke the Mets.

"Do you mind that I hang out with Josh, you know, go to the Yankees games and things?"

"Mind? Why should I mind? You were friends long before I came along. Of course I don't mind."

Darcy melted. *He's so understanding. He's definitely perfect.* She loved a man so sure of his place in the world that he didn't need to be jealous.

They rambled along a few more minutes talking about Blake's residency at Johns Hopkins and then his time in San

Diego, before he turned Darcy toward him, and said, "Now. Enough about me." He placed a soft kiss on her lips, drawing a sigh from her.

She slid her hands up his back to his hair, deepening the kiss. Still not Perfect, she thought, but far from disappointing.

He gently pulled back, looking around at the families and other couples on the street. "We'd better go eat before we make a spectacle of ourselves."

CHAPTER SIXTEEN

Monday afternoon, Josh sat at the kitchen table in Kelly's cozy Harlem townhouse, a cup of coffee in his hand, and a file folder and legal pad at his elbow. Kelly nervously chewed her lower lip, clearly afraid he was there to tell her saving her home was a lost cause.

He reached across the table and tentatively covered her hand with his. "Kelly, I can't make any promises, but I think we can work this out with the bank if you can be patient a little longer."

The cords of tension in her neck released and her eyes filled with tears. "Really?"

"Really."

The door slammed and Kelly's son, Daniel, lumbered into the kitchen, backpack slung over his shoulder. He wore baggy jeans and a T-shirt, a ball chain visible at his neck from what Josh assumed were his father's dog tags. He stopped short when he saw Josh holding his mother's hand. He glanced up at his mother's face then glared at Josh.

"How was school?" Kelly gingerly pulled her hand out of Josh's grasp.

"Great." His flat tone belied the superlative.

"Daniel, why don't you go shoot some baskets while Mr. Ryan and I finish up, then I'll make you a snack?"

"The rim's coming down, remember." There was no hiding the irritation in his voice.

"Oh, hey, I can check it out before I leave," Josh offered. "Maybe I can fix it."

Josh thought he saw a flash of surprise in Daniel's eyes before the resentment flared again. "Don't bother. They're just going to kick us out anyway." He charged from the room and up the stairs, leaving a tense silence in the room.

"Sorry about that. He's been so angry since Dan died." She walked to the doorway and looked up the stairs. "He's getting counseling, but it doesn't seem to be helping."

"Don't worry about it. Maybe what he needs more than anything right now is to know his home is safe. Just a few more weeks and we should be able to make that a reality." Josh gathered his things and slipped them into a leather messenger bag.

"Thanks, Mr. Ryan. I'll never be able to repay you for everything you're doing."

"You can start by calling me Josh."

"Right, Josh." She gave him a warm smile.

"Now, if you have a toolbox and a ladder, I'd be happy to take a look at that rim."

———

On the subway ride back to the office, Josh couldn't get his mind off Daniel. In some ways, he could relate to Daniel's resentment. While his father hadn't been killed in service to his country, he had nonetheless lost his father when he was Daniel's age. His father had died of a massive heart attack at the age of forty-two.

Not that his father had been much of a father while he was alive. Josh's memories consisted mainly of frequent arguments between his parents. Arguments that a young Josh had tried hard to mediate. When his parents weren't fighting, they were hardly the loving couple. His father wasn't abusive, just unapproachable, indifferent. When his father died, Josh felt only relief. You couldn't really miss what you never had.

Janet Ryan had worked hard, but without his father's support, his mother's bank-teller salary often fell short, even with the small life insurance policy his father left them. Josh mowed lawns on weekends, and as soon as he was old enough, got a job bagging groceries at the local supermarket. But his mother had always insisted his grades not suffer, and if they had to give up meat a couple of times a week, he'd quit his job before she'd let his GPA slip.

One thing she wouldn't let him quit was baseball. It was sports, especially baseball, that kept Josh out of trouble, gave him confidence, taught him team work, fair play, discipline, and the benefit of hard work. The fact that his coaches served as role models only sweetened the deal.

A natural hitter, they'd said, with an arm like Hall-of-Famer Ozzie Smith, his mother thought it might be his path to college. A baseball scholarship would be the vehicle for a better life, a successful life.

But much to her and Josh's surprise, he'd landed an academic scholarship, first to NYU and then to Columbia Law. The day he'd graduated from law school at the top of his class, his mother said nothing could ever make her happier or more proud. That meant more to him than all the accolades he'd earned in law school.

When the train reached his stop, he exited the car and climbed the steps to the busy street above. He had to find a way to reach Daniel, and sports might be just the ticket. Maybe he could even enlist Daniel's help with the youth baseball team he coached. Nothing made you forget your own problems like helping others.

Josh checked his voicemail as he walked the three blocks back to his office. One from a stuffy-nosed Miranda letting him know she was going home sick; the other, an awkward one from Darcy.

"Hi, Josh, um, Blake asked me to join him in a friend's box for the game on Saturday, so you can use the other ticket. I hope you don't mind. Anyway, if I don't see you, I'll leave it at the Will Call window. Okay, see ya. Bye."

Just great. He and Darcy hadn't missed a Yankees home game together in years. Blake had only been in her life a month and she was already ditching him.

It wasn't as if he'd have trouble finding someone to go with him. In fact, Chris and Mark might come to fisticuffs over who got to go. But, dammit. He preferred going with Darcy.

Then he thought of Daniel. This would be the perfect opportunity to begin the bonding process. After all, what kid didn't love baseball?

Dodging pedestrian traffic, Josh dialed Kelly's number and got her voicemail. He left a message asking if Daniel could go, and explained he'd take the subway to Harlem, pick up Daniel, and the two of them would head to Yankee Stadium for some guy time, starting with the pre-game batting practice ritual.

Josh tucked his phone in his pocket. The thought of some male-bonding time with Daniel eased some of the disappointment of losing Darcy's company.

———

Saturday's game against the Mets would be a rowdy one. The Subway Series, as the inner-city rivalry was called, would pack the subways it was named for, so Josh wanted to leave early.

He knocked on Kelly's door. The door flew open and Kelly stood there, a dishtowel thrown over her shoulder, looking as if she were the one going to her first live baseball game, instead of her son.

"Hi, Josh! Come in. Daniel's almost ready." Her breathless enthusiasm made him smile.

"Daniel, come on," she shouted up the stairs. "Josh is here." Turning to Josh, she asked, "Can I get you some coffee?"

"No. Thanks."

Daniel clomped down the stairs, taking his time. He could have used a little of his mother's enthusiasm, Josh thought. Dressed in a fatigue jacket two sizes too big, and an off-kilter baseball cap, Daniel's face read like a sullen teenager-to-be.

Kelly walked over and straightened his cap. "You ready for the game?"

"Whatever." Daniel rolled his eyes.

Her smile falsely bright, she continued to gush about how much fun he would have.

"If it's okay, I'll have him home after dinner." Josh opened the front door.

"Oh, sure. You two just have a good time."

Kelly tried to kiss Daniel, but he pulled back with an embarrassed, "Jeez, Mom."

As Josh led Daniel toward the subway, he'd have thought he was leading him to a prison cell. He spoke little on the train ride, only to answer direct questions with one-word answers. *Fine. Whatever. Nothing.*

Once they reached the stadium, however, Josh could feel Daniel's excitement build, although Daniel tried to play it cool.

He bought Daniel a program and while they watched batting practice, Daniel asked a few questions about the players, their positions and their stats, but other than that, the kid just seemed to take it all in.

When they finally took their seats, they were loaded down with hotdogs, nachos, peanuts, and soda. The Mets were up first, and after half a soda and the first few pitches, Daniel appeared to be having a good time, whether he wanted to or not.

Sabathia retired the first two batters, then the Mets hit a pop-up and Jones caught it to end the inning.

"These are awesome seats," Daniel said. "How'd you get 'em?"

"My best friend and I share season tickets."

"Sweet. How come he's missing such a big game?" Daniel asked, his brow furrowed with confusion.

"*She* is in one of those luxury boxes, there." Josh pointed his finger along the third baseline.

"Your best friend is a *girl*?"

"Yep." Cano came up to bat.

"That's weird."

Josh chuckled.

After Cano's base hit, Daniel said, "I'd rather be in the stands."

"You know it, dude!" And he'd bet his Derek Jeter-autographed fielders cap that Darcy would too.

CHAPTER SEVENTEEN

Darcy sat in the luxury box, surrounded by some of New York's *ton,* trying to enjoy the game and guiltily wishing she was in her own seat in the stands. Watching from the box was definitely not all that.

First, no one actually *watched* the game. They were all glad-handing, schmoozing, and otherwise kissing-up. The box's owner was none other than hotel magnate Seymour Holbrook, who had thrown his hat in the ring for U.S. Senate, and everyone wanted a piece.

Second, the food. *I mean, who served non-PC duck liver pâté at a baseball game? Ew!* Where were the hotdogs? The peanuts? The warm beer?

Third, who dressed up for a baseball game? There were women in the box dressed like they were at a gallery opening.

When Blake picked her up for the game, she thought she'd overdressed wearing blue crop pants, navy skimmers, and her white Yankees polo, until she saw him in gray slacks, white open-collared shirt, and navy blazer. Of course, he'd looked über sexy. Tan neck and throat, broad shoulders, muscular thighs encased in expensive tropical-weight wool. The man knew how to dress. But, come on, it was a baseball game, for heaven's sake.

Her eyes roamed the crowded space before she found him. Catching his eye as he spoke to the CEO of some bank whose name she'd forgotten, she smiled at him. He winked back and her insides melted. *Okay.* Maybe this wasn't so bad after all.

She picked up her crudité and delicately stuffed it into her mouth. As she watched Jeter's foul sail toward the first-base stands, right at her and Josh's seats, she nearly choked before she could swallow.

On the big screen she saw Josh jump up and snatch the ball out of the air and away from all the other outstretched hands, fabulous shortstop that he was. After much high-fiving and backslaps from the crowd, Josh handed the ball to some kid in camo.

A wave of disappointment washed over her. A foul ball had finally come their way, and she wasn't there! Aghast, all she could do was stand there and swallow both her carrot stick and her frustration.

———

Josh and Daniel stepped into their assigned batting cage. Josh smiled as Daniel carefully wrapped the foul ball in his jacket before placing it on a bench. He'd politely thanked Josh for the foul ball, but other than that hadn't shown any real excitement over it. Playing it cool again.

After fitting Daniel with a batter's helmet, he handed him a bat and told him to take a few practice swings while he adjusted the machine. Josh frowned as he watched

Daniel take some hard swings. The kid needed to loosen up a bit.

"Okay. You're all set."

After a few missed swings, Josh stepped up. "Daniel, relax. You're swinging too hard."

Daniel just ignored him and swung a few more times, whiffing past the ball, his face a mask of frustration.

"Daniel, here, let me show you."

"I can do it. I don't need your help."

Josh backed off. A couple more desperate swings. The kid swung with all the anger and frustration of a twelve-year-old who'd been handed a raw deal. "Come on, Daniel, you're going to hurt yourself."

Daniel glared at Josh, his face red from his exertion. "You don't want to help me. You just want to tap my mom and you're using me to do it!"

Josh swallowed the anger surging through him, and put on his best lawyer face. "First of all, that's no way to talk about your mother. Second, I am only trying to help you and your mother stay in your home."

"Yeah, well, she's *my* mom. I can talk about her any way I want." He'd assumed a belligerent stance. "And saving our home is a lost cause."

"Daniel, let's get one thing straight. You talk about your mom like that again, and I won't hesitate to put you in a headlock until you remember your manners."

The boy's eyes spit fire and his jaw jutted out in defiance.

"Now, your mother is my client. I don't have . . . relationships with clients."

"Yeah, right. I saw you holding her hand."

"What you saw was one human being comforting

another. Nothing more. I respect your mom. And as the man of the house, I respect you."

Confusion skittered across Daniel's face.

Josh reached out for the bat and taking it from him, pulled a reluctant Daniel down on the bench. "Do you know what ethics are?"

Daniel frowned. "My dad said ethics are what you follow to be a good person."

"That's a good definition. It's a notion of what's right and wrong. As a lawyer, I'm bound by a certain code of ethics. One thing the code says is I can't have a relationship with a client unless that relationship started before she became a client."

Josh waited as Daniel gave it some thought. "So, just as your father taught you to understand the difference between right and wrong, my mother taught me the same thing. She also taught me that actions have consequences, and the consequences of unethical actions were not usually pleasant. She might be small, but my mother packed a wallop." Josh smiled. "I carry those lessons with me today. I may not always get it right, but I always try my very best to make my mother proud."

"Yeah, my mom packs a pretty good wallop, too." He frowned at some memory. "What about your dad? Did he teach you anything?"

Yeah, he taught me how not *to behave,* Josh thought. "I lost my dad when I was your age."

Daniel's eyes grew wide. "You mean your dad died too?"

"Yeah." Josh picked up the bat and turned it in his hands.

"Oh." Daniel hesitated a moment. "Do you want to talk about it?"

"Not really." But he was glad to finally get Daniel talking.

"Okay. That's cool." Daniel nodded in understanding.

"What I want to do is knock some balls out of the park." He shot Daniel a smile as he stood. Grabbing the batter's helmet, he shoved it down on his head, before turning toward the batter's box.

"Hey, Josh?" Daniel twirled the foul ball in his hands.

"Yeah?"

"Did you mean it when you said I was the man of the house?"

"Goes without saying."

A grin spread across the boy's face. The first real smile Josh had seen all day, or ever, for that matter.

"Thanks again for the foul ball."

Josh stepped into the batter's box feeling like he could conquer the world. "You got it, dude."

———

J osh set aside the case he'd been analyzing when he recognized Darcy's number on his phone.

"'Sup, Sunshine?" Josh turned to look out his window at the gloomy skies.

"My, you're in a good mood for a rainy day."

"I kept a single mom with two kids from being evicted today."

"Congrats. Nice snag at the game on Saturday, by the way."

"You saw, huh?"

"Just me and the other fifty thousand fans at the game. Not to mention the replays on ESPN."

"No shit? I missed that." Mark and Chris were probably

green with envy. The fact that they were in court today explained why he hadn't heard.

"Who was the boy you gave it to?"

Josh explained, without violating attorney-client privilege, about Daniel.

"That's a nice thing you did, Josh. Your thoughtfulness has robbed me of an opportunity to rag you for not giving the ball to your best friend in the whole world."

"If my best friend in the whole world hadn't been rubbing elbows with New York's aristocracy, she might have that foul ball in her possession right now. How was it?"

"Oh, it was great!"

Josh hesitated to ask, "So, does that mean you'll be sitting in the box more often?"

"Um, no, I don't think so."

Josh released a mental sigh of relief. "Hey, some of us are going to the South Street Seaport Friday night, grab some seafood. Want to join?"

"I can't. I'm going to a gallery event with Blake on Friday. Rain check?"

"Sure. Some other time then."

"All right. Gotta run. Talk to you soon."

"Yep." Josh hung up with phone with a groan. The unthinkable had finally happened. Darcy had another man in her life who'd inexplicably come straight from her own vivid idealistic imagination. How could he ever compete with a guy who took her to gallery openings and Broadway shows, *and* had friends with box seats at Yankee Stadium?

CHAPTER EIGHTEEN

On Friday evening, Darcy stood in a trendy Chelsea art gallery in front of an enormous black canvas painted with a single white dot in the very center. The plaque below it read: MAN'S QUEST FOR ENLIGHTENMENT.

Huh. Taking a sip of her wine, she tilted her head. *Maybe it's just me, but I don't feel enlightened.* A warm hand settled on her shoulder.

"Do you like this one?" Blake asked, gesturing with his wine glass. "I'm looking for a piece for my study."

"Um, well, I think we should keep looking." There had to be something here that made sense to her. She glanced around, past the eccentric artists, with their multi-colored hair, and the chichi art-collector types, at the display of pricey paintings, most featuring unrecognizable objects, hoping to spot something that resembled art in her mind.

And definitely *not* the one semi-recognizable behemoth that looked suspiciously like a magnified male anatomical part, which should definitely *not* be on display at a children's charity fundraiser. The plaque under that one read:

CAREFUL. OBJECTS IN THIS PAINTING MAY APPEAR LARGER THAN THEY ARE.

Whew. So glad they cleared that up. Where was a nice Renoir when you needed one?

While admittedly Philistine, she didn't allow her opinion of the art, and she used that term loosely, to taint her endorsement of the charitable purpose of the showing. A percentage of the proceeds raised from that night's sale of the art would benefit the Art for Art's Sake program, which supported children's art courses at the city's many after-school programs.

Thus, if in the end, Blake chose to purchase The Dot, at least a portion of the cool six-digit selling price would go to a worthwhile cause.

"Mongrel is an up-and-coming artist." Blake drew Darcy's attention back to The Dot. "Critics are calling his work emotional and intense."

"Mongrel? Seriously? His mother must have *really* hated him."

Blake laughed. "It's a moniker."

"I knew that," she said with a sheepish grin. But really, who *willingly* chooses a synonym for mutt as a nickname?

"Mark my words, one day his work will sell for millions."

Darcy just chose to smile in response. *If you say so.* Her gaze traveled back to The Dot. If that was emotional and intense, she'd hate to see dispassionate and listless.

———

B lake dropped the equivalent of her mortgage on two paintings, including Mongrel's Dot, and another painting of a gray square amid a background of violent purple, called BLANK SLATE.

After arranging for the delivery of his purchases to his apartment, they took a romantic stroll along the High Line. Built on an old freight line above Manhattan's Westside streets, the High Line offered a low-flying bird's-eye view of the Hudson and New York's skyline.

On a soft spring evening, they ambled, hand in hand, through the Chelsea Grasslands with its many and varied flowers in bloom, toward the Meatpacking District, a one-time destination of the historic elevated trains that once traveled the thirty-foot high tracks.

With no destination in mind and no particular time to get there, they stopped frequently for a closer look at the flowers, to point out this landmark or that tableau on the street below, or for no other reason than to kiss. The practice was definitely paying off. The goal of the Perfect Kiss seemed imminently attainable.

Blake gently cradled Darcy's face in his brilliant surgeon's hands, and gazed into her eyes. "Did I tell you how beautiful you look tonight?"

"Yes," Darcy breathed. Mesmerized by the indigo blue of his eyes, she struggled to cobble together a subject and verb to form a sentence. "But you can tell me again if you like. I'm not one of those picky women who mind if you repeat yourself."

The corner of his mouth twitched. "All right." His hands slid to either side of her neck, their warmth sending tingles down her spine. "You are so beautiful. You were the only true work of art in that gallery tonight."

Darcy blinked. *Wow. Good one.* That line was definitely going in the next book.

———

Putting the finishing touches on the chocolate chip mascarpone cupcakes topped with rich chocolate ganache frosting she'd made for Cindy's bridal shower, Darcy realized for the first time in her adult life, she wasn't looking for the flaws in her current, dare she say it?, boyfriend. As if she'd find any. The fact that she'd even gotten beyond a first date said a lot about her feelings for Blake. But then again, he *was* made to order.

After dinner at a swanky restaurant in the Meatpacking District, Blake had taken her to his elegantly furnished penthouse, ostensibly to show her where he planned to hang his recent purchases. The old 'would you like to come up and see my etchings' ploy.

She had fully expected him to put the moves on her once the excuse for the visit was out of the way. And let's face it, she wouldn't have stopped him if he had. But instead, he'd offered her a fine tawny port and a stunning view of Central Park from his basketball-court-sized terrace.

Even so, she had welcomed the opportunity to check out his place. While not her taste, his décor suited his persona, and fit the image she'd had in mind when she'd written him. All clean lines, sleek surfaces, and muted colors. Very tidy and masculine.

He had eclectic taste in art. Everything from abstract modern pieces similar to what he'd purchased at the gallery to Picasso-like cubist works, and chaotic drip paintings not unlike Pollock's. Only, to her astonishment, upon closer inspection she'd discovered that the Picasso-*like* painting was, in fact, a Picasso.

Admittedly, she'd been disappointed at first by his honorable intentions, and while her ego had suffered a minor ding, looking back, she appreciated his gentlemanly restraint. Maybe a little old-fashioned, practically prehistoric by Laura's standards, and certainly out of step with the more adventurous heroines she created, Darcy preferred a strong emotional connection before taking the relationship up a notch, or five.

That wasn't to say things didn't get a little amorous beneath the stars. She smiled at the memory, and licking the creamy chocolate from her fingers, placed a lid on the cupcake carrier, grabbed her gift, her purse, and her keys, and walked out to her stoop to wait for Laura to pick her up.

Notwithstanding the pretentious patrons at the art gallery, well, that, and the missed foul ball opportunity the previous week, Blake was batting a thousand on his dates.

But with the upcoming release of *The Doctor's Dilemma* inching closer every day, and the promotional activities she'd undertake soon, she had her own thorny dilemma. As Laura slid up to the curb in her flashy red Fiat 500 (she'd worked on their latest ad campaign), Darcy wondered how she was going to explain to him, and everyone else, how the guy she's been dating came to be the hero in her latest novel. Or worse yet, vice versa.

———

Amid the champagne punch, elegant wedding-themed wrapping paper, frilly bows, and feminine laughter, Darcy watched wistfully as Cindy, seated in the chair of honor, wearing a sketchy Halloween-costume-of-a-bridal-veil, opened her gifts. She let her imagination take over, and suddenly it was her bridal shower. And the lucky groom? Why, Blake, of course.

The real bride-to-be blushed fifty shades of red when

she pulled the *Fifty Shades of Grey* trilogy from the chic white gift bag.

Darcy rolled her eyes. She didn't have to ask who gave her that as a gift. "Jeez, Laura."

"What? I think of it as a how-to manual. Except in my world the roles are reversed."

Hoots of approval, followed by howls of laughter, only made Cindy blush all the more. But Darcy thought she looked beautiful. She leaned over and whispered that exact sentiment to Laura, who glanced over at Cindy and waved her hand in the air as she replied. "She does have that certain . . . *je ne sais quoi.*"

Darcy drew back with a snort. "Let me guess, a Frenchman this time."

"*Oui. François.*" Laura sipped from her champagne glass. "He's a sculptor. And looks like Michelangelo's *David.*"

"What do you do? Hang out in front of the U.N.?"

"No, but that's not a bad idea, actually. Anyway, François says he wants to sculpt me." Laura's face split into a wide dreamy grin.

"I bet he does."

"So, what's the story on you and Dr. Perfect? You two playing doctor yet?"

"If we were, I wouldn't tell you."

"Liar. And you just did."

"What do you mean?"

"The fact that you didn't blush the same shade as our bride over there when you answered." Laura popped a delicate petit four into her mouth then shot Darcy a knowing smirk.

"Remind me again why I've stayed friends with you since kindergarten?"

"Aw, come on. You know it's because we have a life-long *womance* going." She gave Darcy a friendly shoulder bump.

"Who are you? Elmer Fudd? What the hell's a *womance*?"

"You know, a girl-crush. A straight female romance—the female version of a *bromance*." At Darcy's continued skeptical expression, Laura said, "I love you, girlfriend."

And at the exact moment of Laura's declaration, a lull in the party chatter turned into a stunned silence, before the chocolate-and-champagne-buzzed gaggle erupted into a schmaltzy chorus of "Aws."

CHAPTER NINETEEN

The remainder of May flew by in a blur. Between Blake's busy social calendar and Darcy's busy promotion schedule, work on her next novel suffered. Even on the occasions Blake had to leave for parts unknown to perform surgery, she had difficulty keeping her mind on her work. Dominic, the dashing rough-around-the-edges daredevil stunt-man with the tortured past, began taking on Blake's more polished characteristics. She'd used the delete key so often that the word 'Delete' had rubbed off.

Add to that the somewhat strained relationship with Josh, and she had a lot on her mind. Her work wasn't the only thing suffering from her busy schedule. Josh had called several times about grabbing some dinner or walking through Brooklyn and into Down Under the Manhattan Bridge Overpass (popularly referred to as Dumbo) and meeting her, one of their favorite pastimes—next to watching the Yankees, that is—but she'd already had plans with Blake.

Last time Blake was out of town, she'd called Josh to ask if he wanted to catch a movie or something, but he'd brushed her off with some excuse about working late. Not that she blamed him. She hadn't exactly been available for him. Turns out it was tough juggling work, a boyfriend, *and* friends.

Laura was no exception. With François out of the picture—apparently sculptors were *very* tactile, and enjoyed touching things, especially beautiful women . . . lots of them —she was lonely. As a serial monogamist, Laura also demanded the same from her lovers, even for her short-term relationships. Darcy had had little time to be there for her until the next prey, *er*, hunk came along to take her mind off François.

And now she had no idea if Blake would be home for Memorial Weekend, which was only two days away. Well, at least she'd have time to see her friends. If they'd have her.

A contentious conversation with Gloria that morning about an interview with the *Today Show* hadn't helped her state of mind. She didn't oppose the interview, even though she dreaded it. Not when it would sell more books. She just hadn't figured out how to talk about the hero, especially since she happened to be dating him.

Feeling pissy and generally out of sorts, she abandoned her writing for more relaxing pursuits: shopping and an afternoon at Elizabeth Arden.

———

Early Saturday morning found Darcy on her hands and knees in her little backyard, elbow-deep in garden soil, planting bright red petunias. When the house phone rang, she'd almost decided to let it go to voicemail, before she realized it could be Blake, and kicked it into high gear. Yanking off the gardening gloves, and taking her back steps two at a time, she answered the phone with a breathless, "Hello."

"Darcy, are you all right?"

Darcy tried to hide her disappoint. "Oh, hi, Mom."

"Well, don't sound so excited."

"Sorry, I was hoping it was—"

"Blake?"

"Yes," she said, stunned. "How'd you know?"

"Since my own daughter won't tell me she's seeing someone, I had to hear it from Gloria." Her mother sighed gustily on the other end.

"I was going to. I've just been so busy." Busy keeping *Blake a secret until I could work out a plan.*

"Uh-huh. With Blake."

"And the new book promotion, and my work-in-progress," Darcy added in a defensive tone.

"When am I going to meet this Blake?"

"Soon." Darcy's phone beeped, notifying her of another call. "Mom, I've got to go. That's Blake calling now. Love you. Bye." She clicked over to Blake.

"Blake?"

"I just arrived in New York late last night. Have any plans today?"

"Um, no."

"I'm thinking about lobster tonight."

"Sounds great! Where should we go?"

"Maine."

"Say what?"

"When you're in the mood for lobster, where better to go than Maine?"

Darcy just laughed. "Where, indeed."

———

Never having flown on a private jet, Darcy didn't know what to expect, but the luxurious accommodations didn't disappoint. Buff leather captain's chairs, plush carpet, even a corner sofa, completed the interior. The friendly flight attendant offered chilled mimosas and hors d'oeuvres, while the pilot delivered a smooth flight. Darcy could definitely get used to this pampered lifestyle.

She'd fussed with her appearance for over an hour, trying to decide what to wear. A private jet seemed to call for something a little dressy, but a lobster dinner in Maine seemed to call for something breezy and casual. In the end, she'd compromised with a pair of black pedal pushers, a sunny yellow top, and a white jacket, with some hip jewelry she'd picked up at the GreenFlea Market to dress it up.

For his part, Blake wore khaki slacks, a blue button-down shirt, expensive Italian loafers, and a lightweight navy jacket, *à la* Ralph Lauren. *Yummy.* They were quite the fashion-plate couple if she did say so herself.

A sleek silver convertible Mercedes Roadster waited on the tarmac for the twenty-minute drive into Boothbay Harbor. They drove the Boothbay/Wiscasset Road, the early afternoon sun warm on her face, the cool breeze blowing her heretofore carefully styled hair.

"You warm enough?" Blake asked, his hair fluttering in the breeze. "I can put the top up if you're chilly."

"No, it's great." What the hell, she'd pull her hair back in a ponytail once they arrived at their destination.

The picturesque seaside community of Boothbay Harbor lay nestled amid a craggy stretch of inlets and boasted pretty winding streets lined with quaint B&B's, cafés and restaurants, craft and art galleries, boutiques, and jewelry stores. The sidewalks teemed with tourists, while the shops did a brisk business with the Memorial Weekend traffic.

After strolling down the east side of Commercial Street, perusing shops and galleries, Darcy and Blake relaxed on a bench enjoying a tasty ice cream, soaking up the warm sunshine, and catching the cooling breezes off the Atlantic.

"Having a good time?" Blake asked as he offered her a bite of his butter pecan ice cream.

"Mmm. Yes!" She didn't need a mirror to know that her eyes sparkled with joy. She could read her happiness in Blake's eyes.

He leaned over and kissed her, licking his lips afterwards as if he couldn't get enough of the taste of her. That small gesture sent a frisson of desire coursing through her. Maybe she could join the mile-high club on the flight back.

"What?" Blake interrupted the gutterly flow of her thoughts.

"What, what?" Darcy blinked.

"What's that look for?"

Whoops. Using her napkin to wipe the apparent look of lust off her face, Darcy hedged, "Just thinking about that lobster dinner. Can't wait."

The smirk on his face told her he didn't believe a word she'd said.

CHAPTER TWENTY

As the sun began its descent in the cloudless sky, Darcy and Blake crossed the footbridge connecting the west and east sides of the inner harbor. She'd been covering earlier with her comment about the lobster dinner, but now she really couldn't wait. Between the hors d'oeuvres on the plane and the ice-cream cones, and, oh yeah, the dark chocolate cashew turtles, they'd skipped lunch, and, decadence notwithstanding, those calories had long since given up the ghost. Still, she mentally added another day or two at the gym to her already packed schedule.

The restaurant Blake selected overlooked the Harbor, giving Darcy a clear view of the piers, where sailboats and cabin cruisers bobbed alongside lobster and fishing trawlers, all set against the postcard image of the town beyond with its cedar-shake-covered buildings.

Diners vied for umbrella-bedecked picnic tables where they could unwind and watch the sunset. The hostess offered them a table, and Blake chose to sit next to Darcy so he could view the spectacle as well.

They met thigh-to-thigh on the bench, and Darcy felt a

flush creep up her neck and into her face as her thoughts returned to the gutter.

Blake ordered a magnum of champagne and two lobster dinners with all the trimmings.

"Be sure to save room for a slice of one of our home-made pies," the waitress recommended after completing their orders. "Today we have blueberry and peach."

"Go ahead and reserve one of each," he instructed the waitress.

"Sure thing. I'll be back with your champagne."

As the waitress walked away, Darcy could feel Blake's eyes on her, and the flush deepened.

"There's that look again. You must *really* like lobster," he teased.

"Um." She nervously cleared her throat, her eyes flicking to his lips. "Yeah."

He laughed, rich and deep, before leaning in close, and whispering in her ear. "If it makes you feel any better, I *really* like lobster too."

Darcy shivered as his breath tickled her neck and a sudden warmth settled deep in her belly.

The waitress returned to the table with an ice bucket and two flutes. "Here we are . . . a magnum of our best."

Darcy practically snatched the flute out of the waitress' hand after she'd filled it with the refreshing bubbly, and took a deep gulp. "Whew! Didn't realize how thirsty I was."

"Yeah, all that thinking about lobster really works up a thirst." Blake grinned and tapped his glass to hers. "Cheers."

―――――

Shortly into the flight back to New York, Blake dismissed the flight attendant with an offhand, but polite, "Thanks, Mandy. That will be all. We'll call you if we need anything more."

Darcy relaxed as she and Blake reclined on the sofa, sipping excellent French press coffee courtesy of the now discreetly absent Mandy. Setting his cup aside, Blake reached into his jacket pocket and withdrew a small white box wrapped with a blue ribbon.

Darcy swallowed past the sudden lump in her throat.

"I bought a little something for you today, to remember our time together. I think you'll like it."

Taking the box, she slipped the ribbon off and lifted the lid to find a beautiful hand-wrought sterling silver bangle bracelet with a sand-dollar clasp. The same one she'd had her eye on earlier that day. "How'd you—?"

"Before we left the shop, I signaled to the sales clerk to wrap it up. When you went to the ladies' room, I snuck back and picked it up. Do you like it?"

She looked up at him, awed by his cleverness and generosity. "I love it." She slipped it on. "It's beautiful. Thank you." She leaned in to brush her lips against his.

He cradled her face between his hands and met her halfway, capturing her mouth with his, lingering there, tasting, savoring. As the kiss deepened and the intensity swelled, he grasped her hips and pulled her across his lap, making her inhale sharply when her firm buttocks (thanks to Booty Barre!) met well-muscled thighs.

Darcy grasped his shoulders, pulling him closer still. He slid his hands alongside her ribcage, shifting her body once more until she lay on her back amid the pillows, his lips still firm against hers.

The plane bounced, jostling them momentarily.

Breaking the kiss, he trailed his lips along her jaw, before nipping her earlobe, sending little sparks of electricity along her spine. *Oh yes, mile-high club, here I come.* She giggled at her own pun.

A sudden dip in altitude smothered her giggle and had Darcy gasping for reasons other than desire. But Blake's roving fingers stifled any concern over fiery plane crashes, as his fingers grazed the front of her blouse, unbuttoning the top button.

"Dr. Garrett"—the pilot's voice came over the speakers —"we're experiencing some turbulence from thunderstorms in the area, so I'm going to ask that if you're not in your seats, you return to them now and fasten your seatbelts for the duration of the flight."

Darcy groaned. *So close.*

Blake buttoned her blouse. "Seems we better listen to Captain Southard." He stood, and held out his hand to help her up, pulling her close as the plane hit another air pocket. "Just as well," he whispered into her ear, before pulling back to gaze into her eyes. "When we first make love, it shouldn't be partially clothed on a turbulent flight with only limited privacy. You deserve so much more than that."

Oh my. Way to smooth over an awkward moment. *Dang, he was good.*

CHAPTER TWENTY-ONE

The following weekend, Darcy stood on the lawn of Sunnyside, Washington Irving's historic home on the Hudson River, surrounded by wedding guests.

Cindy glowed in her blush-colored satin gown, while Martin cut a dashing figure in his dove-gray morning coat. The wedding weather gods had smiled on the couple with vivid blue skies, cotton-candy clouds, mild temperatures, and a cooling breeze off the river.

Darcy spied Laura in a royal blue silk charmeuse halter dress and her prized nude Louboutin platform pumps—the very pumps she'd been on her way to purchase the day of her now-infamous run-in with the New York City cabbie. As she turned to laugh at something her flavor-of-the-week date said, her thick blond hair swung across her bare back. Even at another's wedding Laura managed to steal the show.

Josh, surrounded by the other groomsman, looked adorable in his tux.

And there was Dr. Perfect, headed in her direction with champagne for two. Not to be outdone, Blake struck his own dashing figure in a charcoal gray suit, white shirt, and cobalt blue tie. During the lovely outdoor ceremony, Darcy couldn't help but daydream a little, especially when the minister had invited Martin to kiss his bride and Blake had reached over to squeeze her hand.

"Your date abandon you?"

"Not anymore." She smiled as she took the proffered glass of bubbly.

Blake slipped his arm around Darcy's waist, as Laura approached, *sans* escort.

"G'day, mate."

Darcy rolled her eyes. Obviously, Laura's new hottie hailed from Australia. "Blake, you remember Laura. You treated her in the ER."

"Of course I do. How could I forget . . .?"

Laura preened.

". . . the person who brought you into my life?" He pulled Darcy closer, gazing into her eyes.

"Hmph," Laura replied with an unladylike snort, making Darcy chuckle.

"I'll go get us some appetizers," Blake offered. "Would you like a bite, Laura?"

Darcy could see the wheels turning in Laura's head, like a spinning Rolodex, in search of the perfect ribald response.

"No thanks," she said with a smirk, "more for Darcy."

"So, who's that you're with?" Darcy asked after Blake walked away.

"Jake. He's a cowboy and stunt man from Perth, doubling for Daniel Craig in his latest film." Laura found him among the crowd. "Glorious, isn't he?"

"A stunt man? Do you think he'd mind if I asked him some research questions for my current novel?"

"Feel free. Just be sure to give him back when you're done," Laura said with a wink.

Two young women in catering uniforms carrying appetizer trays approached them. "You're Darcy Butler, right?" the shorter, slightly plump one bearing the bruschetta asked. "I'm a huge fan," she continued without waiting for confirmation. "I've read all your books! I follow you on Twitter and Facebook, and I come to all your local book signings."

Darcy mentally cringed, not wanting to hurt the girl's feelings, but most of the time the faces at book signings were all a blur.

"Maybe you recognize my Twitter handle, I'm 'Slutty-Girl,' and this is 'PrincessLeia22,'" she said, pointing to the tall skinny girl with the tray of Brie tartlets.

Laura snorted, then choked on her champagne.

"Um, oh, yes." How could she forget a Twitter handle like that? "I really appreciate all of your retweets, um, SluttyGirl."

"Can you give us a sneak peek of your next book? What's the hero like?" PrincessLeia22 asked.

Laura, now fully recovered from her champagne mishap, turned to Darcy. "Yes, Darcy. Do tell. What's the hero like?"

Darcy briefly imagined strangling Laura with her own Pantene-model-hair and dumping her body into the Hudson, but reconsidered, what with all the witnesses.

"Well, PrincessLeia . . . 22 . . . I'd hate to spoil the surprise I have in store for my fans with this next book. So I'm just going to say you'll have to wait until it comes out. Sorry."

"That's okay," PrincessLeia22 replied with a shrug. "It was worth a try anyway. Tartlet?"

"Sure." Darcy reached for a napkin and a tartlet, figuring it was the least she could do.

PrincessLeia22 and SluttyGirl moved on to the other wedding guests to offer up their tartlets and bruschetta.

Laura took another sip of her champagne, a devilish smile on her movie-star-gorgeous face. "Oh, you've got a surprise in store for your fans, all right."

"Shh. Here's Blake."

"Ladies." He presented a plate piled high with hors d'oeuvres of every shape and color. "I think I've got a little something you'll like."

"Don't say it," Darcy muttered to Laura.

———

Josh watched as Blake wrapped his arm around Darcy's waist and pulled her close, holding out a plate of food with the other hand. Josh tossed back the last of his champagne, longing for something stronger. His opportunity to treat Blake as a hostile witness had finally presented itself.

He'd been busy all morning with his groomsmen's duties, but that didn't mean he hadn't noticed how beautiful Darcy looked in a simply cut green—he guessed some might call it jade—off-the-shoulder deal that fit her slender form perfectly. He could just imagine how the color made her eyes sparkle. Her hair hung loose around her shoulders in soft waves.

He headed in their direction, stopping from time to time to greet colleagues from the firm. Josh gritted his teeth when Blake threw his head back, laughing at something Darcy said. Even his laugh was perfect. Infectious, if you liked that sort of rich-timbered baritone.

"Hi, Darcy."

"Josh." Darcy smiled. "Don't you look handsome in your groomsmen get-up? Blake, you remember Josh."

"Of course."

The two men shook hands.

"Garrett." Josh nodded perfunctorily.

"Nice catch at the Yankees game."

"Yeah, thanks."

"Bloodsucker," Laura greeted Josh in her usual charming way.

"Witch."

"What do lawyers use for birth control?"

"Their personalities." Josh replied, unenthused with their customary banter.

"Damn," Laura muttered. "I've got to get some new jokes."

Darcy just shook her head at Blake's questioning look.

Blake broke the uncomfortable silence. "Laura, how did you spend your Memorial Weekend?"

"Jake and I spent the weekend in the Hamptons."

"The beaches there are wonderful," Blake said.

"If you say so," Laura replied with a wicked grin. "How about you two?"

"We flew to Maine for lobster," Darcy added, as she slipped her hand into Blake's.

"Wow!" Josh drew back in surprise. "Conspicuous consumption in action."

Darcy frowned.

"A man after my own heart." Laura held up her champagne glass in a toast.

"You have a heart?" Josh quipped.

"And they're off," Darcy muttered, while Blake watched

the whole exchange as if he were viewing the final match at Wimbledon.

"Don't you have someone to sue?" Laura thrust.

"Don't you have someone to do?" Josh parried.

"Actually, yes. Excuse me while I round up my Aussie cowboy. Always nice exchanging barbs with you," Laura said, as she nodded at Josh. "Blake, take care of my girl." She kissed Darcy on the cheek and strutted off in the direction of the tent.

"You two always get along so swimmingly?" Blake asked Josh.

"Oh yeah, we're BFFs," Josh replied flatly. "So, Blake, Darcy tells me you're a trauma surgeon, of impeccable pedigree, no less."

"I suppose you could say that."

"Harvard undergrad *and* medical school?"

"Yes."

"Johns Hopkins for residency?"

"Yes."

"UCSD for fellowship?"

"Josh," Darcy hissed.

"Yes, that's right," Blake replied evenly, as if he were accustomed to being cross-examined by his girlfriend's best friend.

"Been in New York long?"

"No. I was in Chicago two years before coming here."

"Where?"

"Mt. Sinai."

"And before that?"

"Josh, stop it!" Darcy stepped between Josh and Blake.

"No, it's okay, Darcy." Blake pulled her back. "I don't mind. We can cover my entire career if Josh is so inclined."

"Well, I'm *not* so inclined. Come on." She tugged at

Blake's arm. "The music is starting, and *I'm* inclined to dance."

She executed a defiant hair flip before turning to glare at Josh, her eyes spitting green sparks, as Blake took the lead in the direction of the tent.

Josh scrubbed his hands through his hair. *Oh boy.* Darcy would make sure he paid for that little confrontation.

Blake pulled Darcy into the circle of his arms. Even their warmth couldn't sooth Darcy's indignation. "I'm sorry, Blake. I don't know what got into him." *Alcohol, perhaps.* "He doesn't usually behave like a rabid lawyer."

"Don't give it another thought. He's only protecting you." Blake tucked her head under his chin, then kissed the top of her head. "That's what friends do. Just forget it."

She closed her eyes and relaxed into Blake, vowing to rip Josh a new one at the first opportunity.

CHAPTER TWENTY-TWO

Darcy's opportunity presented itself sooner than she'd expected when her doorbell rang Sunday morning. She gathered her robe around her and padded in her bare feet to the door, opening it to find Josh standing with two cups from the coffee shop around the corner, a determined expression on his face. He looked like hell. Before she could light into him, he held out the cup like a peace offering.

"I'm sorry."

His abrupt apology momentarily disarmed her. Then her anger flared again when she realized his unexpected remorse had robbed her of the chance to express her righteous anger over his inexcusable behavior.

"That's it? That's all you've got?" She stood with her arm on the door, blocking his entrance to her house, one eyebrow lifted in disdain.

"Well, that and a chai tea, just the way you like it." Nothing. "Look, Darcy, can I come in?" When she didn't move, Josh continued. "I said I was sorry." Still nothing. "I was rude and out of line." Darcy's foot started tapping. "Okay, I was an asshole."

Darcy grabbed the tea, held the door open for Josh to enter, and he followed her into the kitchen where she'd been making tea. When she saw him glance around, she said, "He's not here."

Josh relaxed.

"Which is too bad, since he's the one you should be apologizing to."

"I know. You're right." Josh scrubbed his hands through his hair. "I'll apologize next time I see him. Where is he by the way?"

"He's in Timbuktu."

Josh snorted. "No, really."

"Yes, really. After we got back last night, an international medical charity called about a man who'd been mauled by a lion and needed an amputation immediately." She leaned against the counter sipping her peace offering. She had been keenly disappointed since things had been heating up and she'd planned to ask him to stay the night. "Why?"

"Why what?"

"Why do you want to know where Blake is?"

"Because I wanted to apologize." Josh leaned against the opposite countertop and toyed with his coffee cup. "Why else?"

Darcy narrowed her eyes. "Right."

"So, since you're a free woman for the day, want to hang out? It's a nice day. We could walk to Dumbo."

"I don't know, Josh, I'm behind on my word count." The look of disappointment on his face had her backtracking. "But how about I meet you at the batting cage on Third later and then we can grab dinner after."

"Sure." He pushed off the counter and, leaning down,

kissed her temple. "Again, Darce, I'm really sorry. See you later." He turned and let himself out.

Josh *was* sorry, but primarily because he'd hurt Darcy. Damn, she'd looked so sexy standing there in her skimpy robe and bare feet, hair pulled back in some messy knot, no makeup. The relief he'd felt when he'd learned Blake hadn't spent the night was overwhelming, as if he'd been in an underwater cave and had just come up for air.

He paused on her stoop, unable to bear the thought of going back to his quiet apartment. He'd spent too much time there last night worrying about how badly he'd screwed up with Darcy as a result of his alcohol-fortified interrogation of Blake.

To distract himself, he'd done a little research on Blake via Google, not expecting to turn up anything more than the people-finder agency. But he did come across various articles on his surgical skills and charitable endeavors. He'd performed life-saving surgeries all over the globe, everything from amputations, like Darcy had just mentioned, to *saving* limbs from amputation. If you could believe what they said online, Blake Garrett was some kind of medical saint. And a rich one at that, thinking about the flight to Maine. Yet, his sudden appearance in Darcy's life defied explanation.

Sighing, he shoved his hands in his pockets, turned right, and headed for Prospect Park. Maybe he could pick up a chess match or two. The intellectual exercise would take his mind off Darcy and Blake. If only for a little while.

———

B right and early Monday morning, a little too early by Darcy's standards, she woke up with a horrific toothache in an area where there was no tooth. After getting in to see her dentist, she learned she had not one, but two, impacted wisdom teeth that had to come out ASAP.

According to Dr. Jameson, it was a miracle she'd gone this long without a problem. He'd managed to get her in with an oral surgeon who worked her into his schedule the next morning.

"Now, Ms. Butler, since you're having general anesthesia," the surgeon's nurse explained, "you'll need someone to drive you home after the surgery and stay with you at least for the night. Do you have someone who can help you?"

Darcy ran through her list of friends and family. Her parents were in San Francisco where her mother was speaking at a Jane Austen conference. And, of course, Blake was still in Timbuktu. She'd call Anne or Brandon. One of them would take care of her, they always did.

"Oh, um, yes, I can get someone." A true needle-phobic, Darcy dreaded this surgery like a man dreaded a vasectomy.

"Okay, dear. We'll see you at eight a.m. Don't forget, nothing to eat or drink after midnight."

Right. No worries there, since her jaw throbbed like she'd just taken a right hook. The nurse handed her the paperwork, and asked where she could call in the prescription for pain medicine.

Drowning in self-pity, Darcy walked out of the office and hailed a taxi, wishing desperately that Blake were in town. He'd know exactly how to take care of her.

She called Anne from her cell.

Anne answered with an exhausted sounding, "Hello."

"Hi, Anne. Listen, I have to have my wisdom teeth out tomorrow. Can you come take care of me?"

"Sorry, but Olivia's got the stomach flu. There's no way I can leave her."

Darcy fought back the selfish disappointment. "I'm sorry. Will Olivia be all right?"

"She'll be fine. Just one of those joys of childhood. You going to be okay?"

"I'll be fine." Darcy heard Olivia's feeble voice in the background. "Thanks, and kiss Olivia for me." Sighing, Darcy hit 'end' and dialed Brandon.

"Hey, Darce! How's my favorite baby sister?"

"Well, I've got to have my wisdom teeth out tomorrow. Any chance you could play nurse for a day?"

"Sorry, sis. I'm in Toronto for an engineering conference. Won't be back until early next week."

Darcy winced. If she had to choose between an engineering conference and oral surgery, she just might go with the oral surgery. "Sounds like fun."

"You know it. What about Anne?"

"Olivia's sick."

"Oh. Call Laura then. I gotta run. The session on amorphous metals is starting. Love you, sis."

Great. Just great. There was *no way* she was calling Gloria. She'd try Laura, even though she had more in common with Nurse Ratched than Florence Nightingale.

"*Guten morgen, Freundin.* What's up?"

Jake must have run his course, but Darcy didn't have the energy to ask about *l'amour du jour.*

Darcy got right to the point. "Laura, I've got to have my wisdom teeth cut out tomorrow." She cringed at that visual. "And I need someone to bring me home and stay with me. Are you available?"

"Oh . . . well—blood, needles—not really my thing," she muttered on the other end of the line. "But for you, girl-friend, I'd do it. Problem is, my team is pitching an ad campaign to a pet food conglomerate tomorrow and I can't get away. What about your parents or Anne?"

Darcy explained the circumstances.

"Why don't you call Josh? He'll do it I'm sure, being the *Good Samaritan* and all," Laura said, her sarcastic emphasis crystal clear.

Darcy sighed. "All right. Thanks, anyway. Good luck tomorrow."

"Thanks. Good luck to you, too. I'll come by after work and check on you. Bring you a little something to cheer you up."

Darcy hung up, dropping her phone dejectedly in her lap. This is what boyfriends were for. She'd been completely and utterly abandoned. Grumbling about brilliant surgeons, jet-setting family members, stomach bugs, and pet food, she paid the cab driver, picked up her mail by the door, and let herself in. First stop, the freezer for an ice pack. Flinching as she placed the pack against her jaw, she dialed Josh at work.

"Hey, Sunshine."

"Not so much. More like cloudy with a chance of doom and gloom."

"What's wrong, and why do you sound like you have a mouthful of marbles?"

"Oh, Josh." Darcy teared up then began babbling about how her jaw felt like she'd just lost a bar fight to some guy named Guido, that she had to have surgery tomorrow, and that she was all alone.

"Oh, baby, sounds like you've had a rough day. Want me to come by after work?"

"Yes," she whined. "But I also need you to take me tomorrow and bring me home."

Josh quickly glanced at his calendar. "Done."

"And to stay with me tomorrow night." This last request was met with silence. "Josh?"

"Okay." Josh hesitated. "I can do that."

"Listen, if you have plans, it's really no problem." *Please don't have plans.*

"No. You can't stay alone. I'll stay with you."

"Thanks, Josh. I really appreciate it."

CHAPTER TWENTY-THREE

Josh hung up the phone and rechecked his calendar for Tuesday and Wednesday. A conference call, and a meeting with one of the junior associates tomorrow to discuss a brief due in two weeks, nothing that couldn't wait another day. Wednesday morning he had an appointment with Kelly, but with some juggling he might be able to see her in the afternoon if Darcy felt self-sufficient by then.

He'd always wanted to hear Darcy ask him to stay with her, or words similar to that effect, just not under these particular circumstances.

Unsettled, he stood up from his desk and walked over to his window, looking out over the Hudson River. He'd had a clear view of the Miracle on the Hudson when Captain Sully brought his Airbus A320 in for an emergency water landing. Little work got done that morning at the firm, with everyone crowded into the offices with river views, watching the human drama unfold in the icy river, and praying for the passengers, crew, and rescuers.

In a couple more months he'd be moving to a bigger office, a partner's office, one floor up. He only hoped it, too, had a view of the Hudson. Now that he had the goal in his sights, it didn't hold the same appeal. He sure hoped he wasn't turning into one those people who only wanted what they couldn't have, and when they finally had it, didn't want it anymore.

Would that be the result, he wondered, if Darcy ever reciprocated his feelings for her? Once he had her, would he still want her? Or was his unwavering desire for her simply the product of his unrequited love?

He picked up the case he'd been reading when Darcy had called. If he was going to be out tomorrow, he'd better get a head start on it today.

Missing a day at the office wasn't the problem. He could get some work done at her place. *Her place*. That was the problem. Being around Darcy and hiding the truth was getting more and more difficult, especially now that Blake was in the picture. It seemed he was always fulfilling boyfriend obligations without the boyfriend benefits, he groused.

When she was going through first dates like the Yankees go through baseballs, he could sit back and be the one waiting in the wings. But now, Darcy's clock didn't seem to be the only one ticking like a time bomb. At some point, he had to decide whether to allow Darcy to walk away forever or risk their friendship by telling her his feelings for her. Either way, he could lose her.

———

J osh let himself into Darcy's house early the next morning. "Where's the patient?" he called.

"She's in here," came the frail reply from the living room.

He walked in to see Darcy sitting on the sofa, an ice pack to her cheek. "My poor Darcy. You ready?"

"About as a ready as a cow going to slaughter," she replied glumly.

"Look at the bright side." He helped her up. "At least after you've healed, your mouth won't hurt anymore. Right?"

"I'm in no mood to look at the bright side."

Josh chuckled.

They stepped outside and while Josh went to lock up, Darcy stepped to the curb.

"We don't need a cab," Josh told Darcy. "I borrowed Martin's car." He pointed to a blue Prius parked at the curb. "I didn't think you'd want to do the whole New York cab ride after your surgery."

"Bless you," she said, the relief apparent on her face. "I'd kiss you but it hurts too much to pucker up."

He helped Darcy into the car and walked around to the driver's side. Folding his long frame into the compact space, he glanced over at her. She sat, her head against the headrest, her eyes closed, a frown creasing her brow. He reached over and, squeezing her hand, said, "You'll be fine. And if not, don't worry, I'll sue the pants off 'em."

She didn't bother to open her eyes. "Gee, thanks."

———

Josh juggled a very woozy Darcy, a small bag of medical supplies and post-op instructions, and Darcy's purse as he steered her toward her front steps. After a few miscues, he managed to get her to the door. The surgeon had said everything went well and that in a few days she should be good as new. The stitches would dissolve on their own, and she could begin eating normally as tolerated.

Right now Josh's only concern was getting her in the house without her falling on her face. He leaned her up against the doorjamb while he unlocked the door, then caught her just as she slid sideways.

"Whoops-a-daisy," Darcy slurred, with an inebriated smile, cotton packing peeking out of the corners of her mouth in a way she would find utterly humiliating if she had her faculties.

"Okay." Josh abandoned her purse and the bag by the door, and scooped Darcy up in his arms.

"Wheee!" She wrapped her arms around his neck and cradled her head against him.

The light floral scent of her shampoo drifted to his nose and he closed his eyes briefly against its subtle attack on his senses. Her trim body, even smaller after a couple of days on a liquid diet, pressed against his chest, her waist so small he could practically wrap his hands around it.

He carried her to the sofa and carefully set her down on it, but she didn't release him. "Joth, you thmell thoooo good," she said, doing a fair imitation of her niece, Sam.

"Um, thanks." He gently tried to pry her hands from around his neck. Finally succeeding, he set them in her lap. "Okay. Wait here. Don't move." He held up his hands. "I'll be right back."

He darted back to the stoop to collect her things and close the door. When he walked back into the living room, Darcy still sat, hands in her lap, her eyes closed. He stepped out of the living room and glanced up her staircase. There was no way he was going to get her up the stairs in her present condition.

He took the stairs two at a time and, striding into her

bedroom, snagged a pillow off her bed. As he left the room, he noticed a photo of him at his law school graduation, still wearing his cap and gown, and holding up a bottle of champagne. He never knew she'd framed that picture.

He hadn't been in her bedroom since he and some of the guys had helped her move in almost five years ago. Seeing the photo in her bedroom gave him pause, but sooner or later it would no doubt be replaced by one of her and Blake.

Running back into the living room, he put the pillow at one end of the sofa and eased her back, careful to prop her up like the doctor said, before lifting her legs and stretching them out. He grabbed a throw off the window seat in the bay window and covered her with it.

Darcy snuggled into the pillow and pulled the blanket up to her chin. "I wuv you, Josh." And she was out.

If only she meant those words the way he wanted her to. That one statement—four little words—socked him in the gut, leaving him breathless, not unlike the time Billy Maloney had head-butted him in the belly in football practice. The difference was, he'd recovered from Billy's blow.

———

Darcy woke up, a little disoriented, wondering why it felt like someone had taken a jackhammer to her mouth. Moaning, she tried to sit up.

"Shh. Lie back."

She felt a hand stroking her hair and, opening her eyes, looked up into Josh's warm brown ones.

"How do you feel?"

"Like hell," was all she managed to get out. Her mouth resembled the Sahara and tasted like she'd been sucking on nickels. She shifted a little, and realized she was lying with her head on a pillow in Josh's lap. Some dim memory of Josh carrying her prodded at her aching head.

"Did I do anything . . . strange?"

Josh considered a moment. "No. Unless you count running out your front door naked."

"That would only be strange if it were the middle of winter."

"Then no, you didn't do anything strange."

"Good. How long have I been asleep?" Her words slurred around the cotton in her mouth.

"A few hours."

She closed her eyes again.

"Do you think you could eat something? I'm not worth much in the kitchen, but nuking a can of soup isn't too far beyond my limited capabilities. I saw some chicken noodle in your cupboard."

"Okay. Sure."

He helped her sit up and then propped her up against the back of the couch. "One bowl of chicken noodle coming up. And how about some hot tea?"

"Good." She moaned as the jackhammer picked up the pace.

"And I'm sure you could use a Percocet."

A few minutes later Josh came in carrying a tray, which he placed on the coffee table.

Darcy tried to stand, but a wave of dizziness overtook her.

"Whoa. Where do you think you're going?" Josh steadied her.

"Bathroom."

"Well, hang on." He held out his hands indicating he would help her up.

She hesitated. "You're not going with me."

"I am, at least to the door."

"God, this is so embarrassing." She groaned as she stood.

Josh wrapped his arm around her waist and guided her to the powder bath tucked underneath the stairs.

"Now go away," Darcy croaked.

"Hey, did anyone ever tell you, you do a pretty good impression of the Godfather? Come on, make me an offer I can't refuse." He egged her on by waving his hands toward his face.

If she'd had the strength, she'd have slapped that grin right off.

Instead, she slammed the door in his face.

CHAPTER TWENTY-FOUR

After Josh had Darcy fed, medicated, and resituated on the sofa, her feet in his lap, he picked up the remote and turned on ESPN.

Propping his bare feet on the coffee table, he looked around the cozy living room, Darcy's personality apparent in all the little touches. Photos of friends and family— including some of the two of them, one photo in particular from their first Yankees game together. Knickknacks and throw rugs she'd picked up from her almost weekly haunts of the various open-air markets around Manhattan. An open book, spine-side up on the window seat, and fresh flowers on the end table.

Josh contemplated his own postage-stamp-sized apartment. Darcy and his mom had helped him furnish it, and it was a nice apartment, considering the rent. Charcoal gray walls with white trim. Masculine, clean lines. It served its purpose, and it was close to the office. But it wasn't a home.

He'd grown up in a two-bedroom, two-bathroom cinder block house. Nothing fancy. But it had always been neat as a pin, with colorful flowers blooming in the yard, worn but comfortable furniture, and decorations at the holidays. His mom made sure the house had a warm, welcoming feel. Just like Darcy did.

He felt Darcy's hand on his and glanced over at her.

"Thanks, Josh," she said softly, the absence of the cotton packing making it easier to understand her.

"What are friends for?"

"If you ever get tired of the law, maybe you should consider nursing as a second career."

"Nurse Ryan." He tilted his head. "It has a certain ring to it."

"I really owe you." She glanced over at his feet and cocked a brow. "That's the only reason I'm letting you put your feet on my coffee table."

"Thanks."

Darcy gave a little shrug. "It's the least I can do."

"It's been a pretty tough assignment, so I'll accept your concession." He patted her feet, noticing the pale pink polish. As long as he'd known her, she'd always kept her feet well-groomed and polished. It struck him as just one more reason he thought she was so damned sexy. Even with her mussed hair, dark circles, and slightly swollen jaw, he'd never met anyone who even came close to her fresh, girl-next-door look.

"I hope I didn't throw a wrench in your schedule." She pulled him back to the conversation.

"Nothing I can't handle."

They watched SportsCenter for a few minutes, Josh gently rubbing her feet. The feel of his hands on her feet sent odd little tingles up her legs to her stomach. *Must be the drugs.* She should tuck her feet up under her, but the massage felt so good, so soothing.

Josh could imagine evenings spent exactly like this.

Well, not exactly. Darcy wouldn't have just had surgery. But evenings lying on the sofa together, watching sports, or even a romantic comedy or two. And when he turned off the television, they'd walk up to their bedroom . . . *Okay. Time to get my mind focused elsewhere.*

"So, no more wisdom teeth. Do you feel any less wise?" Josh asked, a slight grin on his face. "I'm not going to have to start exercising some sort of parental authority over you, am I?"

Darcy laughed. "Ow! Don't make me laugh."

The doorbell rang.

"That'll be Laura," Darcy explained. "She said she'd be coming by."

"Super."

Josh walked over to the door and opened it.

"Lawyer," Laura punched as she strolled past Josh.

"Nympho," Josh counter-punched as he followed her into the living room.

"How do you get a lawyer out of a tree?"

"Cut the rope."

Darcy pushed herself to a sitting position with a grimace. "You two will be sniping at one another over my grave."

"How's the patient?" Laura asked as she sat next to Darcy on the sofa.

"Grumpy," Darcy replied.

"Well, maybe this will help." Laura held up a brown paper bag. "Aunt Butchie's famous chocolate mousse cups. One for tonight and one for tomorrow."

Darcy's face went all dreamy. "I have the best friends in the world."

"And for you Josh, a Tiramisu cup."

Josh drew back in surprise. "Really? Thanks. That was . . . uncharacteristically thoughtful of you."

"It's the least I could do after you took care of Darcy." She sniffed as she looked him over. "You do have a few redeeming qualities."

"Gee, thanks." Shaking his head, he took the bag from Laura and walked into the kitchen to make Darcy tea and grab spoons.

Laura laid her hand over Darcy's. "How do you feel?"

"Like Con Ed tried to drill through my jaw."

"They give you good drugs?"

"Yeah. Too good, I think." She frowned over another hazy memory of telling Josh he smelled good. Maybe she'd just dreamed it.

"How'd your presentation go?"

"We got the account!" Laura's eyes lit with pride.

"You should be out celebrating instead of sitting here with me," Darcy fussed.

"What? And leave you with no one but that loser for company?" she said, loud enough for him to hear.

"Hey!" he hollered from the kitchen, where the teakettle had just begun to shriek. "I heard that."

"Hello. That was the point," she muttered, rolling her eyes.

"What is it with you and Josh?"

"What do you mean?"

"Why do you always give him such a hard time?"

Laura thought about it a minute. "Because I can." She shrugged a silk-clad shoulder.

"I bet your committee meetings together are a barrel of laughs."

Laura sniffed, lifting her chin a little. "That's different.

That's business. I'm nothing but professional when it comes to marketing and promotion."

Josh came in carrying a tray with Darcy's tea and the desserts Laura had brought.

"Look at you," Laura said. "Looking all domestic and everything. The next thing you know you'll be wearing an apron and whipping up a soufflé." She smirked as she took her chocolate mousse cup off the tray. She took a bite of the confection, then indelicately licked every trace off the spoon.

Josh ignored the comment and served Darcy her tea and dessert.

Darcy gingerly took a bite and groaned.

Both he and Laura jumped to attention.

"You okay?" he asked.

"Hmm mm." Darcy's eyes were closed. "Just savoring the taste of sin in a cup."

He and Laura sank back in relief.

"Chase any ambulances today?" Laura asked Josh.

"Nope. Sucker any clients?" He turned his attention to ESPN, effectively dismissing her.

"As if," Laura said off-handedly, then ignored him. "Heard from Blake?"

"No." Darcy sighed. "He said it might be a few days before he could call." She got a little teary. "He doesn't even know I had surgery." She dabbed at her eyes. "Must be the drugs making me weepy."

"He'll call. I'm sure he'd be here if he could instead of leaving you here in the incapable hands of a shyster." She lifted the last bite of her mousse to her lips.

As soon as she swallowed her last bite, Josh said, "Enjoy your dessert?"

"Of course." She glanced up at Josh and confusion

turned to suspicion. "Why?" She narrowed her eyes, her spoon poised midway between her mouth and the dessert cup.

"On, no reason." Josh took the last heaping bite of his Tiramisu and smiled in delight.

————

After Laura left, Josh settled in her vacated seat on the sofa and pulled Darcy's feet into his lap again. "Let me know when you're ready for another pain pill."

"Maybe in a little while. Before I go to bed."

Josh picked up the remote and began flipping channels. He paused in his channel-surfing when he came across the movie *A League of Their Own*, one of their favorites.

"Greatest line of all time," he said with a lopsided grin, referring to the line about crying and baseball.

Darcy gave Josh a little shove. "I know, right?" She winced at the painful after-effects of her outburst.

"Darcy. I have something to tell you." He took her hand, as the nagging doubts returned.

"Shoot," she said, shifting positions on the sofa, so that she lay on her back looking directly at him.

He took a deep breath, ready to take the plunge. "I—"

The phone rang.

"Holy hell," he muttered.

Darcy sat up, her face lighting up. "That's probably Blake. Would you mind?" She lifted her feet out of his lap.

"No, of course not." He pulled his hands through his hair, grasping a fistful on his way to the kitchen. "Hello."

"Josh?" Blake's perfect baritone crackled though a bad connection. "Is everything okay? Why are you answering the phone?"

"Hi, Blake. Everything's fine. I'll let Darcy fill you in."

He handed the phone over to Darcy. Her face fairly glowed as she took it.

"Blake? Where are you?"

Josh picked up the tray of dirty dishes and carried it into the kitchen. He wanted nothing more than to toss the dishes into the sink and hear each one shatter. Just like Blake had shattered his opportunity to come clean with Darcy.

Instead, Josh fought his frustration as he rinsed the plates and placed them carefully in the dishwasher, as Darcy's giggle set his teeth on edge.

———

The next morning Darcy straightened up the living room, picking up her discarded book, fluffing the pillows, and folding the throw. A memory flashed in her head of Josh leaning over her, and her snuggling under the throw before telling him she loved him. She winced, then shrugged her shoulders and laid the throw on the window seat. Well, she did love him. She loved both Josh and Laura. Nothing wrong with that.

She gingerly cupped her face. Yesterday's jackhammer had been replaced by a pick-ax, but with some Tylenol she could just about bear it. Sitting on the sofa, gathering her robe around her, she thought about Josh's tenderness. The way he took care of her. Then she remembered he was going to tell her something when the phone rang. He'd looked so serious. Well, if it had been important, he'd have told her after she'd hung up with Blake. Or this morning.

Instead, after preparing a bowl of microwave oatmeal for her breakfast, brewing a cup of tea, and making sure she was self-sufficient, Josh lit out of the house like it was on fire. She didn't know how she would ever repay him for his kindness. It seemed she would spend her life trying to catch up for all the good things Josh did for her. Especially what he did for her after her break-up with Doug.

If she lived to be a hundred, she'd never be able to repay him for his friendship and understanding. Where Laura had been pissed off enough to commit bodily harm on Doug, Josh had turned his attention to soothing Darcy's lacerated heart, with flowers, silly hand-drawn cards, and pints of Ben and Jerry's.

He'd spent so much time with her she worried he'd flunk out of law school. He'd let her cry herself out whenever the pain overwhelmed her, holding a box of Kleenex at the ready, but he never let her feel sorry for herself for long.

He'd listened as she poured her heart out, telling him things she'd never told Laura. With Josh, she was able to stitch up the pieces of her heart, using the threads of his unwavering friendship and support, so that he would always be part of her.

CHAPTER TWENTY-FIVE

Eight years ago, the wedding plans had been in full swing. The date chosen, the venue selected, even the dress was on order. As Darcy left her appointment with the florist to meet Doug for dinner she received a text from him that something had come up and he had to work late.

"Poor guy." He'd been working so hard lately, and she'd been so focused on the wedding plans and her latest book that she'd neglected him.

She texted, No problem. Call me later. XOXOXO.

Crossing the street to the subway station, she had a brilliant idea. She'd pick up his favorite Chinese food, General Tso's chicken and vegetable rice, and a bottle of wine, and take it by his office for a quick dinner, so he can get back to work. Goodness knows if he'd even get to eat otherwise. At least he'd know she was thinking about him.

About a half hour later, she knocked on the glass door of the high-rise building that housed the TV station where Doug worked as a sportscaster, getting the security guard's attention, and showing him the food in her hands.

Frank unlocked the door, "Hey, Darcy! Written that book about the handsome security guard who wins the gorgeous CEO's hand yet?"

"No, Frank, but it's next in the queue," she said with a wink. "I'm surprising Doug with dinner. Poor guy, he's working late again."

"Yeah. He's been doing that a lot lately. I'm sure he'll appreciate the distraction a beautiful lady can bring. He's one lucky guy."

"Aw, thanks, Frank. I brought you a little something too. I hope you like Moo Shu pork."

"Who doesn't like Moo Shu pork?"

"I know, right?" Darcy handed Frank the container.

"Thanks, Darcy." His eyes sparkled with appreciation. "Go on up. You kids have fun."

"We will." Darcy took a quick ride on the elevator to the twenty-ninth floor. Since the news was broadcast from the studio on the forty-fifth floor, the elevator doors opened on a dim, quiet office space.

Darcy walked with a spring in her step, excited over Doug's reaction to the unexpected feast. When she turned left at his hallway, she tiptoed along the industrial carpeting to avoid alerting him to her presence. As she approached his office, she heard deep moans coming from behind Doug's door. Oh my God! Was he hurt?

She dropped the food, throwing open the door to rush to his aid. Her brain momentarily fogged, unable to comprehend the image her eyes conveyed.

Papers were scattered on the floor, Doug bent over the desk, his pants down around his ankles. Beneath Doug, bare buttocks visible below her upturned blue dress, Tawny, the buxom blond meteorologist Darcy recognized from her nightly weather reports, and the office Christmas party, lay facedown on the desk. Her hair disheveled, her arms splayed out wide on the desk.

Apparently the two were still recovering from their, *er*, activity, because neither of them was aware of her intrusion. The gasp escaped before she could flee undetected.

"Darcy!" Doug stood up, before realizing he should pull up his pants first.

Darcy covered her eyes, but the momentary visual of Tawny's bare bottom and Doug's exposed junk would be burned on her retina forever. From some distant place, she knew she should be angry, more than angry. She should be murderous, but she couldn't get passed the humiliation, the abject mortification of seeing her fiancé, the man whose ring she wore, whose children she had hoped to bear, in the throes of passion with another woman.

Her face burned with the shame of knowing she'd been an idiot, a trusting, naïve idiot, as the tears flowed down her face.

"Darcy, I can explain." Doug stood before her, zipping up his pants as he tucked in his shirt.

She couldn't look him in the face. Tawny the Tart had the good graces to beat a hasty retreat, slinking past Darcy, pulling her clothes back into place.

Unable to decide what to do, Darcy stood rooted to the floor. She didn't want to follow Tawny out, and she didn't want to stay here with Doug. The embarrassment mixed with the agony of betrayal and heartache churned in a bitter concoction.

"Darcy, please." Doug touched her arm.

His touch sparked the impetus she needed. Whirling toward the door, she ran down the hall and into the blessedly open elevator, Doug's curses ringing in her ears.

———

Darcy walked aimlessly until she finally caught a cab to her Brooklyn Heights apartment, dazed by what she'd seen. Bloody blisters on her heels, and one on her toe, she slipped off her shoes and collapsed on the sofa. Pressing her hand to her breastbone, where it felt like her heart would literally shatter into millions of pieces, she sobbed.

Questions collided in her brain like cars in a demolition derby.

How long? How long had this been going on? Did it start when he began "working late"? Or had it been going on before that?

How many? How many women had he been with? Was Tawny the Tart the only one, or had there been others?

Had he been safe? Should she worry about sexually transmitted diseases?

And the hardest question of all: Why wasn't she enough for Doug? Why did he have to seek out Tawny and any other women he'd been with?

When her cell phone rang, she ignored it. When the apartment phone rang she ignored that too.

Hours later, she didn't know how long, Doug banged on her front door, calling her name. She cringed away from the sound of his voice, burying her head under a throw pillow. Finally she heard her neighbor, Mr. Bettincourt, threaten to call the police if Doug didn't leave.

She must have fallen asleep, because when she woke, dim, watery light filtered through the shutters. Her eyes burned, her neck ached, and her heart thudded heavily in her chest.

She dragged herself off the sofa when her cell phone started ringing again. She knew she had to face Doug at some point, but not now. Not yet. She needed a little time and distance to figure out what to do. She needed some time to work up the righteous anger she knew she should feel, but simply couldn't at this point. Texting Doug, she asked him to please stop calling and to give her some time.

Laura had enough righteous anger for both of them. When she asked her to come by later that day, she told her the whole sordid story. Darcy practically had to tie Laura down to keep her from going after Doug's private parts with, in her words, "the dullest knife she could find."

While Darcy appreciated the solidarity of incensed sisterhood, she hated to see her best friend imprisoned for Doug's maiming, no matter how much he deserved it.

Darcy agreed to meet Doug a few days later on neutral ground in a quiet restaurant not far from her house. When she arrived, she still couldn't look Doug in the eye. And she knew then she'd never be able to scrub the vulgar image of him and Tawny from her brain.

After trying to kiss her, Darcy told him she'd come to listen to him talk. The touch that had once made her shiver with desire now made her skin crawl with disgust.

"Darcy, what can I do? I'm so sorry. I can't tell you how sorry I am. I haven't slept, I haven't eaten, I can't concentrate. Tell me what I can do to make this up to you?" He laid his hands on the table, palms up, in a placating gesture.

From what she saw, he didn't look worse for wear. He sat across from her impeccably dressed in the expensive suits he favored. Darcy felt sick. He really thought he could make it up to her? Like he'd accidentally spilled coffee on her favorite rug, or broken her favorite vase?

"There's nothing." She couldn't even say his name.

"It's an illness. I'm addicted to sex. I can't help it." He tried to reach for her hand.

She pulled it away. Pressed it to her stomach. Just when she thought it couldn't get any worse. The sex addict defense made it clear that Tawny wasn't the first, but she didn't want to hear the details. She didn't care.

"If I had a drug or alcohol addiction, would you leave me? Just walk away?"

"I'll never be able to look at you the same way again. I'll never be able to trust you. Every time you tell me you have to work late, I'll wonder if you're really working—"

"Darcy—"

She held up her finger. "Don't. I get to speak." There it was. A glimmer of the anger she craved. "Every time you leave town to cover a sports story I'll wonder if you're actually sneaking off with another woman." She suppressed a sob that threatened to bubble to the surface. "I can't live like that. I won't live like that." She took the engagement ring off of her finger, slid it across the table to him, and rose. Turning her back on him she walked out of the restaurant.

"Darcy! Darcy! Dammit! You're such a princess. You think you're so perfect. Well, guess what, you're not. And no one will ever live up to your dreams of perfection."

She wasn't looking for perfection, but she knew one thing, Prince Charming was no sex addict.

CHAPTER TWENTY-SIX

J osh downed his third cup of coffee and it wasn't yet ten a.m. Sleep had refused to put him out of his misery last night. First, he couldn't fall asleep knowing Darcy was only two doors down from him. He'd replayed the scene where he carried her into the house, the one where she buried her face in his neck and told him he smelled good.

Then he'd moved on to the scene where she told him she loved him, certain she'd meant it in a platonic way, but his heart sure didn't take it that way.

When he'd finally fallen asleep she'd haunted his dreams. In one dream, she'd wrapped her arms around his neck, whispering her love for him, as she kissed her way along his throat. The next, she was walking toward Blake, his arms outstretched for her, but she couldn't see the deep crevasse separating Blake from her.

Josh tried to run after her, to stop her before she fell, but his feet felt as if they were encased in concrete. He woke in a cold sweat, just moments after she plunged over the edge.

He didn't need dream analysis to understand what it meant. If he didn't man-up, and soon, she'd be lost to him forever.

———

That afternoon, Josh stood at Kelly's front door, papers in hand. He'd finally gathered all the documents the bank needed to refinance Kelly's house. After she signed them, he'd hand-carry them to the mortgage loan officer that very day. With any luck, Kelly and Daniel's long nightmare would be resolved by Labor Day. Delivering the good news would be a welcome distraction from the Darcy dilemma.

The door swung open and Kelly greeted Josh warmly. "Come in." Madonna blared from speakers in the living room. "Sorry, housecleaning day," she said, a look of chagrin on her face. "It doesn't suck as much when you're dusting to "Vogue"." Kelly walked over and picked up a remote to turn the volume down.

"I know what you mean."

"Really?" Kelly laughed, surprised.

"No." A smile tugged at the corners of his mouth. "Just trying to make you feel better."

"Gee, thanks. Can I get you something to drink?"

"Sure." He followed Kelly into the kitchen. "As promised, I have the papers, and just need your signature in about a million places and your initials in about a million more."

He settled at the kitchen table where they'd conducted all of their previous business, while Kelly poured lemonade over ice. "If it means saving my home and providing Daniel some stability, I'd sign those papers in blood."

"How is Daniel?"

"The same." She sighed. "But now he's having some problems in school." Kelly sat in the chair next to Josh and handed him a glass of lemonade.

"Behavior?"

"No, his geometry class. I may be an accountant, but geometry doesn't fall into my realm of expertise." She smiled sadly. "That was always Dan's job."

"It just so happens I was geometry champ at my middle school."

Kelly drew back. "Really?"

"No, that would have earned me a well-deserved butt-kicking, but I could help Daniel with his homework. I did ace my geometry class."

Kelly contemplated her lemonade a minute before looking up into Josh's eyes. "Josh, I don't want you to feel that you have to take care of Daniel or become some sort of father figure to him. You're already doing so much for us . . ." She trailed off.

"I wouldn't offer if I didn't want to help," Josh said quietly, his gaze locked with hers.

"Okay. If you're sure." She nodded and then picked up her pen. "So, where do I sign?"

———

An hour later, Josh had everything in order. Glancing at his watch, he realized he had plenty of time to get the papers to the bank before it closed.

"I'll call you to set up a time to work with Daniel." As he walked past the living room, he noticed a book lying on the sofa. He'd recognize that cover anywhere—*The Boss' Daughter*—Darcy's fifth novel.

"You like Darcy Butler?"

Kelly looked a little embarrassed. "Yes. Don't tell me you read romance novels?"

"As a matter of fact, I do, and I'm man enough to admit it." He laughed at the dubious expression on her face. "The author happens to be my best friend." *At least for now.*

"Get out!" Kelly shouted. "Seriously? You know Darcy Butler?"

"Yeah. Her new book comes out in a few months. I'll get you an autographed copy." He tried not to think of the living, breathing hero of that novel.

"That would be fantastic—if you think she wouldn't mind."

"Of course not. Hey, what are you and Daniel doing for the Fourth of July?"

"Probably just cooking out with my parents."

"Do you think your parents would mind if you and Daniel did something else?"

"I don't think so. They get so little time to just relax. Why?"

"Why don't you two come with me to Darcy's parents' house for their annual Independence Day cookout?"

"What? Oh, no. I couldn't." Kelly shook her head.

"Of course you could. The Butlers know how to throw a party and their philosophy is the more the merrier. And it would be great to get Daniel out of the city, even if only for a little while."

"I don't know. Are you sure?"

"Definitely."

"Well, I insist on bringing some steaks from the shop. I'll have my dad hand-cut some nice filets."

"If you'd like, but it's really not necessary."

"I'm not showing up empty-handed." Kelly's fist went to

her stomach, then she glanced up at Josh. "Oh God. I'm going to meet Darcy Butler."

"Yes, you are. And you're going to love one another."

CHAPTER TWENTY-SEVEN

J osh pulled up a seat next to Daniel at the kitchen table and reached into his messenger bag for a ruler, two rubber bands, and a measuring tape. Laughing at the look of confusion on Daniel's sullen face, he took a gulp of the iced tea Kelly placed at his elbow.

"Dude, I thought you were helping me with my geometry homework."

"I am. We're going to do a little experiment. Your mom told me you were working on angles in class."

"Yes," Daniel said, clearly still confused.

"Well, we're going to determine the best angle to throw a baseball to get the greatest distance."

"I don't see a baseball."

"Don't need one."

"Huh?"

Josh smiled. "Where's your protractor?"

Daniel rummaged around in his backpack before finding it.

Kelly walked past, her purse on her arm, and tousled Daniel's hair.

"Really, Mom?" Daniel whined.

A smile on her face, she said, "I'll be back later. You boys have fun."

"Whatever." Daniel rolled his eyes and smoothed out his hair.

"Let's get to work." Josh grabbed the ruler, the protractor, and a rubber band.

———

Josh wrestled the rubber band from Daniel's hand, eliciting protests, followed by laughter from Daniel, who turned his back to Josh. He bent over and curled himself into a ball just as Josh launched the rubber band, popping Daniel on the back.

"Ow! Dude, that's harsh!"

"Ha! No harsher than the one you zinged at my arm!" Josh took up a defensive stance as Daniel retrieved the rubber band.

"Boys! I thought you two were studying." Kelly dropped her keys and grocery bags onto the kitchen counter, a smile lighting her features. "Am I going to have to separate the two of you?"

"Mom, we just figured out the best angle to throw a baseball! Next week we're going to put what we learned into action at the park." Daniel's face beamed with excitement.

Kelly cut a quick glance at Josh before returning her gaze to Daniel. "That's great, honey."

"And Josh is going to show me how to throw a curve ball."

"Is he now?" She pulled a gallon of milk and a pack of deli meat from the grocery bags. As Josh gathered his things and placed them back in his bag, Kelly asked, "Would you like to stay for dinner?"

"Thanks, but I'm meeting some friends. Rain check?"

"Sure."

Slinging the bag over his shoulder he looked at Daniel, who stood chugging Gatorade straight from the bottle. "You ever play chess?"

"Chess? Isn't that for geeks?" He wiped his mouth with the back of his hand, then released a thunderous burp.

"Daniel," Kelly admonished.

"Well, I guess if the shoe fits," Josh shrugged.

"Whose shoe you talking about?"

"Yours, big shot. Anyway, it's time you learned. Chess is a game of skill and strategy. It develops logical thinking and spatial reasoning, and improves concentration and memory. It's the game of kings . . . and athletes."

Daniel's face still wore a look of skepticism.

"Kobe Bryant plays chess."

"Okay, all right. I get it." Daniel rolled his eyes. "Chess."

"Daniel, put your things away and get ready for dinner."

Daniel grabbed his backpack and, throwing it over his shoulder, headed to his room. "Thanks, Josh."

"Sure thing."

Kelly touched Josh on the arm, her eyes bright with tears. "I don't know what you did or how you did it, but I haven't heard Daniel laugh like that since before his father died." A tear rolled down her face.

"Hey . . . hey." Josh brushed away the tear with his thumb. If there was anything that broke his heart, it was seeing a woman cry. He'd seen his mother cry so many times growing up he'd lost count. "Don't cry."

"I'm fine. They're tears of joy." She swiped her face

then, grabbing his shoulders, stood on tiptoe and placed a kiss on his cheek. "Thank you. For everything."

Josh felt the heat color his cheeks. Embarrassed to find himself blushing like a schoolboy, he smiled and took his leave.

Whistling as he strode down the sidewalk to the subway station, he touched his cheek. Despite the Darcy Dilemma, his heart felt light. He'd made Daniel laugh and his mother cry. Right now, that was more than enough. That was everything.

———

D arcy had an epiphany. If *The Doctor's Dilemma* was still in copyediting, maybe, just maybe, she could change Blake's name, thus, eliminating the most obvious connection between her latest hero and her boyfriend. Of course, she might still have to explain their similarity of backgrounds, current professions, and appearance, but she'd deal with that later.

Interviewer: "Tell us, Ms. Butler, how is it your hero and your boyfriend are practically identical twins."

Darcy: "Oh, Blake served as my greatest inspiration for Garrick Blaine! Who wouldn't be inspired by the adventurous, philanthropic, and humanitarian life Blake has led?"

She dialed Gloria's cell number practicing her arguments while she waited.

"Gloria Madison."

After exchanging the usual pleasantries, which with Gloria were usually brief, Darcy took a deep breath and spun out her tale.

"I need to change Blake's name."

"What on earth for?"

"Well, it's kind of funny, really." Darcy's stomach started doing backflips. "You remember when Laura was injured and I had to go to the emergency room? The doctor who treated her was named Blake Garrett, and well, now Blake and I are dating."

"You mean to tell me a doctor, who happened to be named Blake Garrett treated Laura in the ER? And now you're dating him?"

"Yes. And Josh said it could be a real issue for the publisher, so I think we should change Blake's name."

"And what do you want to change his name to?"

"I was thinking Garrick Blaine." Darcy heard the clicking of a keyboard on the other end, followed by a rusty sigh.

"And I'm guessing you want me to make this happen?"

"Oh, could you?"

"If the manuscript is still in copyediting, I'll see what I can do."

"Thank you!" Darcy took a deep breath for the first time since Gloria's greeting. She hadn't expected it to be that easy to convince her. Maybe she'd fallen off the nicotine wagon.

"If you weren't my goddaughter . . ." Her voice trailed off, then she shouted for her assistant to get Elise Duncan, Darcy's editor, on the phone. "Now, when do I meet this Blake Garrett?"

CHAPTER TWENTY-EIGHT

D arcy had been both dreading and anticipating this day—the day that Blake would meet her parents. She thanked her lucky stars *The Doctor's Dilemma* was still in copyediting, so they could change her hero's name.

She glanced over at Blake, looking competent and relaxed as he pulled his car into her parents' driveway. Of course he wouldn't be nervous. The cool, calm, and collected Blake Garrett would never get nervous.

He looked handsome and patriotic in his navy polo with its little red polo player and white twill shorts, an expensive TAG Heuer diver's watch strapped to his wrist, while the sunglasses he wore gave him a rakish appearance.

Taking a deep breath to calm her jitters, she opened her door and waited for him to join her. Walking hand-in-hand, she led him through the house and out into the bright sunlit backyard. She'd wanted to arrive a little early to make the introductions before the rest of the guests arrived.

Her dad stood at his station, cleaning the grill with a scrub brush, a holiday-appropriate Sousa march blaring from the outdoor speakers. Her mom stepped out of the summer kitchen, her arms loaded with paper plates.

"Oh. Darcy. I didn't know you were here."

"Just."

Blake quickly stepped forward, relieving her mom of her burden.

"Thank you. You must be Blake." She tilted her head, giving him a careful appraisal.

"Mom, this is Blake Garrett. Blake, this is my mother, Vanessa." *Who knew they made gypsy skirts in red, white, and blue,* Darcy thought, as she made the introductions.

"Blake Garrett. Why does the name sound familiar?" She looked over at Darcy's father. "Jeff. Come meet Blake. Do we know the Garretts?"

Darcy's stomach knotted. Why would his name be familiar? She'd changed his name in the book. Had she mentioned her hero's name to her mother before?

Her father turned from his task and approached her. "Garretts? No, I don't think so."

"Um, Blake's family isn't from around here," Darcy muttered.

"Blake. Welcome. I'd shake your hand, but I can see Vanessa has already put you to work." Her dad wore a big grin as he wrapped his arm around her mother's waist.

"Blake was kind enough to help me with the plates," her mother explained. "Now, why don't you put those on the table over there? What can I get you to drink? I just made a fresh batch of lemonade."

"Lemonade sounds perfect. Thank you." Blake went to place the plates on the table as directed.

Her mother gave her a knowing look, then tossed her long silver tresses over her shoulder and headed into the house. "Darcy, want to give me a hand?"

Here comes the third degree disguised as idle chat. While her mother filled cups with ice from the icemaker, Darcy reached into the fridge to grab the pitcher of lemonade.

"Blake's a real looker. Where'd you two meet?"

Tiptoeing around the truth, Darcy told her mother about Laura's visit to the ER, explaining that Blake had been her doctor, of course leaving out the part about where she fainted because her hero had come to life.

"A doctor?"

Darcy cleared her throat before continuing. "A trauma surgeon, actually."

"Well, my, my. That's different."

"What's that supposed to mean?" Darcy frowned as she poured the lemonade into the cups.

"Well, my little Lizzie"—she patted her on the cheek —"you must admit your past dalliances have been with men more akin to Wickham than Darcy."

"Mom, don't call me Lizzie. Please." Her mother wasn't far off the mark comparing some of her past boyfriends, not to mention her ex-fiancé, to the unscrupulous George Wickham. Not that she'd had that many boyfriends since Doug. But most of the ones she did have had all been . . . what was the word she was looking for? Oh yeah, losers. Except for Steve. Then she remembered Steve as he pulled Miss November up the stairs. Okay. They all were.

She picked up two cups and strode out of the kitchen, effectively ending the conversation.

———

Josh checked Daniel's face in the rearview mirror of the Zipcar he'd picked up for the day. Normally he took the train to the Tarrytown station, but with the cooler of steaks Kelly brought and the other outdoor paraphernalia, the car was a better option.

When Josh turned into Darcy's parents' neighborhood, with its broad, tree-lined streets, multi-million dollar mansions tucked away behind gated entrances, and well-manicured lawns, he thought Daniel's eyes would pop out of his head. If nothing else, he thought Daniel might suffer whiplash, as fast as his head swung from side-to-side, taking it all in.

Josh could relate. The first time he'd been to Darcy's parents' house, he'd thought he'd just stepped into an episode of *MTV Cribs*.

Kelly played it cool. As if she drove past America's castles every day.

"Nice, huh?" Josh asked, catching Daniel's eye in the mirror.

"Your friend a rock star or something?"

"Close enough," Kelly murmured.

"It's not her house. It's her parents'," Josh clarified. "And no, she's not a rock star. Neither are her parents."

Kelly leaned forward for a better look as Josh pulled into the long circular driveway. "It's lovely. Nothing at all like I expected given the rest of the houses."

"Yeah, the house is one of the few originals remaining. All the other beautiful old Colonial style homes were bull-dozed to build the McMansions you see now."

He popped the trunk of the car and gathered Kelly's cooler, his baseball gear, and a couple of bottles of Vanessa's favorite wine that served as his contribution to the party.

"I'm nervous," Kelly whispered as she and Josh followed an excited Daniel up the walk.

"Don't be." Josh laughed and pointed to Daniel. "Clearly, he's not."

"Come on," Daniel urged.

Laughter floated through the house as Josh guided them to the backyard.

"Are there other kids?" Daniel asked.

"Yeah, but they're all younger than you." Josh replied.

"Oh." Daniel's disappointment fled as he looked out at the big lawn and the river beyond. "Whoa!"

Josh felt his own sense of disappointment when he spied Blake talking with Darcy's father. Of course Blake would be here. What did he expect?

"Come on, I'll introduce you to Darcy." Finding her playing in the sandbox with little Olivia, he caught Kelly's hand and crossed the lawn.

———

Darcy glanced up and saw Josh and a woman she knew must be Kelly approach. Her eyes flashed to their clasped hands, and she pressed her hand to the sudden pain in her chest. Must be her dad's famous jalapeno poppers she'd eaten.

Josh introduced the two women. "Kelly is a huge fan."

"Thanks."

"And this is her son, Daniel."

Darcy recognized the boy from the big screen video at the Yankees game. "Hi, Daniel."

"Hi," he replied, a little shy now that he had to interact with strangers.

Josh bent over to pick up Olivia and give her neck a little nuzzle. "Come on, Daniel." He slapped the boy on his shoulder. "Let's go find something to drink. How about you, Olivia, want some juice?"

Olivia nodded, sending her blond curls bouncing.

Darcy watched as Josh walked toward the summer kitchen, rubbing noses with her niece. Something about seeing a guy holding a child made Darcy's heart go all gooey. She gave herself a mental shake. That's Josh holding Olivia, something she'd seen him do hundreds of times. Of course, if Blake had been carrying Olivia in his arms, she'd have had the same reaction, she assured herself.

"He's the best," Kelly said, interrupting Darcy's internal argument.

"Yeah, he's a nice guy."

"He's more than a nice guy. He's a hero. He's my hero, anyway."

Darcy didn't like the dreamy look that glowed in Kelly's eyes.

"And he's fast becoming Daniel's." Kelly tucked an errant red lock behind her ear. "Don't get me wrong, no one can ever replace my late husband, Dan, but Josh has made me, and Daniel, believe in the goodness of people again."

Darcy could feel Kelly's eyes on her.

"But, you already knew that," Kelly said.

"Knew what?"

"That Josh is a hero."

Darcy looked at Kelly as if seeing her for the first time. "A hero?" She'd never considered Josh a hero. A really nice guy, of course. But a hero? Heroes were larger than life. Like Blake.

"Yeah. It's amazing that he's still single. A girl would be crazy not to go after a man like Josh."

The pain in her chest returned. Some antacids were definitely in order. "How long have you two been dating?"

Strange that Josh hadn't mentioned anything about it. Only that he'd met Kelly through the legal aid program.

Kelly drew back in surprise. "What?" Then she laughed. "Oh, no." She shook her head. "We're not dating. He's helping me with a legal problem, that's all."

Darcy exhaled in relief and smiled. "Oh."

CHAPTER TWENTY-NINE

Darcy took the bowl of pasta salad from Blake and made room for it on the table. Her family had been very welcoming. So far, Blake's unexplained existence remained under wraps. She'd seen Blake and Brandon talking over drinks while Will played with the new kitten her mother had rescued. Seeing Blake fit in, she'd begun to relax.

"So, you're the infamous Blake Garrett I've heard so much about."

Gloria's nails-in-a-blender voice cut through Darcy's complacency. This had all the earmarks of a disaster.

"I feel as if I've known you for the last eight months, at least." Gloria continued.

At Blake's questioning glance, Darcy said, "Blake, this is my agent and godmother, Gloria Madison. Obviously, Gloria, you know Blake—I mean I've told her so much about you," she added for Blake's benefit.

Blake politely shook Gloria's hand.

Gloria examined the hand in hers. "A trauma surgeon, I believe."

"Yes, that's right."

"Well, you do right by my girl."

"Yes, ma'am."

"She thinks you're perfect."

"Gloria," Darcy gasped, feeling the heat rise from her chest to her hairline.

"What?" Gloria's painted-on eyebrows shot up. "It's a lot for a man to live up to, and I think he should know what he's up against."

Gloria traipsed off in search of Darcy's mother.

"I'm sorry, Blake," she said, placing her hand on his arm.

"It's okay. Clearly, you have a lot of people who love you and only want what's best for you." He brushed his lips against hers, and she relaxed into his arms.

———

Josh observed their public display of affection and felt sick. Her family welcomed Blake with open arms, but what did he expect? They were by nature inclusive.

The evil Josh would like nothing better than to wing a ball at Blake's head, but unfortunately, the nice Josh won out.

He gathered up his bag of bats and turned to walk out to the makeshift ball field when Gloria tottered past him, muttering, "Did you ever get the feeling you're headed down a path that suddenly ends?"

Josh stumbled, dropping some of the bats, one of which clunked him on the shin. "Ow." *WTF!* Rubbing his abused shin, he stared after Gloria as she sauntered over to a lawn chair in the shade.

"Hey, Josh, the teams are set," Daniel called out as he ran over to help Josh pick up the bats. "Chris, you, and me, against Brandon, Mark, and David. To make things even, Darcy's friend, Blake, agreed to pitch for both teams."

"Super."

———

Darcy strolled over to where the guys were in the second inning, with Josh's team up by two.

Josh got a base hit, and Kelly yelled, "All right, Josh!"

"When did Josh start dating someone?" Laura asked, gesturing with her wine to where Kelly played cheerleader.

"He's not," Darcy said, a little too emphatically, even to her own ears.

"Well, alrighty then." Laura rolled her eyes. "What's with you two lately?"

"Nothing."

After his at-bat, Daniel ran over to his mom and took a bottle of water out of her hand before guzzling it. "Josh is really good!"

"He should be," Darcy interjected, "he played shortstop in high school and was offered a full ride to UCLA."

"No way!"

"Yes way. Said he'd only have to play the mandatory three years before they drafted him into the majors."

Daniel's eyes grew big. "He played college baseball for UCLA?"

"Nope. Got a scholarship to NYU, and took that instead."

"What! Why would he do that?"

"I guess his education was more important to him than baseball."

Josh approached, looking for something ice cold to drink.

"Hey, Josh?" Daniel stopped him. "How come you never told me you played shortstop?"

"That was a long time ago."

"Darcy said you were really something. Could have played in the majors."

Josh reached into the cooler for a beer. "Maybe. No guarantee." He twisted off the top and took a swig. "An education seemed a better bet than taking a chance I might play in the majors."

"If I get offered a scholarship to play ball, I won't pass it up."

Josh reached out and grabbed the bill of Daniel's cap. "You better improve your batting average first." He slapped Daniel on the back and the two walked back to their teammate.

Darcy spied her sister, Anne, sitting alone on a bench beneath the big maple tree. Anne had been overly cheerful all day but now looked completely deflated. When asked by their mother where Matt was, she'd said he was working. Darcy didn't believe Matt would be working and away from his family on the Fourth.

She decided to confront Anne about it while she was alone. Grabbing a couple of diet sodas out of the cooler, she strolled over to the bench, offering one to Anne.

"Thanks."

They sat in silence a few minutes, watching the game. Darcy offered up words of encouragement to Blake when Brandon stepped up to bat with one of her ear-piercing whistles. "Woo! Strike him out, Dr. Garrett!"

When Brandon got a base hit he gave Darcy an obscene gesture.

"Aww, look, Brandon loves me."

"Why aren't you out there playing, Miss Tomboy Princess?" Anne took a deep pull on her soda.

"Don't want to show up the guys." Darcy grinned. "You know, fragile egos. Speaking of the guys, where's Matt? Because I know he's not working."

Anne sighed. "I threw him out."

"What? When? Why?" Darcy stammered, aghast at Anne's news. She didn't know what she'd expected, but that wasn't it.

"We're separated. Since May. We're going through a rough patch." Anne hesitated, staring across the lawn. "And I don't know if we'll make it out the other side."

"Of course you will!" Darcy laid her hand on Anne's shoulder and then removed it, knowing Anne wasn't the most affectionate person. "You guys are perfect together."

"Don't fool yourself, Darcy." Anne's shoulders slumped.

Darcy hated to see her resilient sister so discouraged.

"Marriage . . . relationships . . . aren't fairytales. They take work, especially with a few years, two kids, two careers, and a mortgage under your belt. After you and your prince ride off into the sunset, the real work begins, and you better make damn sure he's up to the task." She gestured with her soda can, pointing her finger at Darcy.

"It's not another woman, is it? I'll personally kick Matt's ass if that's the case."

"No. It's not another woman. He barely has time for the women in his life now." Anne crushed the empty can in her hand. "We just argue all the time, over everything; money, the kids, the house, sex."

Darcy cringed. Her sister's sex life wasn't high on Darcy's list of topics for discussion.

"The two of you will work it out, right? I mean, you still love each other."

Anne sighed as she rose. "Sometimes, Darcy, love just isn't enough." With that, she turned and walked into the house.

Darcy rose to go after her but then dropped wearily back onto the bench. She remembered vividly the day Anne and Matt got married. She thought if anyone's marriage would last, it would be theirs. It was disheartening to think it might not.

———

H ot, tired, and dejected, Darcy sat quiet and moody during the ride back into the city. When Blake asked if she was okay, she blamed it on a headache and turned to stare out her window. She felt a battle brewing inside, looking for an escape valve, and try as she might, she couldn't stop herself.

"Blake, why don't we ever argue?"

He glanced over at her before he focused on the busy road again. "Why would we argue?"

"I don't know. Don't you ever want to do something I don't want to do? Or tell me how to do something? Don't you get aggravated when I eat off your plate or steal a sip of your drink?"

Blake laughed. "No."

No. Just no. That's all he's got to say? "Don't you ever get jealous over the time I spend with Josh?"

"No, why would I? You two are best friends. I understand that." He shrugged.

Dammit! Isn't there anything that torques this guy off? "Well, what if I said Harvard is for brainiacs who can't play sports."

Chuckling, he reached for her hand. "Darcy, you can

say whatever you like about Harvard, I'm not going to sue you for slander." He put his hand back on the steering wheel. "And I'm not going to argue with you over the fact that we don't argue."

When Blake didn't give her the satisfaction of arguing with her, Darcy huffed out a breath and crossed her arms over her chest, patently ignoring him the rest of the way home.

CHAPTER THIRTY

———————

J osh figured the only way he'd see Darcy was to show up at her house unannounced. He hadn't seen her in a couple of weeks, and she'd declined every attempt to get together because she was booked—with Blake, with book promotion, with writing. Too busy to make time for him.

Millie answered his knock. With Blake in the picture, he didn't want to risk using his key and walking in on something he definitely did not want to see.

"Hi, Millie. Hey, are those new glasses?"

Millie touched the brown frames. "Yes." A frown creased her brow. "My mother's dog chewed up the other pair."

"They look very nice. Maybe you should give that dog a treat." Josh grinned and winked at her.

Millie lifted a brow. "Thank you. She's in the kitchen. And she's grouchy."

"Thanks for the warning."

Josh found Darcy preparing a cup of tea, wearing a pair of baggy sweats and an old Columbia Law T-shirt, her hair disheveled and her face worn. She'd had some difficult times with books in the past, but not like this.

He'd come by to rag on her over her neglect of their friendship, but seeing her changed his mind. She needed a pick-me-up instead. Pizza and a movie might do it.

"Hey, Darce."

"What are you doing here?" She paused in pouring water into her teacup.

"Is that any way to greet your best friend in the whole world?"

"Sorry. Tough day in the salt mines."

"Yeah, about that. Why don't we do pizza and a movie tonight? My treat. You can even pick the movie."

"Josh, I don't know. I can't really afford to take the time—"

"From the looks of you, you can't afford *not* to take the time." He leaned his hip against the counter opposite Darcy.

"Gee, thanks." She stirred cream into her tea. "You really know how to sweet-talk a girl."

"Come on. Relax tonight. It might get the creative juices flowing again."

"You know, you might be right."

"Pardon me, Darcy," Millie interrupted. "Don't forget you have an interview with *The New York Times Magazine* in half an hour."

"No, I don't." She stirred a little cream into her Darjeeling tea.

"Yes, you do."

Darcy rounded on Millie. "I don't have an interview! You've screwed up. Haven't I told you to use the iPad I gave you to schedule my appointments? Then this wouldn't happen. You must have put it on my calendar for the wrong day."

Millie replied in an even tone, "I don't need an electronic gadget to do my job, and I don't screw up. You have an interview today, and it is on your calendar for the correct day."

Josh watched the exchange, noticing Millie's clenched jaw.

"That's impossible! That can't be!" Darcy's voice rose in panic. "Look at me! How am I supposed to do an interview in half an hour?"

"Okay, let's just calm down." Josh stepped between Millie and Darcy.

"It's just a magazine interview. It doesn't matter what you look like," Millie said, her arms folded across her chest, her expression that of a mother dealing with an unreasonable child.

Darcy threw her arms up in the air. "Like you would know. I *care* about *my* appearance."

Millie stood her ground even as her hands clenched into fists. "Fine. You better get dressed then." She pivoted on her heel and left the room.

As soon as the words had left her mouth, Darcy knew she'd been unkind, but before she could call Millie back, she heard the front door slam.

Josh paced toward her, then pointed in the direction of Millie's departure. "That woman busts her ass for you, and this is how you repay her. Look, you might be under a great deal of stress, but you don't talk to people that way. The Darcy I know would never intentionally hurt another person."

"Josh, I'm not excusing what I said to Millie, but I'm telling you, Millie made a mistake. She put the interview on my calendar for Tuesday."

"Darcy, today *is* Tuesday." He turned to leave the room, but stopped just shy of the door. "You should be ashamed of yourself. I know I am."

A wave of regret swept through Darcy. Josh's quiet reproach cut her more deeply than any thunderous scolding. Her legs gave out, sending her crumpling to the floor, where she covered her shame-reddened face and cried.

———

The next evening, Darcy raised her hand to knock then, biting her lip, lowered it. It seemed silly to knock when she had her own key, but now was not the time to let herself in with it. *What if he tells her he never wants to see her again? Or just slams the door in her face?* She couldn't bear losing Josh's friendship.

She'd pulled herself together long enough yesterday for the interview she didn't think she had, but when she replayed the scene in her mind she'd cried for hours and gone to bed with a splitting headache. She'd hurt two people she loved, and she was so mortified by her behavior. She'd already made it right with one, now she had to face the other. Taking Lady MacBeth's advice, she *screwed her courage to the sticking-place*, and raised her fist to knock.

Just when she thought he wasn't home, the door flew open. Josh stood, arm braced against the door, wearing nothing but his wet hair and a pair of jeans, unbuttoned at the waist, as if he'd dressed in haste.

Her visceral reaction to him practically knocked her backward. He looked so . . . sexy! The combination of wet, tousled hair, exposed chest, flat stomach, and bare feet sent a shiver of desire up her spine. *Get a hold of yourself,* she admonished. This is *Josh,* for God's sakes. Laura could be right. It *had* been too long since she'd had sex.

"Yes?" Josh raised his brow.

"Hi." It suddenly occurred to her that he may not be alone and that thought hit her like a punch to the gut. "Am I disturbing you . . . anything . . . you?"

"No."

Relieved, she gathered her wits and took a deep breath, and told herself to maintain eye contact—*with his eyes, yes, that was it.* "Josh, I'm really sorry about yesterday."

"I'm not the one you should be apologizing to."

"I've already apologized to Millie. And given her a raise. A substantial one." She gave Josh a sheepish smile.

"Good."

He still didn't invite her in, and his cold demeanor left her with a knot in her stomach. She had to do something to unlock his usual easygoing manner.

"Are we still on for the Yankees game this Saturday?" *Whoa!* So much for eye contact. She found herself looking at that expanse of bare . . . lightly furred . . . well-defined chest. Who knew such deliciousness lay beneath those T-shirts and dress shirts? The thin streak of brown hair down the center of his belly blazed a path to his waist, drawing her eye to where it disappeared beneath the open button of his jeans. Had he always been this buff?

"If you don't have anything else better to do."

Her eyes shot back to his face. That stung. "Look, Josh. I know I haven't been around much lately, but between Blake's social schedule and my promotional schedule it's been brutal—"

"I get it. No need to concern yourself on my account."

She felt tears prick the back of her eyes. She'd really screwed up this time and she didn't know how to make it right. "Josh, what can I do? How can I make it up to you?" She wiped the tear that threatened to fall. "You're my best friend," she whispered, unable to get any more volume past the lump in her throat.

Josh raked his hands through his hair, then reached out and grabbed her shoulders, pulling her into his embrace. "Hey, don't do that. I hate it when you cry. It's okay." He rubbed her back, making soothing circles.

She sobbed in relief, pressing her face to his bare chest, mumbling incoherently about boyfriends and friends, interviews and public appearances. Words that wouldn't come to her. And stress. After a few minutes her sobs subsided and it dawned on her that she had her face pressed to his deliciously warm skin . . . that smelled of soap and virile male, and that her hands caressed his naked . . . muscular . . . athletic back. *Step away from the hunky best friend.*

Digging deep for the willpower, she moved out of Josh's strong . . . capable . . . arms. *Get a grip, girlfriend!*

"All better now?" Josh asked, his voice hopeful.

Darcy brushed the tears from her face and nodded, too embarrassed to look him in the eye.

Josh closed the distance she'd put between them and lifted her chin. "Darcy, I will always tell you the truth, even when it hurts. That's what true friends do for one another."

Her eyes flickered to his lips. She wondered . . . the next thing she knew she'd grasped his neck, pulling his mouth down to hers. She had to know. It was only meant to be an experiment, to test her hypothesis that Blake's kisses were as close to the Perfect Kiss as she could get, but when Josh began kissing her back, he proved her theory so, so wrong.

CHAPTER THIRTY-ONE

t first, completely shocked by Darcy's assault, Josh scrambled to arrange his jumbled thoughts. He hadn't missed the look on her face when she'd raked her eyes over his bare chest. He'd felt the tingle all the way down to his bare feet.

He'd dreamed of the moment when Darcy would kiss him with the passion and intensity he always knew she possessed, but this was far beyond anything he could have imagined. Soft lips caressed his, while her sweet tongue tangled with his.

Her body grew pliant in his arms as their breath mingled in white-hot kisses. Her fingers fisted in his hair, even as his twisted in hers, grasping and holding her lips to his. *But this was Darcy! Nothing but disaster could come from this!*

She trembled in his arms, her soft moans shooting heat straight to his groin where it pooled in his abdomen. Lust so hot and sudden it threatened to scorch his very being. *The hell with it.* He backed into his apartment, pulling her with him, all the while ensuring her lips never left his. Slamming the door, he pressed her against it, breaking the kiss to nip and caress the silky, pheromone-scented skin of her neck. Her moan of pleasure only drove his passions higher.

She slid her hands down his back, grazing him with her nails, before plunging into the open waistband of his jeans and kneading the bare flesh there. He grabbed her face and brought those sweet, hot lips back to his, unable to get enough of her delicious mouth.

Thank God for the summer heat. The little summer dress she wore gave him easy access to her breasts, as he slipped the straps from her shoulders. He caressed one and then the other, as he licked and nipped, until her sighs rasped harshly in her throat. So perfect. So delicious. A dream finally realized.

He felt her hands on his fly, tugging on the zipper. When she slipped her hand inside to stroke him, he thought he would explode. He tugged off his jeans, impatient to touch her again, then skimmed the velvety skin of her outer thighs, eliciting a shiver, before reaching around her bottom and lifting her up against the door. She wrapped her thighs around his waist, nipping at his earlobe, her breath panting in his ear.

Shoving aside her panties, he filled her in one smooth stroke, his world narrowing to the hot, sweet bliss of the moment.

Darcy threw her head back in pleasure so intense as to almost be unbearable. No words were necessary, as if words were even possible. Her breath snagged in her throat and her heart hammered in her chest, making deep throaty moans the only verbalizations possible. Each thrust sent her spiraling higher than the last, spinning out of control until she thought she would surely shatter.

She grasped and clawed Josh's shoulders as his strong

arms supported her, his scorching lips caressing her face, her neck, her mouth. She warred between never wanting this to end and the desire for sweet release. As she approached the precipice, she pulled Josh's mouth back down to hers, swallowing his cries of pleasure even as she soared over the edge.

Nothing intruded into their secluded world but the sound of their ragged breathing. Josh's legs trembled, his body spent from the onslaught, but he still held her, basking in the feel of being inside Darcy. Never in his life had he experienced such mind-numbing ecstasy.

He knew guilt would soon follow. Guilt for shoving his best friend against the front door and impaling her. Even a little guilt for having just cuckolded Garrett—if cuckolding a fictional character were possible. But right now, he didn't care. He pressed his forehead to hers and kissed her nose. "Darcy—"

His cell phone rang. "Damn." If he hadn't been waiting on a call from one of the firm's partners he'd ignore it. He gently lowered Darcy until her feet touched the floor and tugged on his jeans he ran to grab the phone.

"Josh Ryan."

"Oh, Josh," Kelly cried.

"Kelly! What is it? Is it Daniel?" His heart took on a life of its own, threatening to bounce right out of his chest.

"I just got home and . . . and"—she hiccoughed—"there was a Notice of Sale taped to my front door! What do I do? I can't lose my home," she sobbed.

"All right, Kelly. Calm down. We'll get this straightened out." He could hear her still sobbing on the other end. He paced the length of his small kitchen. "Listen to me, Kelly. You aren't going to lose your home. This is clearly a case of the right hand not knowing what the left hand is doing. I spoke to the lender's trustee last week and we have a deal. I'm on my way, but I'm not hanging up until I can get a coherent response out of you."

"Okay, I'm okay, Josh," she sniffed. "Thank you."

"I'll see you soon." Josh hung up. "Son of a bitch!" He strode out of the kitchen, zipping and buttoning his fly.

Darcy stood in front of the door, adjusting her clothes, an apprehensive look on her face.

Damn it! What a time to be interrupted. They needed to talk, but it would have to wait.

"I'm sorry, Darcy, I have to go." He scrubbed his hand through his hair. He didn't know whether to hug her or kiss her, or just leave her alone.

"I heard. It's fine." Her voice sounded tiny, as if she wanted to go unnoticed.

He swore to himself that he'd make it up to her as he dashed into the bedroom, grabbed a shirt and some shoes and got dressed.

When he came out, Darcy was gone.

———

That afternoon, Darcy waited for Laura in the lobby of the fitness center for their biweekly Booty Barre class. Emotionally, she wasn't up for it, but she knew Laura would track her down like a bloodhound after an escaped convict if she didn't show.

Laura walked in, the ever-present smartphone to her ear, looking as if she were one of those TV fitness celebrities in her Lululemon color-coordinated yoga outfit. "Yes, I'm meeting with the client on Monday morning, and I should have the creative brief to the team first thing Tuesday morning. In the meantime, I need numbers on their target audience on my desk later today. I'll swing by and pick them up before my meeting with the airline account. Right. Bye." She shoved her phone into her bag.

"Wow! Look at you, lookin' all . . ." She gasped, staggering back. "You got laid!"

"No, I didn't." Even Darcy could hear the defensiveness in her tone.

Laura waggled her finger at her. "Don't deny it. You've got that JBF look. You and Blake finally did the deed! And recently, judging by the dreamy eyes and the flushed cheeks! Took you long enough. So, how was it?" she asked conspiratorially, elbowing Darcy in the ribs.

Damn Laura and her Super Sex Sensor Skills. "I'm sorry to disappoint you, but no we didn't. Blake's in India, remember?" She fumbled in her gym bag, hiding her face from Laura's scrutiny. "Your Sex Sensor is on the fritz."

"Huh." She scrutinized Darcy once more. "Well, that's a first." She followed Darcy into the fitness room. "Maybe I'm losing my touch."

CHAPTER THIRTY-TWO

Darcy stumbled her way through class, her mind about thirty blocks away in Josh's apartment . . . against his door . . . in his arms . . . having mind-blowing sex. *Stop it!*

Laura said the Perfect Kiss didn't exist. Well, she was Wrong, with a capital 'W'. Darcy had finally experienced the Perfect Kiss and its owner was Josh. He'd kissed her with the ideal combination of heat and tenderness, seduction and devotion, need and fulfillment. What was she supposed to do now?

The guilt she carried around threatened to drop her to her knees under its weight. She and Blake had never said they were exclusive, but they never said they would see other people either. She was a horrible, horrible person. *Slut! Tramp! Tart!* She was no better than Doug 'The Cheating Bastard' Lansing. She groaned. She was Darcy 'The Cheating Ho' Butler.

"You okay?" Laura panted, as she performed her double-time *battements*.

"Tough workout," Darcy huffed.

It had been a mistake on so many levels. First, there was

the whole Blake issue. How could she ever face him again? Second, there was Josh—her best friend—and you didn't have sex with your best friend . . . up against a door . . . or anywhere else for that matter. What must he think of her? What would this do to their relationship? She didn't want to lose him. And really, she was to blame. She'd grabbed him, kissed him, fondled him. Another moan escaped, inviting another look from Laura.

Third, she'd finally experienced her Perfect Kiss. She was ruined for any other kisses. How could she ever be satisfied with anything less again?

———

J osh closed his front door and dropped his keys on the console table in his foyer. Turning, he stared at the door where just hours ago he'd had the best sex of his life. He could still recall the feel of Darcy's legs around his waist, the taste of her skin beneath his tongue. He would never look at the back of his door again without seeing her there, eyes glazed with desire, lips swollen from his kisses.

Releasing a weighty sigh, he went to the fridge for a beer and took a deep, satisfying pull. What a day. He'd gone from one extreme to another. Frustration over Darcy's treatment of Millie, soaring heights of passion with Darcy, instant fight or flight with Kelly, despair over the potential damage to his relationship with Darcy.

He'd told Darcy that he'd always tell her the truth no matter how much it hurt. But that was a lie. He didn't tell her the truth when it came to his feelings for her.

At least Kelly's issue had been resolved. It was exactly as he'd thought. Communication of the mortgage deal hadn't trickled down to the clerical staff. What a cluster fuck. But he'd calmed Kelly down, and decompressed on the subway ride back to SoHo.

He rubbed the back of his neck where the muscles knotted with tension. What he needed was a long, hot shower. Passing the front door again on the way to his bedroom, another memory of Darcy, looking timid and small, flashed through his mind.

He groaned. What had he done? He'd finally fulfilled a deep-seated need, but at what cost?

———

Josh had left five messages for Darcy. Clearly she wasn't taking his calls. He had no other choice but to knock on her door and beg her to talk to him. He had to make this right, and he'd made up his mind to make it right by telling her the truth, once and for all, and let the proverbial chips fall where they may.

He knocked on her door, then shoved his hands in his pockets, hoping to calm his nerves.

The door flew open. "Josh! What are you doing here?" Darcy stood, a surprised expression on her face, wearing a baggy pair of sweats and a ratty T-shirt he recognized from their trip to Ben & Jerry's Factory Tour and Flavor Graveyard almost eight years ago, her hair in a messy twist on top of her head. She looked adorable and very kissable. And exhausted.

"What am I doing here? Why didn't you answer my calls? That's what I'm doing here."

"I've just been busy . . . with the manuscript."

"Can I come in?"

"Um, sure." She left him at the door as she walked into the living room.

"Can I get you something, soda, beer? Oh, I guess it's a little early for beer." She twisted her hands nervously in front of her.

"Darcy, if I wanted something to drink, I'd get it myself, just like I always have."

"Right. Josh—"

"Darcy—"

They both spoke at the same time.

"We need to talk." Josh said, then winced at the sound of it. "I mean—"

"Josh"—she paced away from him—"I'm really sorry about the other day. It was a mistake. I shouldn't have thrown myself at you." She turned back to him. "I plead temporary insanity." She lifted the corner of her mouth in a small, watery smile. "Your friendship means too much to allow this . . . moment of weakness to get in the way. Can we just forget it ever happened?"

Josh felt sick. An eight hundred pound elephant had just stepped on his chest . . . and started bouncing on it. *A mistake? That's what sex with him had been? Forget it ever happened? Not likely. Not ever.* So much for coming clean. He knew now where he stood.

"Josh, are we okay? Please, just say we're okay. I can't lose you." Tears spilled over, running down her face.

He wanted to take her in his arms and hold her, but that was what had gotten him into this mess in the first place, so he just stood his ground, feeling as if gravity were twice what it should be. "We're okay. Please. Don't cry."

"I'm so sorry, Josh."

"Yeah. Me, too. Listen, I'm meeting some of the guys for basketball, so I'll call you later?"

"Sure." She swiped her hand across her face, wiping away her tears.

Josh strode to the front door, looking back one more time at what could have been. But no more. It was time to face reality. And reality declared it was time to move on.

———

A s soon as she heard the door click, Darcy's legs gave out and she crumpled to the floor and burying her face in her hands. She'd ruined everything. No matter how hard they tried, things would never be the same between her and Josh. Maybe one day they'd get over the awkwardness, but there would always be this *thing* between them, a scar on their friendship, a constant reminder of their momentary indiscretion.

And where was Blake in all this? Adding to the layer of guilt she already felt was remorse for having given so little thought to her feelings for Blake and how she should handle the situation with him. He'd be back any day now and she didn't have a clue what to do. She desperately needed someone to talk to, someone who could give her sound advice, but she was too mortified by her actions to share them with anyone, especially Laura. And the painful irony was that she usually went to Josh for sound advice.

Her conscience told her to come clean with Blake, but telling him would strain the already tenuous relationship he had with Josh. Even if she and Blake were to marry, she couldn't just write Josh out of her life. She needed Blake and Josh to at least tolerate one another. That couldn't be if Blake knew they'd had sex.

So far, Blake hadn't shown any signs of a jealous side, then again, she hadn't really given him a reason to. Until now. But fear that he might confront Josh urged her to keep the incident a secret. She didn't want to be the cause of an argument, or worse, a physical altercation, between the two men.

That settled it. She wouldn't tell Blake. The only purpose it would serve would be to alleviate some of her guilt, and she didn't deserve to unburden herself. She deserved to carry the guilt around her neck like Coleridge's Albatross.

Having reached a decision, the knot in her stomach loosened just a bit. But only a bit.

CHAPTER THIRTY-THREE

Two weeks later, Darcy showed the caterer to her kitchen so she could set up for the party and then returned to help Millie with the decorations, doing her best to calm her frayed nerves. The source of her nerves wasn't the party. Darcy could throw a shindig with the best of them. The source of the nerves was the shindig's honoree.

Months ago, Darcy had happily volunteered to throw Josh a party in celebration of his partnership in her father's law firm. But that was before their recent sexscapade. Nevertheless, a promise was a promise.

It wasn't as if she didn't *want* to throw her best friend a party, she did. But did the party have to follow so closely on the heels of their . . . illicit encounter? If she got through it without spontaneously combusting in mortification it would be a miracle.

"Darcy, where do you think we should have guests put any cards and gifts?"

"We can clear off the small console table in the foyer."

"Perfect." Millie carried her ever-present clipboard and

ticked off her schedule of events for the evening. "First, the honoree will say a few words, followed by your father, and the honoree's mother."

Butterflies danced in Darcy's stomach. She loved Josh's mom, but seeing her after having had door-sex with her son would be as mortifying as seeing Josh again.

"Next, we'll open the buffet line. After everyone has filled their plates, we'll begin the slide show—"

With the help of some of Josh's colleagues, and his mother, Darcy had put together a slide show of photos from law school, the day he graduated, the day he passed the bar, and the day he won his first case.

Mixed in were shots from around the office, like the one of Josh's office after his colleagues decorated it in honor of the Yankees' 2009 World Series win, another one of him in one of the firm's conference rooms, the table covered in documentary evidence for an upcoming trial and Josh with his head on the table sound asleep. Then there were the photos of him with clients from the Women's Legal Fund of Harlem, including Kelly, all set to "Razzle Dazzle" from *Chicago*.

"Followed by much drunken revelry, with guests dancing around with lampshades on their heads," Darcy interjected, dryly.

Millie frowned at Darcy. "That's not on the list and you know it."

"Relax, Millie. I bet even if we don't stick to your schedule, everyone will have a good time, and we'll still hit the evening's high points."

"Just trying to be helpful," Millie said, sliding the pen behind her ear.

Relax, she says. A case of do as I say, not as I do, if I ever saw one. How could she relax when every time she looked at Josh her knees turned to Jell-O and her stomach felt as if she were riding Coney Island's Cyclone roller coaster?

Darcy stepped back to review their handiwork. The living room furniture had been pushed up against the walls, leaving space for the partiers. The dining room table awaited trays loaded with some of Josh's favorites, including her gourmet pigs in a blanket.

Through the kitchen, on the other side of the stairs, they'd set up a bar area featuring wine, beer, water, and mixers. The revelers could spill out her back door and into her snug garden, now covered by a tent with tiny white lights that would twinkle once the sun set. The DJ would set up there. She'd promised her neighbors the noise would be over no later than eleven o'clock. The only thing left for Darcy to do was to get dressed. And strap on a pair while she was at it. Yep. Time to put on a dress, and man up.

———

Darcy put the finishing touches on her appearance, hoping her cool blue-and-white Tory Burch dress would soothe her frayed nerves, while Laura sat on her bed and tapped out one email after another. "I'm going to have that thing surgically removed," Darcy said, glancing at Laura in her mirror.

"Just try it," Laura shot back.

Earlier, Laura had peered into Darcy's face and asked if she was okay. Darcy blamed her dark circles on Blake's absence, when really she'd barely given Blake more than a passing thought, which only added to her misery.

Millie knocked and then came in as Darcy slipped on

her strappy fuchsia sandals. "Millie, you can change in the spare bedroom if you'd like."

"Change?" Millie glanced down at her dull brown dress, confusion altering her otherwise unflappable demeanor. "Why would I change?"

"You mean you're wearing that?" Laura asked, her face a study in horror, her smartphone forgotten in the shock.

The shapeless brown dress boasted small sprigs of flowers reminiscent of a 1920's floral wallpaper pattern. Over it, Millie had pulled on an oversized cardigan, in an unflattering cross between mustard yellow and overcooked-asparagus green.

"Yes." She lifted a brow in defiance. "I don't understand the question."

"Where ever did you find it?" Laura asked, looking as if she'd just swallowed a bug. "Never mind. There must be something we can do." She walked into Darcy's closet and began pulling out and discarding various belts. Settling on a narrow gold belt, she wrapped it around Millie's diminutive waist and fastened it. Standing back, her hands on her hips, she assessed Millie's shape. "You actually have a figure hiding under those baggy clothes you wear."

Turning back to the closet, she found a sunny yellow shrug and ordered Millie to take off the yellow-green monster and put on the shrug. Millie rolled her eyes, but complied.

Darcy and Laura stepped back. Darcy cocked her head, thinking Millie looked quite put-upon. And schlumpy. Schlumpier than she had without the belt and shrug. Darcy cut Laura a look, made a face, then shook her head.

"Okay. Fine." Laura removed the items and tossed them on the bed and snatched up her phone. "You win. For now.

But your day is coming. Consider yourself warned," she tossed over her shoulder as she left the room.

Josh's feelings ran the gamut. Satisfaction in having attained a long-held goal. Joy at having his mother here to celebrate with him. Dread at seeing Darcy again and facing the reality of his decision to move on. How could so many divergent feelings exist in a person at once, he wondered?

Josh glanced over at his mom and smiled. She had a death-grip on the door of the taxi as it sped through traffic. She gasped as the taxi stopped barely inches from the bumper of the car in front of them.

"We're going to be killed. How can you sit there so calm?"

"You get used to it."

He hadn't seen Darcy in two weeks. Not since he'd left her house determined to move on. The question he'd failed to answer during that time was how did he move on and yet still keep her friendship? You couldn't find an answer to that question in law books.

"We're here."

"Thank God," his mother breathed.

Josh tossed the driver some bills and helped his mother out. He hesitated before reaching for the brass doorknob on Darcy's front door.

"Are you all right?" his mother asked.

"Yes. Just nervous."

"Well, for heaven's sake, what do you have to be nervous about? These are your friends, and they're throwing you a party."

"Right." He opened the door, calling out "Hello" as entered.

"Josh. Hi." Darcy didn't look him in the eye, choosing instead to gaze beyond him at the painting hanging in the foyer. Her stomach executed a perfect somersault.

"Hey, Darce." He didn't reach for her, just maintained a safe distance.

"Hi, Janet." *I had sizzling hot door-sex with your son.* "It's so good to see you!" Darcy hugged his mom, who then held Darcy at arm's length.

"I think you get more beautiful every time I see you. Doesn't she, Josh?"

Darcy could feel Josh's eyes on her face as her cheeks burned.

"Every time," he muttered.

Laura sauntered up. "Vampire."

"Succubus."

"What's the difference between a lawyer and a vampire?"

"A vampire only sucks blood at night."

"Damn," she muttered, before turning to his mom. "Hi, Janet, how are you?" She leaned in and brushed her cheek.

Long used to Laura and Josh's barbs, Josh's mom returned Laura's kiss and let her lead her into the living room, leaving Josh and Darcy alone.

The tension, as tangible between them as any wall, tormented her. How do they get back to just Darcy and Josh?

"Thanks, Darcy." Josh broke the silence. "For doing this." He took her hand and held it, his touch casual and friendly, but the frisson of desire his touch brought her intensified the flush.

She gave him a hesitant smile. "Of course. It's my pleasure."

She could see a sliver of light through the tiny crack that just opened in the wall.

CHAPTER THIRTY-FOUR

Josh good-naturedly accepted the hearty backslaps, the hugs and kisses, and the drinks one person after the next pressed on him, all the while roaming the party keeping Darcy, beautiful as always, in his sights.

Her usually straight hair hung thick with waves, just begging to be touched, but the blush that rose to her cheeks when she'd greeted him couldn't hide the dark circles under her eyes.

He wondered if she could lay the blame for her sleepless nights on him, Blake, or the party. Whatever the reason, he hated to see her so distressed.

He'd never be able to convey how much he appreciated all the effort she'd put into this party. When she'd offered to throw him a bash, he'd been honored. She's always been there for him—a little less now with Blake in the picture—but for the big things, she hadn't let him down.

He owed it to her to be a good friend—to be there for her no matter what—to put their momentary heart-pounding, blood-pulsing lapse in judgment behind them. *If that's what she wants, I can do that.* Her laughter floated across the room, sultry and sweet, making his heart stutter. *Or not.*

———

The drinks flowed, the food vanished, the conversation hummed, and the music pulsated. Darcy took a spin around the tent outside, ensuring Josh's guests were having a good time.

The video was a hit, with the throng *oohing, ahing,* and laughing over the photos. Toasts were made, jokes told, and congratulations offered. The initial anxiety notwithstanding, Darcy declared the party a huge success.

She and Josh avoided any close contact all evening, reducing the anxiety to a manageable level. He looked so sexy in his white button-down and dark-wash jeans. Had he always been that sexy and she'd just never noticed? Or did having mind-altering sex with him, well, alter her mind? What difference did it make, how or when it happened? She had to get Josh out of her head.

Darcy watched as Cindy and Martin, still wearing their newlywed glow, danced as if they were the only two people in the world. Her heart ached at the sight. Happy for them, confused for herself.

Her father gave Janet a spin, while her mother cut the rug with Mark. Her mom had rhythm, Darcy had to give her that. Kelly boogied with Daniel, who looked as if he wanted to be anywhere but on the dance floor with his mother. Gloria did a little bump-and-grind with Chris, who'd apparently had one too many.

Check that, Darcy thought, as he made a grab for Gloria's ass, *more like twenty too many.*

Laura sidled up next to her, champagne glass in hand.

"I think Josh's friend there is wasted." She pointed to Chris with her glass. "Wonderful party, Darce. You going to throw a big shindig for me when I make VP?"

"Of course. But wouldn't you rather have it at your parents' house?"

Laura leveled her 'How long have you been on this planet?' look at her.

"Right."

Darcy frowned when she spied Millie standing on the fringes of the party, as if she wanted nothing more than to fade into the night. Before she could make up her mind to go talk to her, Josh approached her. Darcy watched as Josh held out his hand for her. At first Millie shook her head no, but Josh flashed his boyish grin and she relented. Taking his hand, she let him lead her to a corner of the dance floor, away from the crowd, away from the spotlight.

Darcy's vision blurred as Josh gathered a reluctant Millie into his arms for a slow dance. In that instant, Darcy knew. She loved Josh. She loved his generous heart, his benevolent soul, and his beautiful mind. She loved his capacity for empathy and his limitless determination to not only be a better person, but to inspire those around him to want to do the same.

She pressed a hand to the fluttering in her stomach.

"Are you okay?" Laura studied Darcy's face.

"Yeah. I'm having a moment." She gestured to Josh and Millie, blinking away her tears and covering the real reason for her reaction.

"Aww." Laura tilted her head. "Even I can see why you're having a moment. How sweet is that!"

Darcy couldn't respond, too afraid her voice would reveal the depth of her emotions. Remembering the champagne in her hand, she took a sip.

"So what's up with you and Josh? You two are circling one another like a politician and a reporter over a sex scandal."

Darcy choked on her champagne, sending bubbles up her nose. Coughing and wheezing, her eyes watering even more, as Laura patted her on the back.

"You're supposed to drink it, not snort it. Here, have some water." She snatched a bottle from the passing waiter.

Darcy waved the water away and used the incident as an excuse to avoid responding to Laura's too-close-for-comfort observation. Having narrowly made her escape, Darcy dashed up the stairs for a few moments to allow herself time to regroup and adjust to tonight's startling revelation.

Finding the solitude of her bedroom, she closed the door and paced her room. The music thrummed down below, as the muted sound of laughter floated up the stairs.

She realized, with stunning clarity, that she'd never loved Doug, because she didn't feel one-tenth of what she felt for Josh. She'd only been in love with who she *wanted* Doug to be. He'd hurt her, no doubt about that. But when you trusted someone and they abused that trust, of course you ached.

Darcy picked up the photo of Josh at his graduation, holding up a bottle of cheap champagne someone had given him. Just when she thought things couldn't get any more complicated. How long? How long had she loved him? Setting the photo back on the dresser, she took a deep breath, then released it.

What now? What should she do about it? Josh had never indicated he felt anything for her but friendship. Well, except for the sex. But lust and love are two different things, and you didn't need the latter to feel the former.

Armed with this new knowledge, she'd just . . . be patient. See if Josh threw off any vibes. If impulsive sex wasn't enough to botch a perfectly good friendship, then a one-sided confession of love could send it right over the cliff to an untimely death.

Satisfied with her decision, she touched up her makeup, ran her fingers through her hair, and headed back down stairs. She stopped in her tracks at the bottom of the stairs, her hand to her mouth. *Jiminy Cricket!* She'd forgotten about Blake.

CHAPTER THIRTY-FIVE

"There's my girl."

Josh froze, as he watched Blake gather Darcy in his arms and bury his face in her hair, before pulling back to plant a searing kiss on her lips.

She might as well have flung a dagger at his heart. The crushing jealousy at her warm 'welcome home' made Josh stagger back a step.

But what did he expect when Blake returned? That Darcy would realize she didn't have feelings for him? That she would break it off with him? Blake may come from *Fantasyland*, but Josh didn't.

After they finally broke their liplock, Blake said something to Darcy that made her blush, and then, holding her hand in his, he and Darcy walked over to him.

Blake extended his right hand. "Congratulations, Josh. You must be gratified by your accomplishment."

Josh didn't want to take his hand, but in fairness to Blake, he had no idea the turmoil his mysterious existence created for Josh. "Thanks."

"Our Darcy's very thoughtful to throw you a party."

Blake wrapped his arm around Darcy's waist and pulled her close, before planting a kiss on the top of her head.

Josh's hands curled into fists. She's not our Darcy. Clearly, she's your Darcy. "Yeah."

Darcy wouldn't look at him, suddenly finding the foyer rug fascinating, as the color rose in her cheeks. He had to get away before he did something that would embarrass them both.

"Speaking of the party, thanks. I really appreciate it. My mother is pretty wiped out—jet lag—and the party's winding down, so I'm going to take her home." When did he turn into such a liar? Last time he saw his mom she was shaking her groove thing with one of the firm's slightly inebriated senior associates.

"Sure. I hope you both had a good time."

"Goes without saying. I can come by tomorrow after I take Mom to the airport and help clean up."

Darcy waved him away. "Don't be silly. The caterers will handle most of the clean-up, and Millie and I can handle the rest."

Josh hesitated, then leaned over and kissed her cheek before snapping back like he'd been stung. He said his good nights and went to round up his mother.

———

L ate afternoon sun glinted off the water of the Hudson River, as pleasure boats and sailboats gave way to ferries transporting tourists to Ellis Island. Josh had achieved his goal. A partnership and a corner office with a view of the Hudson.

The offices were dark and silent on a Sunday afternoon, especially on the partners' floor. Any junior associates who'd come into work that day were two floors below.

As he unpacked boxes of files and placed them in the drawers of his new desk, Josh wondered why, if this was what he'd wanted for so long now, he felt restless. Was it the bitterness of Darcy's rejection that dispelled the sweet taste of success or was it truly dissatisfaction with his job?

Over the past few months, he'd been mediating disputes for clients of the legal aid organization, and he'd enjoyed it. He had a knack for it, too. Maybe in all those years attempting to mediate disputes between his parents, he'd learned a thing or two. One thing he'd learned from his recent mediation experience, he liked mending fences better than he liked tearing them down.

But the firm had trained him to litigate, and he was damn good at that too. It's what he'd dreamed of since before entering law school. He'd devoured courtroom dramas like *Law and Order*, *The Practice*, and reruns of *L.A. Law*.

He'd always felt he'd been born to litigate, to seek justice for his clients. His style didn't tend toward the slick, smooth-talking Arnie Becker of *L.A. Law*. He simply wore his opponents down, backing them into corners with motions hearings, like a chess master wearing down his opponents.

Tossing aside the empty box, he reached for another one filled with office supplies and began sorting and placing them in drawers and cabinets. His secretary had offered to set up his office, but he preferred to do it himself. Right now it gave him something to do while he sorted out his thoughts.

He'd brought his mother by to see the new office earlier, on their way to the airport. Having her here for this celebration meant a lot to him. She'd sacrificed so much. She deserved to see the results of all those years of making do with less.

When he'd brought her into his new office, she just stood quietly, looking around, then turned to him, her eyes bright with unshed tears and said, "I never thought I could be more proud of you than the day you graduated from law school, but I was wrong."

He couldn't help it, he'd gotten choked up at his mother's words. Sighing, he opened another box, this one filled with his diplomas and his bar admission certificates for the entire tri-state area. Against the wall stood a couple of framed prints that Darcy had helped him pick out when he'd decorated his first office.

Dragging his fingers through his hair, he looked around the box-cluttered office. He could really use her help now. She had an eye for what should go where. He'd just have to do the best he could with what little skill he had.

Moving on to a box of weighty law books, he hoped that one day soon he and Darcy could mend their fences, and put all this discomfort and self-consciousness behind them. But he knew, even once mended, those fences would never be the same.

———

A blank computer screen glared at Darcy, mocking her, daring her to type something, anything. She glared right back, willing it to display words that formed sentences that in turn, created paragraphs, producing pages, and eventually a completed manuscript. No luck. Fifteen thousand words behind and not a thought in her head.

Dominic had morphed from an alpha-male stunt man

with a dark past, to Blake's polished sophistication, to Josh's boy-next-door charm. As if that wasn't bad enough, she'd been halfway through a love scene before she realized she'd written a hot door-sex scene.

She lowered her head and gently banged her forehead on the desk in frustration. In the immortal words of Rose Castorini, her life was *going down the toilet*.

She'd had sex with her best friend, cheated on her perfect boyfriend, then fallen in love with said best friend; her novel was destined for the Great Recycle Bin in the Sky; and Dr. Perfect had lost his luster.

When Blake came home, she'd been so certain the planets would realign and life would get back to normal—if having a fictional character who comes to life as your boyfriend was considered normal. But that was before her emotional epiphany. Now, she felt restless and cross.

Blake handled her mood swings with the same aplomb with which he handled reattaching severed limbs, which only frustrated her more. She wanted him to react, to show anger or confusion or something besides superb composure.

Josh would have given her a metaphorical slap on the back of the head by now and told her to get over herself.

"Darcy, I've got those edits you requested," Millie said as she entered the room, a pen stuck behind her ear, carrying pages of Darcy's dreadful manuscript. "Great sex scene. Who doesn't love Suspended Congress?"

Darcy's brows winged up in surprise at Millie's reference to the *Kama Sutra*.

"I've corrected some of your word usages," Millie said, then she released a gusty sigh. "But the problems with it go much deeper than just words. You've got real issues with your character development, especially your hero. He's either bipolar or has multiple personality disorder—or maybe he has a secret twin."

"I know, I know." She rose to pace the room. "I'm blocked. For the first time in my career I'm completely and totally blocked. Look at that thing." She jabbed her finger at the blank computer screen as if she were pointing to a freak of nature. "It just sits there, taunting me."

"The best way to tackle a problem is to divide it up into manageable pieces and take them one piece at a time. Once you've corrected the problems, the rest will follow."

Millie handed Darcy the manuscript. "With that in mind, I made a list of the inconsistencies and color-coded them on the manuscript. I suggest you take them one at a time and either make your hero an alpha or a beta."

Darcy reluctantly took the marked-up pages from Millie. "Writing is not a checklist to be ticked off one item at a time," she said, indignant. "It's a creative process born in the imagination, crafted with love and artistry."

"And how's that working for you this time around? I'll bring up a pot of tea. You're going to need it."

Groaning, Darcy sat back down at her desk, fingers poised over the keys and waited. And waited. Nothing. She stuck her tongue out at the screen in contempt before propping her chin in her hand. So much for love and artistry.

Outside her window, the dove's nest sat empty, their offspring having long since fledged the nest. Yet, she was no closer to happily-ever-after now than she'd been before—in either her manuscript or her life.

CHAPTER THIRTY-SIX

E lated, Josh's feet barely touched the ground as he strode down the sidewalk to Kelly's house, whistling a cheerful tune. This kind of news required face-to-face inter-action. He bet on her being home since Daniel's school day was over. The Friday before a holiday weekend, what better day to give good news?

He knocked on the front door, tapping his foot to a lively internal beat, waiting for Kelly to open it.

"Josh."

Without saying a word, he grabbed her up and swung her around in a circle.

"Josh! What are you doing? Have you lost your—" Her eyes opened wide. "You did it didn't you? You closed the deal on the house!"

"Signed, sealed, and delivered." He released her before handing her a packet of papers. "You no longer have the foreclosure ax hanging over your head. You have payments you can afford, at a reasonable interest rate. Your closing date is in two weeks."

"Thank you, thank you, thank you!" She kissed him on

each cheek and then the mouth, laughing and crying at the same time. "I'll never be able to thank you enough, even if I live to be a hundred years old!"

Josh's spirit soared at the heartfelt gratitude. "It was my pleasure. Just seeing you so happy and relieved is thanks enough."

"Oh my goodness! I have to tell Daniel!" She turned to enter the house, then grabbed Josh's wrist and pulled him along. "Come on!"

Once inside the house, she shouted up the stairs, "Daniel! Come here."

Daniel poked his head around the corner. "What'd I do?"

"Nothing," she laughed, bouncing up and down like an excited child.

Daniel plodded down the stairs. "'Sup, Josh?"

Josh just rocked back on his heels and smiled.

Daniel looked between his mom and Josh. "Have you been sneaking into the liquor cabinet like Grandpa Rudy?"

Kelly grasped Daniel's hands, her eyes bright with tears and excitement. "We're home, Daniel!"

Perplexed, Daniel threw up his hands. "Of course we're home. Where else would we be?"

Kelly giggled. "No, we don't have to worry about losing our house anymore. Josh fixed everything!"

Understanding dawned on Daniel's face as he glanced at Josh. "No kidding? You did it?"

Josh nodded.

"That's epic, dude!" Daniel raised his hand for a high five.

Instead of returning the high-five, Josh grabbed Daniel into a bear hug, slapping him on the back. Daniel hesitated a moment before hugging him back, but when he did, Josh saw the look on Kelly's face as she raised her hand to her mouth and smiled.

"What do you say about going out to celebrate?" Josh asked as Daniel recovered his teenage composure. "Dinner and ice cream on me!"

"Sweet!" Daniel said, already headed out the door.

You said it, kid.

Kelly placed a hand on Josh's arm. "Daniel has really come out of his shell. Helping you with the little league baseball team, making good grades in school, even trying out for his school's basketball team."

"And his chess skills are coming along too. Won't be long before he beats me." Josh rocked back on his heels.

"It's all your doing. I owe you so much."

Josh looked down at his feet a moment, before gazing into Kelly's watery eyes. "I get far more than I give."

————

Summer ended on a quiet rainy note with a simple Butler family dinner *sans* Anne's husband, Matt. The two were still separated, leaving Darcy to wonder if they would ever patch up their differences.

Darcy set the table as Josh bounced a fussy Olivia on his hip, trying in vain to get a smile out of her. He was so good with the kids, never losing his patience, even when the toddler displayed a trait she'd inherited from her mother —contrariness.

Speaking of contrariness, Anne and her mother argued in the kitchen over whether to make balsamic or mustard vinaigrette dressing for the salad, until Josh suggested they make both.

Her father stood out in the summer kitchen firing up

the grill for fish as the rain fell in a light mist beyond the cover of the porch. Brandon and David supervised Will and Sam as they played *Super Mario Galaxy* 2 on the Wii.

Most people wished for sun on Labor Day, but Darcy was content with the rain. It lent a cozy feel to the gathering and encouraged closer familial interaction. She and Josh had finally reached some sort of unspoken accord with one another. Neither of them brought up the incident, and they went about their business as friends, both to Darcy's relief and dismay. Josh hadn't given any sign that he might have feelings for her beyond those of a friend.

Yankee games were still a regular outing for them, as was the batting cage, but they were both careful not to touch one another. She missed the easy affection between them, but she supposed it was for the best.

Even if Blake weren't in the picture—and currently he wasn't, since he'd left for Tasmania several days ago—the whole friends with benefits arrangement rarely worked out, and she didn't think she could handle having sex with Josh knowing she loved him and he didn't reciprocate those feelings.

She had just put the finishing touches on the table setting when she heard the front door slam.

"Where is she?" Matt asked, his coal-black hair glistening with raindrops.

Darcy stood mute, then pointed toward the kitchen before following her brother-in-law in the same direction. Josh, Brandon, and David fell into line behind them.

Matt planted his feet in front of Anne. "I want to come home."

Anne faced off, hands on her hips, and fire in her eyes. "And I want a body like Heidi Klum, but we can't always have what we want." She went back to her salad dressing, whisking it with a vengeance.

Her father drifted in from the porch, apparently having heard the commotion.

"You never want to have sex anymore," Matt blurted out.

Her father groaned and exited stage left, while Brandon snickered.

"All right. Time to go." Darcy turned to the rest of her family, trying to herd them out of the kitchen. Like her father, she sure didn't want to hear a discussion of Anne and Matt's sex life, or lack thereof. "Josh, you coming?"

"Because I'm exhausted all the time," Anne replied. "Maybe if you helped around the house more I wouldn't be so tired."

"I'm working seventy to eighty hours a week trying to grow my construction business!" Matt replied.

"Yeah? Well, I have a business to grow, too. Then I come home and work some more."

"Okay, maybe we can find some common ground here," Josh interjected.

"Butt out, Perry Mason," Matt said.

"Hey, Bob the Builder!" Darcy poked Matt in the arm. "Who are you calling Perry Mason?"

"Darcy, it's okay," Josh cajoled.

"No. No, it's not okay. Nobody calls you a name and gets away with it," she said, indignant.

"I don't mind being called Perry Mason. It's kind of flattering, actually."

He grinned as Darcy rolled her eyes.

Matt ignored the exchange.

"You take me for granted," Anne said.

"What? I— What's that supposed to mean?" Matt spluttered.

"Exactly what I said. I buy the groceries, I cook the meals, I do the laundry, take the girls to their doctor's appointments, dance lessons, piano lessons, and I don't get one word of gratitude. It's as if it's expected!"

"I don't expect all that!"

"Well, I don't see you offering to do any of it! If I didn't do it, it wouldn't get done."

"Look, guys, I think there's a solution to this. Don't throw away ten years of marriage over something that can be easily fixed."

Anne and Matt glared at Josh.

"It sounds like the two of you need to clear the air, then take a step back and analyze the issues. That's what you both do at work, right? You analyze problems and solve them."

"Yeah," Matt muttered.

"Okay," Anne said.

"Great. So, Anne, you feel like you're underappreciated. Am I right?"

"*Un*appreciated," Anne corrected. "The applicable prefix is 'un'."

"Okay. And Matt, you feel like you're, um, lonely."

"Damn, right."

"Now we're getting somewhere. Let's sit down and work this through."

Darcy watched in stunned silence as her often intractable sister followed Josh and Matt into the living room.

Her father reappeared. "What's going on?"

"Josh is playing marriage counselor."

"Better that than sex therapist," her father mumbled as he returned to the grill.

———

J osh wiped his hands on the dishtowel after loading the dirty dishes into the dishwasher. The satisfaction he'd felt over resolving Kelly's mortgage problem settled over him again when he thought about Anne and Matt.

The Butler's dinner had waited over an hour while Anne and Matt hashed out their issues. After tears and angry outbursts, accusations and pent-up frustrations, it had all boiled down to complacency. They'd both become so busy with their daily lives—work, kids, chores, errands—that they'd forgotten to take time for themselves.

After divvying up the chores to take some of the burden off Anne, Josh had suggested they do one nice thing a day for each other—and schedule a date night each week. And Matt promised to take care of the kids one night each week so Anne could have some downtime.

And Vanessa and Jeff had been more than willing to keep their granddaughters one night a week to give Anne and Matt some alone time.

Josh had quietly suggested to Vanessa that she take the girls that night since Matt and Anne could barely keep their hands off each other during dinner. They left shortly after dinner, skipping out on dessert.

At least someone's love life had hope.

CHAPTER THIRTY-SEVEN

J osh nervously adjusted his black tie, scanning the room for anything that might be amiss, as the hotel staff put the finishing touches on the table settings for the Silver Linings Ball to benefit the Women's Legal Fund of Harlem. The Grand Ballroom at the Waldorf Astoria sparkled like the grand dames of old who once frequented its luxurious accommodations.

He glanced at his watch. The guests wouldn't begin arriving for another half hour or so, leaving plenty of time to correct any problems that arose. He'd never taken on an endeavor of this magnitude. As the event's working chair, he'd put together a committee of dedicated volunteers who, like him, had put their heart and soul into this event, and it showed.

He felt a hand on his shoulder and turned to find the Legal Fund's Executive Director, Sherry Stevens, and the Mayor's wife and Honorary Event Chair, Meredith Stokes. Both wore broad smiles to complement their elegant evening gowns.

"Josh, what a job you've done!" Sherry said, assessing

the room's silver and white décor. "It's more than I ever could have imagined. We hope to raise a good deal of money for the Fund tonight—more than we've ever raised."

"I can't take credit," Josh replied. "I have the event committee and Mrs. Stokes to thank for their hard work and constant support." The Mayor's wife had been instrumental in recruiting New York's well-connected movers and shakers. Laura had also been crucial to the event's great attendance because of her many business connections.

This was the first year the gala had such a high-profile honorary chair. Being introduced to her by one of the firm's senior partners at the opera in April had been the first step to getting her on board.

He glanced up to see Laura gliding toward them in a silver lamé gown reminiscent of something out of the classic Hollywood movies his mother loved to watch. The dress swirled around her like liquid silver, hugging her long legs and voluptuous body. The Veronica Lake hairstyle she wore added to the Hollywood effect.

Every head turned to observe her entrance. Of course he'd noticed her beauty before. What man wouldn't? But tonight she looked stunning. It was her personality that rubbed him the wrong way.

"And here's who we have to thank for the elegant venue," he said, indicating Laura as she approached.

He introduced Laura to Mrs. Stokes and Sherry. "Laura served as the chair of the marketing and PR committee. Her advertising agency recently wrapped up a PR campaign for the Waldorf, and Laura convinced them that holding a fundraiser at their hotel for such a worthy cause would be good PR."

"That's marvelous, Laura!" Sherry said. "Thank you."

"My pleasure," Laura said with a smile.

"Ah, there's Senator Briggs." Mrs. Stokes turned to Sherry. "Let me introduce you."

Josh watched as Sherry and Mrs. Stokes approached a portly man with a comb-over.

Laura leaned in and whispered, "Ass kisser."

Not tonight, Josh thought. He wasn't going to spar with her tonight. "Goddess."

Laura recoiled as if she'd been slapped. "What?"

He gazed into her blue eyes. "You look like a movie star from Hollywood's glamour days."

"Who are you, and what have you done with Josh Ryan?"

He laughed. "I'm too excited to fight with you tonight. In fact, I don't think I've told you what a terrific job you did heading up the PR committee. I really appreciate it."

"Thanks." She waved her hand, dismissing the compliment. "It's what I do. But don't think for a minute that when this is all over I'm not going to go back to loathing you."

"I wouldn't expect anything less." He offered her his arm. "And why do you loathe me, exactly?"

"Because you're just too nice a guy," she said, as if it should be obvious.

———

J osh had just completed a final circuit of the ballroom when he saw Darcy and Blake approach. Darcy was the glam to Laura's glitz. Draped in a dress the color of dark plums, her graceful petite body left him longing to pull her into his arms. She'd piled her golden brown hair on top of her head, leaving some curls to float around her face, and her green eyes sparkled with excitement and wonder.

He'd meant it when he told Laura she looked like a movie star, but Darcy looked like royalty. Blake, on the other hand, gave a good impression of 007 in his white dinner jacket. *Always got to one-up everyone.*

The awkwardness between him and Darcy had waned but lay just beneath the surface of good manners and appropriate public behavior. He still couldn't look at her without thinking about the taste of her lips or the silkiness of her skin. And he couldn't bear to see Blake's arm around her without feeling jealousy's bite. His inner caveman yelled, 'Mine!'

"Wow! Josh, this is *amazing!* Really." Darcy scanned the room as she spoke.

"She's right, Josh. It's impressive," Blake confirmed.

"Thanks. You know the saying, 'It takes a village.' Well, it truly took a village to put this together."

Darcy stretched to place a kiss on his cheek. "I'm so proud of you."

Josh's cheek burned where her lips touched him, and he resisted the urge to touch his face to see if she'd branded him with her kiss.

"The table is this way." He led them to the front of the stately room, near the stage. "Laura's already here, and so are Kelly and Daniel. You should see Daniel," he continued. "He looks very handsome in his suit, but you'd think someone forced him to wear a noose the way he keeps pulling at his collar."

The large round table would seat Darcy and her family, Blake, Laura, Kelly, Daniel, Mark, Chris, Martin, Cindy, and himself, giving them an uninterrupted view of the evening's speakers, one of whom was Kelly.

Several women who have used the Legal Fund's services planned to speak briefly about what it meant to them, followed by former Jets' defensive tackle, Jordy Jacobs, whose late mother was a recipient of the Fund's services when Jordy was just a teenager.

"Mom, are you nervous?" Daniel asked.

Kelly looked around the crowded room, and placed a hand to her chest. "God, yes!"

Darcy took the seat next to her and, grasping the hand in Kelly's lap, gave it a squeeze. "You'll be great. Just speak from the heart. Oh, and picture everyone naked."

Daniel's eyes grew big. "What? Ewww!"

"It's just a little speaker's trick to calm the nerves," Josh explained as he took the seat on the other side of Daniel.

"That wouldn't calm *my* nerves. It would make me want to hurl."

"Daniel," Kelly admonished.

"Darcy, thanks again for contributing to the auction." Josh gave her a warm smile.

"You're welcome. I don't know how much money it will bring, but I'm happy to help."

Kelly's eyes lit up. "What did you contribute?"

Laura chimed in as she sat down, "Dinner with *NY Times* best-selling author Darcy Butler."

"I have to bid on that." Kelly shook her head. "Oh, but I'm sure I can't bid enough to win."

Darcy lifted a glass of champagne, a look of confusion on her face. "We're friends. Why should a friend have to bid on dinner? We can have dinner any time."

"Aw, thanks Darcy," Kelly replied, her eyes bright with pleasure.

"Told you we'd get $500 a ticket," Laura whispered, as she adjusted Josh's tie.

Josh glanced around the room quickly filling with wealthy patrons. "Yes, you did. And you were right."

"Joshua Michael Ryan, this is no fun!"

"The event?"

"No. You being so agreeable. I can't wait for this night to end so we can get back to normal."

Josh just grinned as he took a sip of champagne.

CHAPTER THIRTY-EIGHT

The evening was in full swing when Darcy slid into the empty chair next to Josh and leaned over to whisper in his ear, "Wow, Josh. You have to be proud of what you've accomplished tonight. I know I am." She scanned the room full of New York's Glitterati. "This could be *the* social event of the year." Being close to him, inhaling his crisp, clean scent flooded her brain with sweet, sexy memories. *Down, girl.*

"Thanks, Darcy. That means a lot to me." He gazed into her eyes and she momentarily forgot about Blake, and the roomful of people, until Josh broke the spell. "Did I tell you how beautiful you look tonight? But, then again, you always do."

Darcy could feel the warmth of his compliment all the way down to her toes. Was that a sign, or was he just being nice? Unable to answer, she turned her attention to the ballroom.

Blake was speaking to the Mayor. Daniel and his mom were out on the dance floor looking adorable . . . and relaxed, Kelly having already delivered her speech. When she'd finished, there hadn't been a dry eye in the room, including Darcy's.

She recognized members of the media working the room, in search of valuable photo ops and sound bites. Laura was talking to a reporter from the NBC network, in her element as the center of attention, however momentary that fame might be.

Darcy had noticed Laura and Josh getting along. When Laura had adjusted his tie, Darcy thought she'd entered an alternate universe—one she didn't like. Their constant harping on one another was oftentimes grating, but this open friendliness got on her nerves. *Don't bring it up. Don't bring it up.*

"You and Laura are getting along well." *You just had to bring it up.*

"Yeah. She's very professional when the situation calls for it. I have to admit she's been . . . pleasant all evening. And she did a terrific job with the marketing. I couldn't have gotten all of these people here without her help." He gestured to the elegantly clad assembly. "She's been my right arm for the whole event, from planning to execution."

"Who's been your right arm?" Laura pulled out the chair on the other side of Josh and sat, the slit in her evening gown revealing her long, Victoria's Secret model legs.

"You, who else?" Josh patted her arm.

Darcy felt an irrational stab of jealousy.

"Well, well, if it isn't Thelma and Louise."

Darcy's heart stopped. "Doug!" His tie was slightly off-kilter and he reeked of bourbon.

Josh and Laura stood, shouldering in front of Darcy.

"If it isn't Doug Lansing, Cheating Bastard," Laura said. "What are you doing here? Hell spit you out?"

"I'm here to claim my prize. Dinner with *NY Times*

best-selling author, Darcy Butler," he said in derision as he swayed on his feet.

"She's not having dinner with you," Josh ground out. "We'll gladly give you a refund."

"Don't want a refund. Want my prize," he slurred, reaching out to grasp Darcy's arm.

"Touch her, and you'll draw back a nub," Laura warned through clenched teeth.

"What's going on?" Blake joined the group, pulling Darcy back and into his arms.

Doug aimed his blurry glare on Laura, grabbing her by the wrist. Josh noted that for a drunk guy, his reflexes were quick. "You bitch. Still fucking anything that moves?"

"All right, that's it." Not wishing to cause a scene, Josh grabbed Doug's arm and twisted it behind his back, restraining him, before signaling to security. "Mr. Lansing has had too much to drink and could use an escort to a taxi." He released his grip on Doug's arm and handed him off to the burly security guard. "We wouldn't want him to *become* the news story, now would we?"

Doug chose the better part of valor and went with the security guard, but not before a parting shot at Darcy, "You always were a little princess," he spat. "Too good for everyone else."

An awkward silence fell among the group, but the other nearby guests hadn't caught wind of the near scuffle.

"That was fun," Laura muttered, as she rubbed her offended wrist.

Josh took Laura's wrist and examined it. "You okay?"

"Oh sure. Asshole is nothing I can't handle. Thanks, though."

———

"**Y**ou okay, Darcy?" Josh asked.

Darcy noted the look of concern on Josh's face and nodded. "I'm fine." *Sort of.* Her insides shook like a martini shaker in a bartender's hands. She hadn't seen Doug in person in years and he had to pick Josh's event to resurface in her life.

"Good," Josh said before turning to Laura. "Want to dance?" he asked, as he slid his hands up Laura's arms to her shoulders.

Laura looked at Josh in surprise. "Um, sure."

Darcy watched as Josh escorted Laura out onto the dance floor with his hand on the small of her back, a dull ache beginning in her chest.

"How about you? Are you sure you're all right?" Blake kissed her temple.

"Yes. I'm fine."

"Who was that guy, anyway?"

"No one important." Darcy didn't feel like drumming up the past by discussing what Doug had done to her.

"Come on." He led Darcy out to join the other couples swaying to a romantic waltz-tempo and pulled her into the circle of his arms. She leaned her head against his chest, but she couldn't take her eyes off Laura and Josh. Her two best friends were finally getting along, so why wasn't she happy about that?

——

Josh and Laura swayed to the music, her arms around his neck, his around her waist, but a respectable distance between them. In her heels, she stood face-to-face with him.

"What a dick," Laura muttered.

"If you're talking about Doug the Dick Head, no argument there."

"Cheating Bastard."

Josh snorted. He hated what Doug had done to Darcy, but as far as he was concerned, Doug didn't deserve her anyway. "You really hate him." It was a statement, not a question.

"What's not to hate, after what he did to Darcy?" Laura turned in Darcy's direction. "I wanted to reach my hands down his throat and pull his balls out."

Josh winced, but couldn't argue with that reaction.

"Her self-esteem took a big hit, and to this day, she won't watch that network's news."

Josh remembered all too well the changes he saw in her.

"I didn't know what to do to help her. I'm not sure if you've noticed, but I'm not exactly Dear Abby when it comes to love."

"You're a good friend to her," Josh said. "That's all that matters."

"There you go again, being nice to me. Cut it out before I start to like you."

Josh laughed and gave Laura a quick spin before pulling her back in his arms. "I'm surprised you don't have some international hunk on your arm tonight."

Laura huffed out a laugh. "I'm working. Men and work don't mix."

After a few moments, Josh asked, "Why do you do it?"

"Do what?"

"Sleep with one jerk after another?" Josh felt Laura go stiff in his arms but he just held her tighter.

"Well, so much for Mr. Nice Guy," Laura grumbled.

"I'm serious. You're worth so much more than you give yourself credit for."

Laura's brow furrowed in thought, a flicker of confusion, before she laughed it off. "He's ba-ack."

CHAPTER THIRTY-NINE

D arcy sliced into eggs covered with Hollandaise sauce, while Laura signaled the waiter for another mimosa. She wasn't up for the post-mortem brunch, but she'd promised Laura last night when she left her and Josh to "put it to bed," whatever that meant. She'd spent a good bit of the ride home trying to figure out if that could mean anything other than closing out the event.

Just as Blake kissed her good night, his cell phone rang— a ten-car pile-up on I-95. Dr. Blake Garrett swung into action, and Darcy sighed in relief that she didn't have to come up with an excuse not to invite him in.

Laura was saying, "I think notwithstanding the unwelcome appearance of Cheating Bastard, the event was a tremendous success. What do you think he was doing there, anyway?"

"Probably there to interview Jordy Jacobs." Darcy pushed the eggs around on her plate.

"Oh yeah, you're probably right." Laura gestured with her mimosa.

Laura continued with her animated discussion of the

evening. Who made an appearance, what they wore, and who they snubbed. Darcy listened with half an ear, feeling out of sorts. She couldn't even lay the blame for it on Doug's behavior, although seeing him had been a shock.

She'd like to blame it on her sleepless night, but even that wasn't the reason either.

"I couldn't believe how Josh came to my rescue last night," Laura said, interrupting Darcy's glum musings. "It was very, well, chivalrous of him. I'm beginning to see why you like him so much."

Yep. There it was. The reason for her morose mood. Darcy pushed her half-eaten Eggs Benedict away. "Yeah, he's a prince." She flashed a lame smile.

"Hey," Laura reached her hand across the table and squeezed Darcy's fingers. "You okay? You look a little pale."

"I'm fine. Just a little hung over."

"You didn't have that much to drink. Oh, you mean a *love* hangover?" She waggled her eyebrows. "You and Blake play doctor until the wee hours of the morning?"

"No," Darcy said a little too emphatically.

"Oh, girl. Did you two have a fight?" Laura patted Darcy's hand. "It'll be fine. Anyone can see he's crazy about you."

Guilt knifed through her. *Great.*

———

Children swarmed the lawn like an invading army, their squeals, laughter, and shouts muffled by the heavy soul-sucking August air. Darcy sipped ice-cold lemonade and wiped the sweat from her face as she watched her Great Aunt Rosie, whose bounteous progeny had gathered to celebrate sixty-three years of wedded bliss, accept a kiss from her oldest granddaughter.

The adults gathered under the shade of an ancient white oak, the brood of some forty-eight children, grandchildren, and great-grandchildren, far too large to hold the festivities in the old house Aunt Rosie and Uncle Al had lived in since 1955.

So, everyone dressed in the lightest clothing possible and resigned themselves to sweating through the party. Even Aunt Rosie dabbed at the perspiration on her upper lip with a lace-edged handkerchief like a trooper.

"Vanessa tells me you're seeing someone," her aunt said, drawing Darcy's attention away from the game of torment-the-family-dog.

"Um, yes. Blake."

"And he's a doctor?"

"Yep."

"And a hunk?"

"Oh, yes."

"But the important question is, does he make your heart sing and your toes curl?" She winked at Darcy.

Aunt Rosie had always been a favorite of Darcy's. She was . . . well . . . cool, hip, with it. When Darcy would come to Poughkeepsie to spend time with her cousins in the summer, her aunt played dress up with them, took them to the latest teen heartthrob movies, bought them fake nails and lip gloss in bright red. All things Aunt Rosie's sister, Darcy's grandmother, would never do.

She didn't know how to answer that question. Blake wasn't the man who made her heart sing. Her toes curl. *He was perfect—so why didn't he?*

Before she could answer, Uncle Al approached with a glass of lemonade in his hand. He still stood at over six feet and maintained the build he'd acquired playing football for Yale.

"For my bride." He bent and kissed Aunt Rosie's raised lips. "She's even more beautiful than the day I met her." His eyes glowed as he gazed at his wife's face. "I'm the luckiest man alive."

Darcy stared at the hem of her halter-top as if it was the most fascinating thing she'd ever seen, feeling like an intruder on a moment too intimate for public view. When she glanced back, Aunt Rosie was patting her uncle's face and laughing, the corners of her eyes crinkling, the look of love on her face making her appear decades younger than her eighty-three years.

"Pop-Pop," a dark-haired little girl said, tugging on his shorts, "Mandy won't let me ride the scooter."

Uncle Al reached down and picked up the little girl. "Then Miss Jenny, why don't we do something more fun?"

"Like what?"

He glanced around. "Well, like playing horsey."

"Yay!"

Uncle Al galloped off with Jenny clinging to his neck, giggling as he tickled her belly. Double knee replacement hadn't diminished his athleticism.

Aunt Rosie took a sip of her lemonade, smiled, and said, "What a gem."

Darcy's gaze drifted over the three generations of cousins who'd made their way from all over the country to celebrate a marriage that had survived six decades, at a time when the average marriage didn't last one. Despite the distance, the family had a close, loving relationship—so close, they made Norman Rockwell look like the Simpsons.

To spend time with Aunt Rosie and Uncle Al was to see first-hand what two people still in love after all those years looked like. Even as a child, Darcy had noticed the little gestures of affection, the flirtations, the sparkle in their eyes when they gazed at each other. The deep respect they had for one another made her hope for that very thing when she reached those same milestones in her own life.

Uncle Al never hesitated to say that he'd married the love of his life, and he always made it a point to tell her how beautiful she was and how thankful he was that she loved him.

"How do you do it?" The thought was out of her mouth before she even thought about asking the question.

"Do what?"

Now that the words were out, she might as well ask what she really wanted to know. "Not only stay married, but stay so obviously in love?"

"I love Al for who he is. Can he get on my nerves sometimes? Of course, as I'm sure I get on his. No one's perfect." She tilted her head in thought.

Darcy picked a honeysuckle flower from the vine wrapped around the fence and held it to her nose. The sweetness was almost unbearable. Like Aunt Rosie and Uncle Al.

"Even if perfection were possible," Aunt Rosie continued, "I think it would get, well, boring, maybe even tedious. Who wants to be reminded of their own imperfections on a daily basis by an irritatingly perfect person?"

Darcy hadn't thought of it like that.

"But the other reason I think we've stayed in love all these years is because we never take each other for granted."

Darcy nodded, remembering Josh's comments to Anne and Matt. She took another sip of her drink.

"And of course, I married my best friend."

Darcy coughed as the tart liquid went down the wrong pipe.

"You okay, dear?" Aunt Rosie patted her on the back.

"I'm fine," Darcy choked out around her coughs. "Swallowed wrong."

Aunt Rosie graciously fanned her face with a vintage Babe Ruth paper fan—*yes, being a Yankees fan was a genetic trait*—giving Darcy time to catch her breath and organize her thoughts.

"Thanks." Darcy reached into her bag for a hairclip and twisted her hair up to allow what little breeze there was to cool her neck. "Were you and Uncle Al friends *before* you fell in love?"

"Best buddies since junior high. We hung out with a group of friends, doing what teenagers do. It wasn't until our senior year in high school that we realized we had the hots for one another." Aunt Rosie smiled at some memory.

One of the balls the kids were playing with rolled next to Darcy's feet. She bent to retrieve it and throw it back, thinking about what her aunt had said. "Aunt Rosie, can I ask you a *really* personal question? You don't have to answer if you don't want to."

Her aunt glanced over, a look of concern on her face, and she patted Darcy's hand. "Whatever it is, Darcy, I'll try my best to answer it."

Darcy bit her lower lip, opened her mouth, then closed it. Drawing in a calming breath, she went for it. "Did you and Uncle Al, um, sleep together before you were married?"

Aunt Rosie smiled. "I know it's probably hard for you to believe, but we did have sex back in the Dark Ages, even pre-marital sex. Caroline is the result of one of those romantic trysts."

"You mean you and Uncle Al *had* to get married?" Darcy saw her Aunt in a whole new light.

"Well, no, not really." She laughed. "We'd already decided to marry. Caroline just moved the date up a bit."

Darcy looked over at her cousin Caroline as she chased after one of her grandchildren. *Wow. Cousin Caroline. A love child. Who'd have thunk it?*

Another question popped into Darcy's head. One she shouldn't ask, but curiosity got the better of her. "How was it . . . with Uncle Al?"

"Earth-shattering." She hesitated a moment, then winked at Darcy. "Still is."

———

D arcy sat in the back seat of her parents' car for the hour-long ride back to their house. The party had ended with an enormous cake, complete with Aunt Rosie and Uncle Al's wedding picture from 1950 in icing displayed on top. Their oldest grandson had played "Stardust," by Nat King Cole, on his iPod, while the two danced like teenagers in love.

Aunt Rosie had said neither their marriage nor their life had been perfect. She'd also told Darcy that she'd miscarried their second child, a son, and that their third child, a daughter, had died shortly after birth. No, not what anyone would call perfect, but maybe the beauty of their life and their relationship was that they'd had each other through it all.

"You're awfully quiet, Darcy," her mom said in the dark interior of the car. "You okay?"

"I'm fine."

"You should stay with us tonight. I worry about you taking the train back to the city this late."

"Your mom's right," her dad chimed in.

"Okay. Sure."

Silence enveloped the occupants of the car once more, allowing Darcy to return to her ruminating. Her aunt and uncle have been married sixty-three years and could boast four children, eleven grandchildren, and eighteen great-grandchildren. Quite a legacy.

Her own dreams of princes and white horses, of perfect alpha-male heroes and being swept off her feet seemed childish and silly when compared to what her aunt and uncle had. Mr. Right didn't have to be perfect. He just had to be perfect for her. Like Uncle Al was for Aunt Rosie.

It suddenly occurred to Darcy that fairytales weren't found in books. They were found in real life—everyday life, with both its triumphs and its tribulations. And her aunt lived that real-life fairytale every day, while she had been wishing for the wrong fairytale all along.

CHAPTER FORTY

D arcy dreaded making this call. She glared at her phone, hoping it would die a sudden and tragic death, giving her an excuse to procrastinate a little longer. No such luck as her phone blinked to life. She groaned. Might as well get it over with. Pulling up a chair at the kitchen table, Darcy hit the call button.

"Hey, Darce."

"Hi! How goes life in the legal stratosphere? You growing accustomed to the thin air up there on the forty-second floor?"

"Well, you know, it took a while to acclimate, but I'm quick to adapt. What's up?"

Darn. So much for idle chitchat. "Um, well, you know those division series playoff tickets we have for Monday night? Well, um, I can't go."

"What? Why not?"

"Well, it's pretty exciting, actually," she said, coating her response with a little more enthusiasm than she felt. Not that she wasn't excited and proud of Blake, a little like a proud parent, especially since *she* wrote the humanitarian work he was being recognized for. But who scheduled an award ceremony the same night as the first game of the American League Division Series? *Hello.*

"You see, Blake is receiving the International Medical Society's Humanitarian of the Year Award, and the ceremony is that night."

"I see."

"I'm really sorry, Josh. But I can't miss it."

"No, no. Of course you can't."

"I'm sure one of the guys at work can go, right?"

"Yep. I'll have no problem finding someone to take the ticket. Listen, Darce, I've got to run to a meeting. I'll talk to you later."

"Right. See ya."

That wasn't so bad. Darcy lowered her head to the kitchen table. Yes. Yes, it was. In fact, it sucked!

———

J osh wrapped up the post-gala committee meeting, satisfied with the results. The Director had been so pleased with the event that she wanted to make it an annual fundraiser, and the meeting would help make the event even better next year while everything was still fresh in everyone's minds. The committee members offered up suggestions for improvements, discussed what worked and what didn't, and started work on the plans for next year.

Laura had agreed to stay on and head up the PR committee, while many of the other committee members had also agreed to stay on in their roles. The continuity would be a benefit, avoiding the whole reinventing-the-wheel thing.

Josh's phone buzzed, signaling a text. Frowning, he read

the text from Mark saying he couldn't go to the game—his parents were in town. Well, so far none of the usual suspects could go to the game. *Great.*

"What's wrong? Another ambulance get away?" Laura said as she gathered her belongings.

"Ha. The jokes never end with you. Anyone ever tell you, you should consider stand up?"

"Actually, yes." Throwing her tote bag over her shoulder, she continued, "No, seriously, what's up?"

Josh looked up from his phone in surprise. "Really?"

"Sure." Laura shrugged.

"Well, since you asked, I have two tickets to the first game of the division playoffs tomorrow night and no one to go with."

"Where's your sidekick? Oh right, Blake's award ceremony."

"Yeah." Then Josh had a thought—a crazy one, but what the hell? "How about you? You want to go?"

"Me? Why?" she asked, an edge of suspicion in her voice.

Josh contemplated the answer. "Three reasons: the Yankees, the playoffs, and my charming company. Make that four. We can discuss the idea you had for Darcy's gift. What more could you ask for?"

Laura snorted.

"Come on. Come cheer on your hometown team."

"Doesn't New York have two baseball teams?"

"Yes. But only one is in the playoffs."

Laura considered it a moment. "Oh, all right." She held up her hand. "But only because I've got nothing else on my calendar."

"That's fair. I'm only asking because I don't have anyone else to go," Josh countered.

"Be still my heart." Laura placed her hand on her heart. "And they say lawyers aren't romantic."

———

The speaker droned on about life in the Congo and as Darcy tried desperately to appear alert and oriented. It wasn't the speaker's fault she was so bored. Certainly everyone else must be fascinated by the statistics on bacterial dysentery. Well, with the exception of the elderly gentleman next to her who gave an Oscar-worthy impersonation of a bobblehead doll.

The Grand Ballroom of the Pierre hotel dazzled, its impeccable five-star service impressed, and its superb food amazed; yet as she plucked at the satin skirt of her fabulous emerald green evening gown, she couldn't help but wonder about the baseball score. She barely resisted the urge to pull out her phone and check it. If she weren't seated at the head table, she might chance it.

Okay, if she was completely honest with herself, she really wondered which of the guys went to the game with Josh and whether he was having more fun with them than he had with her. Or whether he missed her company as much as she missed his.

Truth be told, she'd much rather be wearing jeans and her Yankees shirt, eating peanuts, and drinking beer than wearing an admittedly gorgeous evening gown, eating Lobster Thermidor, and sipping fine champagne.

She immediately felt a wave of remorse. Blake sat next to her looking every bit the hero and humanitarian. This was his moment, and he deserved her unwavering attention and adoration. He reached over and grasped her hand in his, giving it a little squeeze. Her heart squeezed in response. Or maybe it was the cucumber and salmon appetizers she'd eaten. Hard to tell.

Once they got to the actual award presentation, she'd be the attentive, supportive girlfriend Blake deserved. But for now, her thoughts were just six short miles away in Yankee Stadium, Section 113, Row 16, Seat 23.

———

The next morning, Darcy trudged up the stairs to her office hoping the writing muse would pay her a visit and hang out for the day. She'd been absent so long, Darcy wasn't sure she'd recognize her if she came up and bit her on the ass.

The awards dinner had ended on a disappointing note, with Blake leaving in a rush for the hospital. He'd placed her in the care of his driver, kissed her good night, and hailed a taxi.

When the emcee had introduced him, she'd beamed with pride in his accomplishments, many of them she'd written. His acceptance speech had been brief but heartfelt. When he returned to his seat next to her, he'd pulled her into his arms for what should have been a toe-curling kiss, accompanied by the *oohs* and *ahs* of the audience. Sadly, the kiss didn't compare with Josh's.

The phone rang just as she hit the second-floor landing. Hoping it might be Josh, she dashed into her bedroom to grab it. "Hello?"

"Hey, what's cooking?"

Laura. Hiding her disappointment, she said, "I'm hoping a little hot and heavy sex is cooking."

"Oh! It's about time you and Blake got horizontal."

"Not me and Blake. Dominic and Ashley."

"Who?"

"My hero and heroine."

"Oh." Laura's disappointment rang clear in her voice. "It's a sad state of affairs when you write more sex scenes than you actually experience. How was the award ceremony?"

"It was fine. Good. I mean the keynote speaker could have picked a topic other than digestive ailments for a dinnertime talk, but I was proud of Blake."

"Where is Dr. Perfect?"

"He had an emergency right after the dinner, so he's probably at the hospital." Darcy heard a loud thud, followed by some shouts and applause. "Where are you?"

"Checking out the hotties at the cross-fit gym on East Eighty-Fourth. Speaking of hotties, you won't believe what I did last night."

"I really don't want to hear about your kinky sex life."

"It wasn't sex. It was baseball. I went to the game with Josh."

"The Yankees game? Like a date? Why?" Darcy tried to wrap her mind around Josh and Laura doing anything together, much less going to a Yankees game.

"No, not a date. Get real. He couldn't find anyone to go with him since you threw him over for Blake, so I went. At first I just felt sorry for him—"

"Wait, you felt sorry for Josh?"

"Yeah, crazy I know. But then I actually had a great time. He's kind of . . . I don't know . . . fun, you know?"

"Yeah, I know," Darcy muttered.

"Anyway, we went to this batting cage afterwards and then to some dive called Yankee Tavern."

The omelet she had for breakfast took on the characteristics of a brick, sharp and heavy in her stomach. Josh took

Laura to all the places they go. How could he? First he defends Laura at the gala, then he takes her to a baseball game and the batting cage! What next? She didn't want to go there.

"Darcy? You there?"

"Yeah. Sorry." *Don't say it.* "You and Josh going to start hanging out now?" *Of course you had to say it.*

"Pfft. I doubt it. It was just a one-time thing. Ooh, I gotta go. The hottie in the chest-hugging T-shirt just gave me a come-hither look. See ya."

Darcy started to throw the phone down on the bed but remembered what happened last time she did that and restrained herself, placing it in the cradle instead.

She didn't know what to think of Laura's revelation. It sounded innocent enough. But one thing was certain, *she* would not be missing anymore Yankees games.

Impulsively, she picked up the phone and dialed Josh. She wanted his take on the 'not a date' date.

"Hey, sunshine. Boy, did you miss a great game last night!"

Darcy rolled her eyes as Josh painstakingly described every at-bat. Before he could get to his exposition on the Yankees' pitching line-up, she interrupted him. "Yeah, thanks for rubbing it in. So, you and Laura, huh?" She let the question hang in the air.

"Oh . . . yeah. None of the guys could go, so after the committee meeting I had a wild idea and asked Laura. And surprisingly, it wasn't bad at all. Beneath that brash exterior, Laura is . . . fun."

There was that word again. "Well, I'm glad it worked out. But you haven't given away my seat have you, because I'm not planning to miss any more games."

"Of course not. We're on for tonight then, right?"

"Absolutely."

"Great. I have to meet Laura at Lexington Bar and Books to return her keys. Want to join? We could have a pre-game beer."

Her keys! "Why do you have Laura's keys?"

"Oh, it's the funniest thing—"

I just bet it is.

"On the way out of the stadium after the game, a Twins fan bumped into Laura, making her drop her purse. Boy!" Josh laughed. "She's got quite the mouth on her—she could give a sailor a run for his money—but I'm sure you already know that."

Yeah, yeah. Laura Potty-Mouth Armstrong.

"Anyway, in the scramble to pick up the contents before they—and we—were trampled, I scooped up her keys and stuffed them in my pocket. I forgot I had them until I got a call from her later when she couldn't get into her apartment. Turns out security let her in, so no worries."

"No worries." We wouldn't want Miss Priss inconvenienced. "What time should I meet you?"

"I told Laura I'd meet her at six."

"Okay. I'll see you then." Maybe seeing the two of them together would alleviate some of her concerns. If Josh and Laura fell back into their same punch-counterpunch routine, to use Josh's words, no worries. She refused to consider the other possibility.

CHAPTER FORTY-ONE

D arcy dodged people on the crowded sidewalk. Running late as a result of the extra subway traffic for the game, she strode into the dimly lit interior of Bar and Books. After taking a second for her eyes to adjust, she scanned the room for Josh and Laura.

She heard Laura's laugh and glanced to her left to see Josh and Laura at a corner table, yukking it up and looking quite cozy. Laura had her hand on his forearm, while Josh chuckled at something she said.

Hurt, angry, and a little shocked, Darcy froze, wondering what she should do. Brush it off? Make a joke? Sneak away and text Josh that she'd meet him at the game instead?

"Hey, Darce!" Josh waved his hand. "Over here."

Too late. She waved back as she made her way through the crowded room to the table.

"Am I interrupting?"

"Of course not!" Josh said.

"Pfft!" Laura waved her hand, before conveniently scooting closer to Josh to make room for Darcy.

To Darcy's mind, the two were just a little too nonchalant.

"Sit," Laura said as she patted the seat next to her. "We were just talking about how bad my swing is."

"I think the word is abysmal," Josh said. "Just stick with volleyball."

Darcy remembered Josh helping her with her own stance at the batting cage once, grabbing her hips and nestling up behind her. The memory triggered a quick flash of him impaling her against his door while she moaned in pleasure. She wondered if Josh had similarly helped Laura with her stance last night.

"Yeah, those hooker heels Laura wears makes batting practice difficult." *Wow. Talk about snarky.*

Josh laughed, clearly remembering his same remark to Darcy. Laura, on the other hand, glared at Darcy.

Then Laura's ever-present phone buzzed. "I've got to take this call. Thanks again, Josh." She pecked him on the cheek. "See ya."

Yeah, well don't let the door hit you in the ass on the way out.

"You two seem to be getting along swimmingly," Darcy remarked, her voice just a little too bright.

"Under that tough-girl exterior, she's nice." Josh shrugged. "I see now why you two have been friends for so long." He reached over and patted her hand. "I know that makes you happy . . . to see us getting along, I mean."

Ecstatic.

Darcy strained so hard for the words to come she thought she'd burst a blood vessel. In search of a distraction, she popped over to Facebook, liked a few posts, then skipped over to Twitter to retweet and reply, before checking her inbox.

Seeing an email from her editor with the subject line 'Holly's Heroes' and an exclamation point marking it as urgent, she opened it.

Darcy, we need to talk.

Never a good start to an email, especially from your editor.

Is there something going on with you that I need to know about? Are you ill? Has there been a death in the family? Clue me in here, because the first few chapters you sent me earlier this spring were fantastic, some of your best work, but these last few . . . P.U., do they stink. At this rate, I'm thinking your deadline is toast. Am I right?

And, not to pour salt in the wound, but I just received the review of The Doctor's Dilemma from the upcoming issue of RT Times. It's attached. Not good. Not good at all.

We need to talk about some strategies to help you get your mojo back. Give me a call ASAP.

Elise

Darcy didn't need her editor to tell her the last few chapters were crap. She already knew that. If it hadn't been for her deadlines, she wouldn't have sent them to her editor at all.

And now a bad review. Of course not everyone liked

her books—that was fine—it was all part of the business, but the worst reviews she'd ever received were mediocre.

With dread, she clicked on the attachment. *Two Stars! Holy crap!* That was *RT Times* code for 'has problems.'

Sadly, Darcy Butler's latest book, The Doctor's Dilemma, is DOA . . . Dead On Arrival. Trauma surgeon hero Garrick is flat and a little too perfect to be believable, while NGO-worker heroine Valerie is a simpering simpleton who couldn't think her way out of a paper bag. The plot is predictable, containing the timeworn trope of knight-in-shining-armor rescues damsel-in-distress.

What happened to Butler's smart, sassy heroines, fully capable of fighting their own battles while single-handedly saving the wrongfully accused hero from spending his life in prison?

On a positive note, the setting is exotic and the pace is dynamic. Too bad my two pet goldfish have more depth than the hero and heroine.

Maybe Butler needs a kiss from Prince Charming to awaken her from her stupor.

Darcy laid her head on her desk after reading, unquestionably, the worst review she'd ever received. Her life wasn't *going* down the toilet; it was down the toilet and heading to the sewer.

What next?

There were few ailments a spa day couldn't cure. Crappy manuscript, abysmal review, guilty conscience, unrequited love—all these things faded away, at least temporarily, under the capable hands of the massage therapist and aesthetician. Now Darcy lay on the warm tile lounger, wrapped in a cozy terry robe, cool cucumber slices over her eyes.

Laura stretched out with a sigh on the lounger next to her, tapping out something on her phone.

"Will you put that infernal device away?" Darcy could see why Gloria hated the things.

"Sorry." Laura laughed. "Just replying to a text from Josh."

Josh! Snatching the cucumber slices off her eyes, Darcy sat up and looked at Laura like she'd sprouted another head. "Josh?"

"Well, yeah," Laura replied, clearly taken aback by Darcy's reaction.

"Since when do you and Josh exchange texts?" So much for the relaxing effects of the massage and facial.

"Since when do you care who I exchange texts with? Jesus, Darcy. What is your problem? I haven't forgotten the snarky remark the other night about my 'hooker heels,' you know."

Darcy ignored Laura's comment. "What's going on with you and Josh?"

Laura narrowed her eyes. "What's it to you? Since when are you my or Josh's keeper? And I thought you wanted us to get along."

"He's not your type."

Laura sat up. "What the hell does that mean?"

Seeing the Cold Room empty but for her and Laura,

Darcy got up to pace. "He's not one of your international boy-toys or a one-night stand. Josh deserves more than that."

"You mean he deserves more than a nymphomaniac?"

"No. That's not what I mean."

"Sure sounded like that to me."

"He needs someone who wants to settle down, have children, grow old with him. I don't want to see him hurt."

"I see. And that's all I'm capable of—hurting him?"

"Laura, your track record isn't exactly that of long-term relationship material."

"Now there's the pot calling the kettle black. You think I don't see it? Your feelings for Blake aren't what they were at the start. Is he failing to live up to your fairytale notions like all the others?"

Darcy winced. *Ouch.* The truth hurts. "We're not talking about me and Blake."

"No. And we're not talking about Josh and me. We're talking about you and me. You think I'm capable of only hurting someone like Josh?"

Darcy turned her back to Laura. She couldn't let her see the jealousy she knew was tattooed across her collagen-masked face. "Just stay away from Josh."

"I see." Laura strode to the door. "I guess that says it all." Her hand on the door handle, she glanced back at Darcy. "I know you think I'm a hard-hearted, emotionally distant woman who likes to sleep around, but I've always wanted whatever you've dreamed of to come true. That includes the husband, the kids, the happily-ever-after you write about in your books. And I know you think there is *always* something better, but you don't have always." She closed the door with a quiet click.

This time Darcy didn't ask what was next. She was afraid of the answer.

CHAPTER FORTY-TWO

Josh shoved some files into his messenger bag for the trip. The conference in Dallas didn't mean he could let his other work slide. The weeklong conference couldn't come at a worse time. He had two cases going to trial soon, and another one in the discovery phase. After spending the days in conference sessions, his evenings would be spent reading and responding to emails, reviewing documents, and communicating with clients.

And he'd get in just hours before Darcy's big thirtieth birthday bash—provided there were no flight delays.

But he couldn't pass up this chance to attend the Alternative Dispute Resolution Conference. He'd made up his mind to become a certified mediator, and this conference offered the perfect opportunity to network with other mediators, talk about the pros and cons, get some training under his belt. Once he'd accomplished certification, he had a plan cooking for his future at Butler, Lukeman, and Michaels.

His carry-on stood next to his desk, ready to go. Only one thing left to do—call Darcy to let her know he'd be out of town but would be there for her birthday.

Disappointed to get her voicemail, he left her a message. Knowing the week ahead would be an exhausting blur, he didn't make any promises to call her. He'd just see her at her party.

————

Coming up for air, after methodically working through her marked-up, color-coded manuscript—yes, Darcy had broken down and followed Millie's advice—she ran down the stairs to get her heart rate up, get the blood flowing, and take a mental break.

She couldn't say it was going well, but she had made some modicum of progress. Taking a swig of diet soda straight from the can, she picked up her phone, which she'd purposely left downstairs to avoid the distraction. She'd been as obsessed as Laura with her phone, desperately hoping to receive an email, text, or voicemail from her friend.

The other day in the spa hadn't been a shining moment for her. She'd said some things to Laura out of jealousy and pain—things she, of course, regretted now. An overactive imagination—that's what she had. Too bad that over-activity didn't come in the form of ideas for her manuscript. She'd tried to call Laura to apologize, but she'd only gotten her voicemail. Maybe she didn't want to talk to her, which only made Darcy feel worse.

Seeing a voicemail from Josh, she listened to it first. The short message left little to be desired. No promise to call—no explanation about where he was going. Just that he'd be back in time for her birthday. "He'd better be," she groused.

Her phone buzzed and she saw a text from Laura. *Finally.*

IN CASE YOU CARE, I JUST THOUGHT I'D LET YOU KNOW THAT I'M GOING OUT OF TOWN SO YOU WOULDN'T THINK I'D BEEN KIDNAPPED. BUT IF I'M STILL INVITED, I'LL BE BACK FOR YOUR BIRTHDAY PARTY.

Darcy got a sick feeling in her stomach. Josh and Laura leaving town at the same time? It had to be a coincidence. *Pfft. Of course it was.* Laura and Josh wouldn't go away together, would they? Recalling the confrontation with Laura, she realized Laura never denied there was anything between her and Josh, and she never promised to stay away from him either. Laura never made promises she couldn't keep. Did that mean Laura couldn't stay away from Josh?

The diet soda boiled in Darcy's stomach like hydrochloric acid. What would she do if her two best friends became lovers, or worse, already were?

D arcy needed air. Her comfortable brownstone had suddenly become an airless tomb. Grabbing a jacket, she ran out of the house as if flames dogged her heels. Where to go? Not Dumbo. Too many memories of Josh. Turning in the opposite direction, she walked with no destination in mind.

She passed families walking dogs, lovers strolling hand-in-hand, joggers, power walkers, people scurrying home to a late dinner. None of them held any interest for her. Deep inside her head, she strode the streets of Manhattan. What had she done? Had she fallen in love with Josh only to realize it too late? How had she overlooked her feelings for him all these years? Surely she didn't suddenly fall in love with him when he danced with Millie. She must have been in love with him for years. Perhaps it happened so gradually she didn't see it.

She thought of Josh's intervention with Anne and Matt. He'd said they'd taken each other for granted. Grown complacent in their relationship. Is that what she'd done? Taken Josh for granted, believing he would always be there, no matter what?

She'd been looking for something she was so afraid to find that she couldn't see what had been right in front of her. The question was whether Josh could love her.

All the years of complaining to him about the guys she'd dated. She couldn't have made a relationship with herself any less desirable than if she'd had bad hygiene.

And what about Laura? Would she let this come between her and her childhood best friend? Right now, she couldn't answer that question. Every time she thought about Josh and Laura together, she wanted to scrub her brain with radioactive sulphuric acid. Unbearable.

She finally found herself on the High Line. Wrapping her jacket closer around her to fight against the chilly wind, she stopped and looked over the rail at the view below, then at the lights of the city beyond. She remembered walking with Blake along this very stretch of the High Line, her feet barely touching the ground in her bliss. Recalled his kisses, his romantic lines, his hero-perfect features, and his larger-than-life image.

It all paled in comparison to Josh's Perfect Kiss, his frank opinions, his boy-next-door charm, and his quiet heroism.

Maybe deep down she knew Blake wasn't real—couldn't be real. That was why she hadn't felt the same fear, the same need to bail before things got serious with him, because a fantasy could never be serious.

What now? Turning her feet toward home, she knew the answer. Even if she couldn't have Josh, she couldn't continue with Blake. It wasn't fair to him. She didn't love him. Didn't think she ever could. She still didn't know how he'd come to be in her life, and she guessed she never would, but she knew it was time to send him back to wherever he'd come from.

———

The next morning, Darcy wiped the sweat from her palms as she walked to the front door. The hour of reckoning had come. She opened the door to Blake Garrett, a man most women would kill for, a man she once thought was the perfect man for her. Of course he looked handsome, even in his hospital scrubs, his hair disheveled from his surgical cap.

She'd left a message for him earlier, telling him she needed to see him. She'd received a text message from him asking if she was okay and that he was in a case but would come over as soon as he could. She'd texted back that she was fine so he wouldn't worry. That was three hours ago. She'd been pacing ever since.

"Darcy, are you okay?" Blake ran his hands through his hair as he stepped into her foyer.

She sidestepped his attempt to kiss her, instead walking into the living room.

"I'm fine, Blake."

He followed her into the room. "I'm afraid I can't stay, I have to get back to my patient."

"I'm sorry to take you away from the hospital, but this won't take long." She'd never been so nervous breaking up with someone before. Then again, she'd rarely let the relationship progress to this point. She took a deep breath, turned back to Blake, and said, "I don't think we should see each other anymore." She exhaled in relief after the words were out.

"I see." His brow furrowed in confusion. "Is it the hours I keep at the hospital, or my trips abroad?"

"No." Her voice held steady.

"Oh. Well." His phone buzzed, but he ignored it. "Then, what is it?"

"It's nothing. It's everything. I just don't . . . I don't love you, and I'm not sure I ever could. I'm so sorry, Blake. Truly sorry."

He wore a pained expression. "I could reduce the number of medical missions I go on. Spend more time with you."

"No, Blake. It's your calling. It's what you're meant to do."

"But, Darcy, we're so perfect together. Isn't there anything I can do?

She walked up to him, and cupped his face. "You're perfect, Blake. You're just not perfect for me."

His phone buzzed again. "Dammit."

"You have to go. Duty calls." She smiled gently at him.

"Darcy"—he grazed his fingers along her cheek—"you're one exceptional woman. Don't ever let anyone tell you differently because whoever wins your heart will be the luckiest man alive."

She shivered at the memory of her Uncle Al's words.

"You're pretty exceptional yourself." Tears welled up, despite herself.

Blake's phone buzzed again, then he leaned down and

brushed a soft kiss across her lips, before snatching it out of its holster and striding to the door.

"Dr. Garrett," he answered.

And with that, he walked out of her life.

CHAPTER FORTY-THREE

arcy checked her watch once more.

"They'll be here," her mother admonished. "Go enjoy your party. You only turn thirty once."

"Thank God for that," Darcy muttered. She knew her mother was right, but she didn't feel much like celebrating. The day she'd been both dreading and looking forward to had arrived, and with it, the realization that dreams don't always come true.

No sign of Josh or Laura anywhere, and no word from them either. Maybe Laura was still angry with her. Or maybe they were having too much fun together to break away for her party.

Her mother handed her a tray of food and shooed her out of the kitchen, "Go. Mingle. Eat. Drink. Be merry. It's what one does at parties, especially when one is the guest of honor."

Darcy stepped out onto the patio then into the enormous tent rented for the occasion. Several tall kerosene heaters chased away the October chill, white twinkle lights provided illumination, and a local DJ spun the latest dance tunes, while a caterer supplied delicious appetizers and bite-size desserts.

Speaking of the caterer, she looked down at the tray of food in her hands. Why was *she* serving the food?

"Mom," she said under her breath as she found room for it on the food table.

Anne and Matt emerged from the darkness, clothes disheveled, hair mussed. They'd been incorrigible since their reconciliation.

"Hey there, Birthday Girl!" Matt called out.

"Hey, Matt. You might want to zip your fly," Darcy said.

"Oops." He turned his back as he tucked his shirt in and zipped up.

Anne didn't miss a beat as she plucked a goat cheese appetizer off the tray Darcy had carried out. "Worked up an appetite." Winking at Darcy, she took a bite then stuffed the other half in Matt's mouth when he turned back around, before kissing him.

"Get a room," Darcy muttered and stalked off.

Brandon and David chatted with Aunt Rosie and Uncle Al, while Will and Sam slow danced together.

How cute is that! Even in her heartbroken state, she could still delight in puppy love.

Her parents had certainly spared no expense, and friends and family had come in from all over the East Coast to celebrate her birthday. The least she could do was make a show of enjoying herself. Her father helped in that endeavor when he pulled her into his arms for a dance.

"How is it my baby girl is thirty today? Where did the time go?"

"I don't know, Dad." She sighed as she laid her head against her father's chest, his arms a comforting band of strength around her. "It seems like yesterday we were fishing off the dock and I hooked that striped bass."

She heard her father's chuckle deep in his chest. "The fish was so big I had to help you reel it in. You were so proud! You couldn't stop talking about that fish for a month. Drove your brother and sister crazy." He chuckled again, a soothing, familiar sound. "You must have been, what, twelve?"

"Ten."

"Twenty years ago. Time does fly."

Inexplicably, tears burned her eyes. She'd wasted so much of that time searching for a fictional Prince Charming —at least the last few years of it. She cleared her throat. "Dad. How did you know Mom was 'The One'?"

He drew back and looked into her eyes before gathering her back for a hug. She'd told her parents before the guests began arriving that she broke up with Blake. Oddly, her mother had seemed relieved. And her dad, well, he'd seemed sanguine. "Oh, sweetheart. Just because it didn't work out with Blake doesn't mean you won't find love."

She didn't tell him that she'd found love only after she'd lost it.

———

The party grew louder as the alcohol flowed. Drunken revelers lined up for "The Electric Slide" as the DJ called out words of encouragement to those less inclined to make fools of themselves.

Darcy skipped out on the line-dancing fun and crossed the lawn to the river. Away from the warmth of the heaters, the fall air nipped at bare skin, sending goosebumps down her arms. Undeterred, she continued to the spot above where the lawn sloped down toward the river. Her breath puffed out in white clouds before dissipating in the dry air.

Stars winked in an ebony sky, no moon to dim their glow, while the river lapped gently against the bank and swished a little, as it wrapped around the dock pilings.

Still no Josh or Laura. Her eyes filled as she held back a sob. Even if they were a couple, she knew she wouldn't forsake their friendship. Her birthday felt meaningless without them to share it with. She knew her life would feel the same.

They'd been there for everything. Especially Laura. The terrible teens, the crush she'd had on Billy Bradenton, the rejection letters from publishers, and the devastating blow when she'd caught Doug cheating on her. How could she have a life without Laura? Or Josh? She couldn't.

———

L aura held a hundred-dollar bill up against the Plexiglas partition. "This is for you if you can get me to Riverdale in forty-five minutes or less."

"You got it, lady," the cab driver responded, an avaricious gleam in his eye and stepped on the gas, pinning Laura against the back seat.

She closed her eyes. What a day! Her trip to Chicago had netted her a potential lead for a client (and some celebratory shopping on the Magnificent Mile), but the journey home had been fraught with one snafu after another. She wouldn't miss her best friend's birthday party. Come hell or high water, she'd be there. And she'd beat Josh to a pulp if he gave Darcy her gift without Laura there.

On the bumpy flight from Chicago, she mulled over the argument she had with Darcy in the spa last week. Darcy's reaction had been completely out of character for her. Laura had chalked it up to the stress of her book promotions, the fact that Blake Garrett would be coming out of the closet, so to speak, with the book's release, and her writer's block. Then it'd hit her like a jolt of turbulence. Jealousy, plain and simple. Jealousy over her and Josh, which could only mean one thing.

Darcy Butler loved Josh Ryan.

She'd been so wrapped up in her own drive for success that she'd missed all the signs. She and Darcy had known one another for so long, they were open books to one another. Laura had simply failed to read what was there in black and white.

Did Josh know? she wondered as the taxi sped down I-87. Did he love Darcy? God, she hoped so. She'd hate to have to kick his ass for breaking Darcy's heart.

———

Josh stashed his luggage and messenger bag in the coat closet and made his way through the throng in search of the Birthday Girl. Talk about a day of 'if something could go wrong it did.' He'd missed his connecting flight in Boston due to weather delays in Dallas, and he'd had to wait around until the next flight. He'd begun to think he'd arrived without his luggage, since his made it onto the belt long after everyone else's.

Then the train from Grand Central to Tarrytown stopped for about twenty minutes due to problems with the tracks. His phone battery gave up the ghost, so he couldn't even send a text. The short taxi ride from the station to Jeff and Vanessa's seemed interminable.

He only hoped he hadn't missed the cake and the toasts.

He'd given a lot of thought to his relationship with Darcy over the last few days. His days had been packed solid. So much to learn about mediation, so many contacts to follow-up with, and so many documents to review for his upcoming trials, but none of that had managed to keep thoughts of Darcy at bay. He loved her, and only her. He had to tell her. If she told him she didn't love him, then he'd deal with it, but at least she would know, and so would he.

He didn't see Darcy or Blake as he scanned the crowd in the tent.

"About time you got here." Gloria's unmistakable gravel-pit voice came from behind him.

"Hi, Gloria. Have you seen Darcy?"

She pointed with her martini. "Last time I saw her, she was walking in the direction of the river. Alone."

"Thanks," he called over his shoulder as he hurried off to find her.

CHAPTER FORTY-FOUR

C hilled to the bone, Darcy turned toward the house and saw someone striding across the lawn, someone with Josh's height and build. Her pulse quickened, first with excitement, then with fear. The moment of truth. She stood, frozen to the spot. What should she say? How should she say it? *Hey, Josh. Did you and Laura enjoy your secret tryst?*

"There you are!" He scooped her up and swung her around. "Happy birthday, Darcy!"

Dizzy from the spin, she grasped his jacket sleeves to steady herself. "Josh! I was beginning to think you weren't coming."

"Are you kidding? Nothing from a dead cell phone to a train wreck could keep me from getting to your birthday party."

"Where's Laura?"

Josh pulled back in confusion. "What do you mean, where's Laura? How would I know where Laura is?" He laughed. "I didn't know it was my day to watch her."

"You mean, but I thought—" Darcy laughed in relief.

Josh shook his head. "Mean what? Thought what?"

"Oh, nothing." So they hadn't been together? Or maybe they had, and they'd had an argument.

"My God, Darcy, you're cold as ice." He chafed his hands up and down her bare arms to warm them. "Let's go inside." He took her hand, gave it a gentle tug.

"No. I mean, in a minute. I need to talk to you first."

"I need to talk to you, too, but let's go somewhere warmer."

Darcy relented, pointing to her father's boathouse that served as a guest cottage when needed. Josh removed his jacket and draped it around her shoulders, engulfing her in his scent, his warmth. She shivered.

An awkward silence fell as they both crossed the dock leading to the entrance of the boathouse, not touching.

Josh flipped the light switch on a bedside lamp and gave the well-appointed one-room efficiency a cursory look before turning back to Darcy. "You warming up?"

"Mm hmm."

"Darcy—"

"Josh—"

They both chuckled, a nervous sound.

"You first," Josh said.

"Oh. O-okay," Darcy stammered. Her mouth suddenly went dry. *Deep breath. In through the nose, out through the mouth.* She'd practiced a long thought-out speech but suddenly couldn't remember it. She'd waited too long to say the words. *Don't back out now.* Her old fears surfaced. Fears she'd tried to face since Doug broke her heart. Fears of rejection.

What if they start dating, and it was great, and then it just . . . petered out? What if her track record continued and she bailed? Not such a big deal when it was a blind date, but devastating if it was Josh. Wasn't it better not to start something only to have it crash and burn?

But they'd already started something, weeks ago in his hallway, in his apartment, against his front door, she reminded herself. *So just say it.* "I love you." *How's that for blunt?*

———

Josh's eyes widened and his breath snagged in his throat. "You love me, how?" he asked, his mind a jumble of confusion and skepticism.

"I love you," she said, taking a slow, deep breath, "like a woman loves a man."

The confusion deepened. "What about Blake?"

"I broke up with him." She took his hand, and before he could respond, rushed on. "Josh, it's you I love. I guess it happened so gradually, I . . . I don't know when it happened. I've loved you for so long." Her voice trailed off as a tear slid down her cheek. "But I've taken you for granted, too, and I'm so sorry. Please, tell me I'm not too late."

"Even if you don't love me, I can't lose your friendship over my selfish behavior. I had to tell you. You had to know."

Josh gently cupped her face, his thumb catching the tear. "My God, Darcy. I've waited so long to hear you say that and mean it the way you do. Not just as a friend, but . . . the way I love you."

She looked up at him in surprise. "You love me?" More tears threatened to spill as her eyes filled.

He pulled her to his chest, his arms wrapped around, held

her close. "I've loved you for years, almost since the day we met." His confession spilled out. "I'd finally worked up the courage to ask you out on a date, and the next thing I knew you were engaged. When Doug broke your heart, I wanted to both pulverize him and send him a thank-you gift—you were free, but I knew you needed space and time to heal. We became so comfortable with one another in such a short time. Best friends. The fear that I would lose your friendship if I told you how I felt, and the thought that it either might not work out or you wouldn't feel the same, kept me from telling you."

"Oh, Josh! How stupid and blind I've been. Can you ever forgive me?"

He tilted her chin up, brought his lips to hers, a butterfly kiss. "Nothing to forgive." His gaze held hers, as he grazed her lower lip with his thumb. "I'm as much to blame for all this wasted time. I promised you once, that I'd always tell you the truth, even if it hurts. Well, I didn't keep that promise. I kept my true feelings from you, and not telling that truth hurt. Hurt us both. I won't do that again. I love you, Darcy Elizabeth Butler, and I intend to make up for lost time."

She wound her arms around his neck as his jacket fell to the floor. "And just how do you plan to do that, Mr. Ryan?" She laughed through her tears.

"By making every second count." He kissed her, this time with passion and heat, love, and want. His hands slid up her back then back down again, squeezing her bottom. "And by taking my time," he murmured against her lips before slanting his mouth across hers, encouraging her to let him in, to caress his tongue with hers.

Her fingers skimmed the back of his neck, raising goose-bumps, before fisting in his hair. She pressed the length of her lithe, delicious body against his. He moaned when she made contact with his erection.

"I want to learn, touch, taste, every inch of you." He licked and kissed, caressed and nipped at the tender flesh of her neck, her bare shoulders, the delicious skin along her collarbone, as her head rolled back to allow him unimpeded access. "I want to make love to you in every way possible, until every curve, every dip and hollow of your body is engraved in my memory."

"Oh God, Josh," she moaned. "I haven't been able to forget what happened in your apartment, at your door, with you. I've never experienced anything like it."

He choked out a laugh. "I haven't forgotten it either. It's burned in my brain forever. But I can promise you something, this time won't be a partially clothed quickie against a door. I want to see you. All of you." He spun her around, swept aside her hair, and unzipped her ruby-red dress as he pressed hot kisses on her bare back.

Her dress floated to the floor as she turned to face him, wearing nothing but red lace panties and stilettos. She went all shy, the blush rising from her toes to the roots of her hair.

"Okay, I see the fascination with those stilts. My God, you're sexy!"

A throaty laugh bubbled up, sending a shot of heat straight to his groin. He'd never heard such a sensual sound coming from Darcy's lips, and he hoped to hear more of that and other sounds of pleasure coming from her from this night forward.

CHAPTER FORTY-FIVE

J osh's sharp intake of breath sent shivers of pleasure down her spine. She felt beautiful, erotic, under his heated gaze as it traveled the length of her. Darcy hooked her fingers in the front of his khakis and pulled him toward her. "No fair. If I'm naked, you have to be naked, too." She unbuckled his belt and couldn't resist slipping her hand inside to stroke him, shivering as he groaned in pleasure.

Josh grabbed her wrist, holding her at bay. "Not yet." Scooping her up, he carried her to the guest bed, remembering another time he'd carried her in his arms and how he'd wished it had been under different circumstances. Laying her gently on the bed, he pulled off his shirt, toed off his shoes, and dropped his pants and boxers to the floor as she watched, an avid gleam in her eyes.

The bedside lamp lit her skin with a golden glow, casting shadows beneath her beautiful breasts, and contrasts of light and dark along her shapely body. Josh couldn't wait to touch and taste her. He crawled up the length of the bed, settling between her thighs. Rocking against him, she wrapped her legs around him. The intimate contact almost proved his undoing as he remembered how it felt to be inside her.

Clamping down on his self-control, he pressed his lips to hers and sucked her bottom lip in between his, then nipped it before grazing his tongue across it. He slid down her body, kissing her fragrant skin, inhaling the scent of flowers and pheromones.

His fingertips skimmed up her hip and across her stomach, setting off a wave of quivering as he made his way to her breasts. He groaned as her nipples hardened beneath his touch. "So beautiful." He took one into his mouth, lathing his tongue across its pink surface, as she arched her back into him. He moved to her other breast, her panting breath ruffling his hair.

His mouth drifted down her belly as her hands fisted in the bedding. She reared up when his mouth met the wetness of her panties. Raspy sighs escaped when he slipped them down her gorgeous legs. She reached out to him. "Josh . . . Now . . . Please."

He'd restrained himself long enough. Her hoarse plea sent him over the edge.

———

Darcy watched as he crawled back toward her, his lids heavy with desire, the muscles in his arms bunching. She opened her arms to him as he positioned himself over her. When he thrust into her, she melted into the bed, her limbs liquid and boneless. He kissed her as he drove into her again and again, deep and slow.

Scraping her nails down his back, she returned his kisses with a frenzy of passion and need. Wondering how she could have denied herself this bliss all these years. Wondering how she could have been so blind.

He clasped her hands in his, pulling them over her head. "Darcy, my God," he exclaimed, his voice husky with desire.

This wasn't the flash of fire she'd experienced in his apartment, but a slow, delicious burn that started in her center and radiated from there, up her body, down her legs, making her curl her toes. She breathed his name as he buried his face in her neck, nipping her earlobes, his driving thrusts more urgent.

The climax burst upon her like fireworks, leaving shimmers of light in its wake, even as he cried out her name.

———

Josh rolled off of her, pulling her into his arms, nestling her head on his shoulder, and they lay silent and content, waiting for their heartbeats and breaths to return to normal. Sounds of laughter and strains of music drifted down to the boathouse. Certain she'd been missed by now, Darcy could have cared less. As far as she was concerned, she'd be happy to lie in Josh's arms all night.

"Why did you ask me where Laura was?" Josh asked, interrupting her thoughts.

"It's nothing." She buried her face in his neck, trying to distract him with little kisses.

"Come on. Or I'll tickle the truth out of you." He reached for her ribs, having just learned how deliciously sensitive she was there.

"No!" she shrieked. "Okay, okay. I confess." She traced little circles on his chest, hesitating. "I thought you two had something going."

Her confession was met with silence, and she tensed, thinking maybe she'd been right. Then Josh burst out laughing.

"You thought Laura and I"—he chuckled some more—"were, what, sleeping together? Wait a minute." He pushed back from her to look her in the eye. "You were jealous?"

"Well, yeah. You two had gotten pretty friendly since the gala. The Yankees game, meeting up at the bar, texting. What was I supposed to think, especially given your previous animosity toward one another?"

"Trust me, she's not my type. Besides, I only had eyes for you." He kissed her nose.

"How was I supposed to know that at the time? So then, why were you two spending so much time together?"

"She'll kill me for spilling the beans, but I can't have you jealous of your best friend. We were spending time together because we were working out the details of your birthday gift—a trip for you, to Sonoma and Napa Valleys. All expenses paid."

Darcy raised herself up on her elbow to look Josh in the face. "What?"

"It was her idea. She said you told her over lunch some months back that your next series would be set in Sonoma and Napa and that you needed to take a trip out there, learn about winemaking and culinary training. So that's your gift. A week under the tutelage of one of Sonoma's top winemakers, and a week at the Culinary Institute of America in Napa. She pulled some strings with the winemaker, one of her accounts."

"Wow! I don't know what to say. That's an extremely thoughtful and creative gift! And expensive. You two really shouldn't have spent so much money." And to think she'd been jealous of Laura. Guilt over their last words to one another rocketed through her. Boy, did she owe her big time!

"The day you met us at Bar and Books, I needed to pay her my half of the trip."

"So you didn't need to return her keys?"

"Nope."

"You two are pretty sneaky."

"Well, you better act surprised."

"I will. I promise." She hugged Josh. "I'm the luckiest woman alive. I have the two best friends in the whole universe."

"Speaking of gifts, Birthday Girl, we should probably rejoin the celebration. They've likely sent out a search party for the guest of honor, and it wouldn't do to have them find her wearing nothing but her birthday suit."

———

Hands clasped, Darcy and Josh crossed the lawn toward the lights and noise of her birthday party. Darcy snuggled beneath the warmth of Josh's jacket, inhaling his fresh citrus scent, wondering why she'd always written heroes that smelled of spice and woods.

Giggling like teenagers as they'd dressed, barely able to keep their hands off one another, Darcy remembered her sister and Matt's rumpled appearance after their little tryst. Would it be that obvious to everyone at the party? Darcy nervously ran her fingers through her hair once again.

Stepping beneath the twinkling lights of the tent, her father was the first to greet them. "There you are! We wondered where you'd gone off to." His eyes drifted to their clasped hands, then back up to their faces. A slow smile spread across his features, followed by a flush. "Oh. Well. Hey, Van, look who decided to join her own party."

"Darcy! Where on earth have you been?" Her mother stood, hands planted on her hips, a pose Darcy remembered well from childhood. "We've been looking all over for you."

Her father cleared his throat and thrust his chin in the direction of their clasped hands.

"Oh. Oh!" Her mother clapped a hand over her mouth before a giggle escaped, laughter dancing in her eyes.

Laura sauntered up, a glass of champagne in her hands. "It's about time!" She stepped back, gasped, and pointed her finger in an accusatory manner. "You two had sex!" She wagged her finger in Darcy's face. "You can't deny it this time. My sex sensor is *not* on the fritz."

Darcy could feel the blush to the roots of her hair. "Jeez, Laura."

Laura's eyes narrowed and she pulled Darcy in. "This wasn't the first time, either!"

"Shh," Darcy hissed.

Gloria had joined the group. "'Bout damn time, too," she muttered before walking off in the direction of the bar.

"We're in love." Josh reached out to cup Darcy's face, kissing her.

Her father clapped Josh on the back. "I can't think of anyone better for my little Tomboy-Princess."

Her mother hugged Darcy to her. "I'm so happy for you both."

Laura faced off against Josh. "You ever hurt her, and remember what I said about Cheating Bastard? That would only be the beginning."

Darcy saw Josh cringe and wondered what Laura was talking about.

"Hey, everyone," her father belted out over the music.

"My daughter is in love!" As if her love life were breaking news.

The revelers erupted in applause.

"Dad," Darcy muttered in embarrassment, but the elation she felt over her family's acceptance of what must appear to be a rash development quickly overshadowed any discomfiture over the public announcement.

Brandon, David, Anne, and Matt gathered around to offer their congratulations as if people didn't fall in love every day.

"Damn, sis, I thought you'd never find someone good enough for you," Brandon gushed. "I mean, we had all given up hope of ever seeing you get the happily-ever-after you're always writing about. David and I were just saying the other day, if your life were an Austen novel, you'd be Miss Bates—"

"All right, I get it." Darcy shoved her brother.

His face wore a broad grin. "Seriously, Darcy." Holding her by the shoulders, he looked into her eyes, his own serious. "Josh is the perfect man for you."

CHAPTER FORTY-SIX

After the most awesome thirtieth birthday in history, she and Josh quickly fell into a comfortable rhythm, a mix of the thrill of newfound love and the comfort of the years they'd shared. It hadn't taken long before Josh's things ended up in Darcy's house, his own apartment all but abandoned. Never much of a morning person, it quickly became Darcy's favorite time of day. Waking in Josh's arms, skin against skin, legs entwined, often led to slow, languorous lovemaking.

Evenings were spent in front of the fireplace, catching up on SportsCenter or watching a romantic comedy that usually ended with a pile of discarded clothes, heated making out, and passionate sighs.

Yankee games were a new experience. Every accomplishment was celebrated with a kiss, from home runs to base hits to double plays. Sadly, the Yanks lost in the seventh game of the World Series to the Atlanta Braves.

While Josh went to work as the partner in charge of the firm's new mediation division, Darcy focused on rewriting her work-in-progress, pleased with the results. Millie had proven so helpful with her previous manuscript problems that Darcy now had her read each chapter as she completed it. Her insights and critiques were always right on target.

Two weeks after her birthday, Darcy overheard Josh on the phone with his mom, telling her that he and Darcy planned to come see her for Thanksgiving. He'd paused, listening to her response, then added, "I'm glad you're happy for us, Mom. I love Darcy more and more every day."

Warmth had spread from her head to her toes. Darcy felt truly loved and cherished. This is what she wrote about, this is what she'd dreamed of. And now she had it for herself. Josh's unconditional acceptance of her opened her eyes to her real dream of happiness. Not her falsely bright superficial fairytale, but the deep, rich mutual love and respect that lasts a lifetime. Some day in the future they'd celebrate their sixty-third wedding anniversary just like Aunt Rosie and Uncle Al.

———

Josh's days at the office were insane, between interviewing for potential mediators and secretarial staff, to reviewing and approving the marketing materials for the new division, to meeting with the Director of Finance about budgets. Even with the busy days, he'd take a few minutes to call Darcy, see how her day was going and how the manuscript was coming along. And he thought about her throughout the day, looking forward to the time when he walked through the front door to take her in his arms and kiss her until they both became dizzy with want.

His secretary knocked on his door, interrupting his daydream. "Your two o'clock is here."

"Right." Josh stood, pulling on his suit jacket and straightening his tie. "Bring him in."

Yep, he'd never been happier or more fulfilled in his life. His mentor and father-figure supported him, Kelly and Daniel had their home, and Darcy Butler loved him. There was just one thing missing, and this appointment was one step toward filling in that missing piece.

Josh approached the stout man wearing a camel cashmere coat and extended his hand in greeting. "Mr. Workman, thank you for coming."

"Mr. Ryan. Where would you like to conduct business?"

Josh indicated the sofa and chair around the coffee table.

Mr. Workman set his heavy case on the coffee table and worked the lock's combination, before opening the case to a dazzling display of diamonds of all shapes and sizes. "Now, tell me about your fiancée-to-be, and we'll pick out the ring meant for her."

In celebration of their six weeks together, Darcy planned a special picnic-style dinner in front of the fireplace. After laying out the cashmere throw that would serve as a picnic blanket and placing pillows on the floor, she tidied up the living room, plumping throw pillows and sofa cushions. Lifting one of the sofa cushions, she noticed a bit of cobalt blue peeking out from beneath the neighboring cushion. Pulling on the fabric, she realized it was one of Blake's ties. She remembered the night of Martin and Cindy's wedding when they were on her couch and were interrupted by the call from the medical charity.

He must not have missed it. Even so, she wanted to let him know she had it and if he wanted it, she'd leave it for him at the hospital.

Calling his cell phone, she got a voicemail that wasn't his. *Hmmm. Did he change his number?* Wanting to resolve this, she dialed the hospital, asking for the emergency room charge nurse.

"Metropolitan Hospital ER, Nurse Buchanan."

"Yes, could I leave a message for Dr. Garrett?"

"Who?"

"Dr. Blake Garrett."

"We don't have a Dr. Garrett on staff."

"There has to be some mistake." Darcy didn't want to tell the woman she'd dated him, created him, even. "He, um, he treated my friend."

"No, there's no mistake. Is there something else I can help you with?"

"But— Did he leave?"

"Miss, I've been here for twenty years and we've *never* had a Dr. Garrett on staff. Now, for the last time, unless you're bleeding from a knife or gunshot wound, or having a massive coronary, I have patients to take care of."

The phone clicked. Darcy held the phone up and looked at it like the device had just insulted her. "She hung up on me!"

She didn't know what to think. How could she explain that the man she'd created, who'd suddenly appeared in her life, had apparently disappeared just as suddenly? If it weren't for the Hermès tie she held in her hands, she'd almost believe she'd dreamed the whole thing. Was it possible? Like Cinderella's coach-and-four, was it really possible that Blake Garrett's very existence had been magic?

Feeling dizzy, her legs quivered and she sank to the sofa

at the thought. "Pfft. Impossible. Nurse Ratched was just having a bad day."

―――――

"**H**oney, I'm home."

Darcy checked the temperature on the roast, Josh's favorite, before skipping out to the foyer. How she loved greeting Josh at the end of the day. Today, she'd taken special care with her appearance, right down to the purple lace panties and bra she wore beneath the rich purple cashmere wrap dress—easy on, and, better yet, easy off.

"Hi, Honey! How was your day?" She stepped up on tiptoe to plant a firm kiss on his lips.

"Look at you, lookin' all June Cleaver."

Josh's gaze traveled the length of her, warming her inch by inch.

"But June was never this sexy." He hung his coat on the rack. "My day was fine, but I can see my night is going to be even better." He snagged her around the waist to pull her in for another kiss. "Do I smell pot roast?"

"Yes, with carrots and potatoes, just the way you like it."

"What's the occasion?"

"Our six week anniversary of course. And we're having a carpet picnic by the fire."

Josh followed her into the kitchen where she handed him a glass of Merlot. "Mmm. Good wine."

"To us." She raised her glass to his in a toast.

"To us." Taking another sip of his wine, he backed her into the counter, and setting his glass down behind her, brought his lips to hers. "Mmm. Even better wine." He licked the taste of her from his lips, sending a shiver of desire through her.

"You keep that up and your roast will be shoe leather before we eat it."

"I could use some new shoes." He nuzzled her neck, while she giggled in response.

"Take the wine and go sit down. I'll bring your plate," she said, with a half-hearted push.

"I like a woman who waits on her man." He swatted her on the bottom as she turned to take the roast out of the oven. "Keep 'em barefoot and pregnant, I always say." He tossed a grin over his shoulder as he headed to the living room.

Darcy followed shortly with two plates. Sliced roast, baby carrots, and roasted potatoes, with green beans on the side.

The fire threw flickering light across one side of Josh's face, leaving the other half in shadow, but she couldn't miss the gleam in his brown eyes. Nickelback sang about never being alone, while the world outside continued its frenetic pace. But for now, she and Josh could savor this time together.

After dining on the succulent roast, enjoying the excellent Merlot, and talking over the events of their day, Josh settled back on the pillows, lounging like the Sultan Suleiman. "That was delicious. Thank you."

"You're welcome. Wait 'til you see dessert—Tiramisu."

"Woman, are you trying to make me fat?"

"Nope. Trying to make you happy." She winked.

"You already make me happy." Josh's gaze grew serious. "Come here."

Darcy's heart performed a little stutter step at the look in Josh's eyes. She moved to kneel in front of him while he sat up.

"Darcy, I know we've only really been dating—well, essentially living together—for six weeks now, but we've been together for almost ten years. In those years we've gotten to know one another about as well as any two people can."

The stutter step became full-fledged tachycardia.

"In keeping with my promise to make up for lost time." He reached into his pocket and pulled out a little white box.

The breath Darcy was holding left in a rush.

"Darcy Elizabeth Butler, will you marry me, have children with me, grow old with me?" Opening the box, he took the heart-shaped diamond solitaire out.

Darcy sat speechless for a moment as tears blurred her vision. Once his words sank in, she threw herself at him, knocking them both to the floor. "Yes, yes, yes!"

He caught her face in his hands and kissed her with all the heat and tenderness, seduction and devotion, need and fulfillment she could wish for.

EPILOGUE

THE FOLLOWING MAY

Darcy's satin slippers floated three feet above the lawn of her parents' house, Josh's hand clasped in hers. Everyone was there, all the people who meant so much to her, especially her Aunt Rosie, who'd opened her eyes to the true meaning of love and happily-ever-after. Even she couldn't have written such a wedding celebration. In the space of a single baseball season, Darcy's fairytale had come true. *Check that.* Her dream had come true.

The picture-perfect sky, all rich blue and white fluffy clouds, complemented the white bedecked tables and chairs set around the lawn beneath canopies strung with pale coral, turquoise, and green tulle. Alabaster roses topped the tables, matching the flowers in Darcy's posy bouquet. The photographer followed along snapping memories—some candid, some posed. Champagne flowed like water, and the delicious hors d'oeuvres were served by none other than PrincessLeia22 and SluttyGirl.

She waved to Kelly as she and Brandon made their way to the dance floor. Kelly and Daniel had become members of their extended family, and Darcy counted her among her dear friends. Millie stood on the fringes, as she always seemed to do, talking with David. Anne looked beautiful in her bridesmaid's gown, her face aglow as she and Matt swayed to Lifehouse.

Darcy had already performed the traditional wedding dance with her father and her first dance with her husband. Now free to enjoy the reception until the cake-cutting ceremony and bouquet toss, she walked with Josh, sipping champagne and secretly toasting her good fortune.

Josh had managed to completely surprise her. When she'd stepped out of her parents' house on her father's arm and onto the runner for her walk down the aisle, she blinked in confusion. At the end of the aisle, just in front of the flower-covered arch sat Josh on the back of an enormous white horse, Daniel standing next to him as best man.

A giggle had escaped her, and she whispered to her father, "Did you know about this?" His knowing grin had said it all.

Darcy thought about all those years daydreaming about her knight charging across the lawn to whisk her away, making her dreams come true, and there he sat atop his white horse.

Once she'd reached the arch, Josh dismounted and gave her a sweeping bow, as a young man led the horse away.

Now, as they strolled toward the enormous main tent where guests danced to the "Cupid Shuffle," she gave her Prince Charming's hand a squeeze and he glanced down at her, a question in his eyes. "Thank you," she said.

"For what?"

"For loving me so perfectly."

Josh stood mesmerized by the love shining in his bride's eyes. Love for him and him alone. She'd chosen him, without a word from him, without knowing if he returned her love. She'd chosen him, and he vowed never to make her regret that choice.

When she'd walked down the aisle in a cloud of white, her golden brown hair a cascade of curls around her shoulders, he thought he'd died and gone to heaven. No bride had ever looked so beautiful. His legs shook and he thought he'd fall trying to dismount. He hadn't ridden since summer camps as a boy and feared the horse would bolt, or he'd get his foot caught in the stirrup and do a face-plant. But seeing the brilliance of Darcy's smile when she saw him made any fear worth it.

He bent to brush his lips across hers. "Ditto, Mrs. Ryan." He tasted her lips once more, then retreated a step. "You keep looking at me like that and the honeymoon will start sooner than planned."

"You'll get no argument from me," she said with a lusty grin.

———

Gloria watched the festivities with a sense of satisfaction in a job well done. Darcy looked every bit the fairy princess she'd always dreamed about in her white tulle confection, the white Swarovski crystals sprinkled about the skirt, catching the sun and tossing it back. Josh stood beaming by her side, an arm around her waist, dapper in a gray morning suit. One down, two more to go.

Gloria scanned the crowd until she found Millie, looking very un-Millie-like in her turquoise chiffon bridesmaid's gown, her usually drab brown hair gleamed in an elegant twist, her lips a luscious Merlot color. "She cleans up well," Gloria murmured to herself, though she'd heard

Laura practically had to cuff her to the vanity chair so the stylist could work her magic.

Speaking of Laura, she scanned the crowd before spotting her, ever-stunning in her customary stilettos, her blond hair back in a sleek ponytail that fell almost to her waist, her coral bridesmaid's gown showing off every curve.

"No rest for the weary," Gloria said to herself as she rose and moved to stand next to Laura and her father and mother. Milton might as well have stayed home for all the attention he paid to the ceremony and reception. She'd have to give him a swift kick in the pants if he did this at Laura's wedding. But right now his addiction to his smartphone worked to her benefit.

———

Spying her maid-of-honor across the dance floor with Cherise and Milton, Darcy wove her way through the guests, accepting warm congratulations along the way. The photographer had announced the bouquet toss, and she wanted Laura front and center. Not that she expected Laura to settle down any time soon, if ever. Still, she'd like to see Laura catch it. Her height and athleticism gave her a definite advantage, but Darcy planned to aim well. Her friend deserved the same happiness she had found with Josh.

Milton looked up from his phone just as Darcy joined them, and said, "I just received an email from Jackson Jeffries, CEO of Imperial Cruise Lines—one of the largest luxury ship lines in the world, and our best customer—" he added for Darcy's benefit. "They fired their advertising agency."

Laura choked on the mouthful of booze she'd just swallowed.

"Laura, can't you swallow your drink without making a scene?" Cherise chided. "If you can't handle your alcohol, you shouldn't be drinking it. Gracious, where are your manners?"

Darcy patted Laura's back and offered her some water.

Milton turned to Cherise. "Doesn't Mitchell McCutcheon's son own an ad agency in Manhattan?"

"Now why on earth would I know something like that? Laura, do you know?"

Milton went back to his phone, fingers tapping on the screen.

Finally able to catch her breath, Laura blurted out, "I *work* for an ad agency! Why would you tell my competitor?"

Her father waved his hand dismissively. "Your agency could never handle such a large account."

"Giddings-Rose is one of Madison Avenue's oldest ad agencies. Of course we can handle the account."

"Doesn't matter now, I've already forwarded the email to Mitch."

"We'll see about that," Laura muttered.

"What's that? Speak up when you talk." Cherise patted a hair back into place.

"Time for the bouquet toss." Laura set her drink on a passing waiter's tray.

Darcy shot a worried glance at Laura. Instead of the anger and frustration Darcy expected to see, she saw a predatory gleam in those cool blue eyes. *Ruh-roh*, she knew that look and it didn't bode well for anyone who got in her way.

"Alrighty then." Darcy gathered up her skirts in one hand and her bouquet in the other. "Let's do this."

————

J osh and Darcy dashed through a shower of birdseed to the waiting limo emblazoned with the words JUST MARRIED across the back window. The wedding guests crowded around the car shouting best wishes for eternal happiness, salted with a few bawdy comments about the honeymoon activities.

As the car drove away with Josh and Darcy kissing in the back seat, Gloria raised her glass in a silent toast to happily-ever-after.

REVIEWS

Did you enjoy this book? Please let other potential readers know.

Reviews are the most powerful tool in an author's toll box when it comes to gaining new readers–more powerful even than the most expensive ads. Honest reviews help bring them to the attention of other readers.

If you enjoyed this book, I would be grateful if you could take a few minutes to leave an honest review on the retailer's website. Even a short review can help.

Thank you!

SHIP OF DREAMS

EXCERPT FROM BOOK 2 OF THE DREAMS COME TRUE SERIES

Laura Armstrong strode toward the building housing the New York offices of Imperial Cruise Lines. Her stiletto heels clicked a staccato on the sidewalk as she tested the limits of her snug pencil skirt.

Tapping out a message on her smart phone, her mind five steps ahead, she nearly took a header when the heel of her shoe plunged into a sidewalk seam. The text message all but forgotten, she twisted and turned, unable to dislodge the stubborn heel.

Risking a tear in the cherry red patent leather of her sky-high Louboutin ankle-straps — the ones with the plunging vamp revealing her sexy toe cleavage — wasn't an option. But between the ankle strap and her figure-hugging skirt, she couldn't slip out of the shoe, nor could bend over and unfasten it either.

Perfect. She'd be late for her meeting with Imperial's CEO.

Daddy Dearest thought Giddings-Rose couldn't handle an account the size of Imperial. Check that. He thought she couldn't win an account the size of Imperial.

Determined to prove her father wrong, she'd get the account and the corner office. That is if she could pry her heel out of the sidewalk.

Bustling New Yorkers in suits and skirts just stepped around her, dodging her like an out-of-place trashcan. "Well, sh—"

"Hold still, Sugar, or you'll break the heel." The masculine voice called to mind the mellow sweetness of the fine Kentucky Bourbon she'd once sipped at the Derby. Rich and mellifluous, with a hint of Southern graciousness. Even so, there was no denying the authoritative tone. "And that would be a damn shame." The hand that wrapped around her ankle from behind was broad and masculine, but well-manicured, topped with an elegant Cartier watch.

Not her type. She preferred her men with a little more grit than polish. So why did tantalizing warmth spread up her leg?

With adept fingers, he unbuckled the ankle strap and lifted her foot from the still-lodged shoe. Having no other choice to avoid either resting her bare foot on the filthy Manhattan sidewalk or the humiliation of falling on her face, she reached back and grabbed his shoulder.

Hmm. No padding there. Nothing but muscle beneath that expensive tropical weight wool suit. She caught a glimpse of charcoal gray fabric, dark hair, and Italian shoes in rich mahogany leather.

But she'd yet to lay eyes on her rescuer's face.

Nathan Maxwell took advantage of the up-close and personal view. Trim ankles met shapely, muscular calves, and judging from the fit of her skirt, a firm derriere topped off those swimsuit-model legs. Beneath his touch, soft skin beckoned further exploration. Long honey-blond hair hung almost to her waist in a sleek ponytail. The fragrance of her haute couture perfume drifted over him, reminding him of magnolia-scented summer nights.

Focusing on the task at hand, he gently pried the heel from the sidewalk seam and examined it. "No harm done." He grasped her ankle and settled her foot back into the shoe and fastened the strap, but not before noticing the firecracker red nail polish. He laughed. "Here you go Cinderella."

The warmth of his laugh slid over her, knocking her a little off balance even though she'd placed her foot firmly back on the ground. "Thank you, uh . . ." She turned and looked up into golden brown eyes the color of that same sweet Kentucky Bourbon.

"Nathan, Nathan Maxwell. My pleasure, ma'am." He flashed a devastating grin, igniting gilded sparks in his eyes.

There was that Southern drawl again — subtle, like the peach undertones of a fine Pinot Gris. "You're not from around here, are you?"

"My accent give me away?" Her sardonic smile weakened Nathan's knees more than any toothy grin ever did.

"No, your courtesy."

Nathan chuckled. "My grandmother would have expected nothing less." Her eyes, cool blue like the May sky overhead, captured his and held. No shrinking violet, this one, he mused. A full, determined mouth painted to match the red of her toenails set off an arresting face with high cheekbones, a stubborn chin, and aquiline nose.

"Well, thank you, Nathan." Maybe she should add suave polished men with a hint of Rhett Butler to her menu, Laura thought. Her phone, all but forgotten in her hand, buzzed. "I, uh, I've got to go. Thanks again, Nathan Maxwell." Something about the way his name rolled off her tongue. She answered the phone as she walked away, "This is Laura."

Nathan watched as she strode down the sidewalk, hips swaying to some inherent rhythm. "Come on, Laura, glance back." She turned and gave him what he wanted, another look at that bold, beautiful face.

"It's going to be a great day." Glancing at his watch, satisfied with the outcome of the errand that brought him to this part of Manhattan in the first place, he hailed a cab back to his office.

ABOUT THE AUTHOR

Rebecca Heflin is a bestselling, award-winning author who has dreamed of writing romantic fiction since she was fifteen and her older sister sneaked a copy of Kathleen Woodiwiss' Shanna to her and told her to read it.

Never quite sure what she wanted to be when she grew up, Rebecca didn't attend college until age 30, and earned her bachelor's in literature, before going on to complete her law degree.

Ever the late bloomer, Rebecca finally turned her attention to fulfilling her dream of writing, and published her first novel at age 48. When not passionately pursuing her dream, Rebecca is busy with her day-job at a major state university.

She and her husband are also co-founders of a non-profit organization, which raises money to help cancer patients and their families.

Rebecca's pen name is an abbreviated version of her great-great grandmother's name: Sarah Anne Rebecca Heflin Apple Smith. Whew! And you wonder why she shortened it.

Rebecca writes women's fiction and contemporary

romance, and she is a member of Romance Writers of America (RWA), Florida Romance Writers, RWA Contemporary Romance, and Florida Writers Association. Rebecca and her mountain-climbing husband live at sea level in sunny Florida.

Sign up for Rebecca's monthly newsletter, Rebecca's Readers, for all the latest news on upcoming releases, appearances, and contests.

facebook.com/RebeccaHeflinBooks

twitter.com/RebeccaHeflin

pinterest.com/rheflinbooks

bookbub.com/authors/rebecca-heflin

ALSO BY REBECCA HEFLIN

THE PROMISE OF CHANGE

RESCUING LACEY

DREAMS COME TRUE SERIES

SHIP OF DREAMS, BOOK 2

DREAMS OF HER OWN, BOOK 3

STERLING UNIVERSITY SERIES

ROMANCING DR. LOVE, BOOK 1

WINNING DR. WENTWORTH, BOOK 2

EDUCATING DR. MAYFIELD, BOOK 3

SEASONS OF NORTHRIDGE SERIES

A SEASON TO DANCE, BOOK 1

A SEASON TO LOVE, BOOK 2